MW01234327

Stardust

MIMI STRONG

BOOKS BY MIMI STRONG

For a current listing of books and
series, visit www.mimistrong.com

CHAPTER 1

I wasn't always a magnet for hot guys, but then one day I fell into Dalton Deangelo's arms, and my whole life changed.

I was standing on a wooden stool, inside the bookstore where I worked, trying to solve one of my two major problems. A tempting cupcake smell kept wafting in the air vent. I couldn't take it for another minute. My very smart plan was to tape over the vent.

My other problem was that I didn't have a date for my cousin's wedding that afternoon, but it was too late to do anything about that.

The bells on the front door jingled, and a guy came running into the store, breathing heavily. I could tell instantly he was not a local. If there'd been a guy that yummy in the small town of Beaverdale, I would have known.

He didn't see me standing on the stool, and slammed into me with his gorgeous body. It was more contact than I'd had with a man recently, so I didn't mind one bit. And he was so cute! Two points for Peaches.

The stool wobbled. I tried to catch my balance, but there was nothing to grab onto.

I toppled off the stool and fell.

Right into his arms.

The handsome stranger didn't just catch me.

He held me.

He held me like I belonged to him, and he didn't want to let me go.

I stared into his gorgeous green eyes, wondering if I was dreaming. The light from the window made his dark brown hair glow like amber, a honey-hued halo around the face of my angel.

And then, he opened his mouth and said the most captivating thing: "What kind of an idiot stands on a stool when there's a perfectly good ladder available?"

"Ladders are overrated. And it's good to challenge yourself."

He grinned, still holding me in those amazingly strong arms. "You've got a lot of opinions."

"And you've got a lot of... biceps."

He chuckled at my compliment. He cradled me tenderly, like I was a lost kitten who'd fallen from a tree, and not a curvy twenty-two-year old in a bridesmaid dress.

The smell of his skin reached my nose. Oh, mercy, he smelled as good as he looked. Better than the wicked cupcakes from next door. Better than anything or anyone I'd ever smelled.

I glanced around, glad the two of us were alone in the little shop. My employee was due to show up at any moment, and it would ruin my authority as Boss to be seen getting held like a kitten.

"You can set me down anywhere," I said, even though I didn't *want* to be set down.

"Anywhere?"

"Yeah. Any time." I stared at his lips. *Please don't stop cradling me like a kitten.*

"I'll set you down," he said, "but no more standing on chairs. Promise?"

"I'll use the ladder."

"There's my girl." He set me down gently, but didn't step away. We were so close, we could kiss.

I couldn't stop staring at his lips. And his square jaw. And those green eyes. If he wasn't from Beaverdale, why did he look so familiar?

He said, "Do you have a storage room where I could hide out for a few minutes?"

"We have a washroom, but it's for customers only."

He glanced over the New Arrivals table and grabbed a book at random.

"I'm buying this," he said.

It was a book for ladies with bladder control issues.

"Excellent choice," I said with a straight face. "The washroom's at the back, through the bead curtain. The light switch is in the last place you'd expect it to be."

He raised one sexy, dark eyebrow. "Should I take a flashlight?"

"Just grope around in the dark until you get lucky."

He raised his eyebrow even higher. "It's been a while since a beautiful girl's said that to me."

I resisted the urge to melt into a puddle of giggles. I just smiled, playing it cool.

He glanced over to the front windows, where I could see a bunch of people approaching.

"I'm trying to shake someone who's pure evil," he explained as he turned back to me. "If anyone asks, I'm not here." He held my eyes with his hypnotic gaze. "We can trust each other."

"Um, can we?"

There was a ruckus outside the front door, and people running back and forth. A big guy whizzed by with a video camera on his shoulder.

I stepped out from behind the counter to look out the window. When I turned back, the hot guy was already gone.

"That was odd," I muttered to myself. I picked up the fallen stool and returned it to behind the counter.

The front door crashed open, and suddenly a whole TV news crew came rushing into Peachtree Books.

At the front was a woman with bright red hair and way too much makeup. She gave me a disappointed, disgusted look.

"It's just some boring girl," she said, sneering.

I put on my professional retail smile and said sweetly, "Anything I can help you with?"

The woman turned and asked her crew, "He wouldn't come in here, would he? I doubt he's ever read a book."

The cameraman chuckled. "Meat puppets can barely read their cue cards."

A guy with a boom mike said to the cameraman, "You're just jealous because you're not a pretty boy with screaming fans."

The rude redhead was now looking around Peachtree Books. The store was my pride and joy, and she had her upper lip curved up in a sneer. "I thought all the bookstores were closed," she said.

Even though I knew not to argue with people of apparent low intelligence, I said, "You're standing inside a bookstore now, so unless this is a dream, we can deduce that not all the bookstores are closed."

"Huh?"

"Simple logic." I flashed her my biggest grin.

She snorted, as if I was the stupid one, not her.

I continued patiently, "You see, we have all these shelves full of books because this is a bookstore."

The woman wrinkled her nose and sniffed the air contemptuously. "Thanks for nothing. Good luck with the, uh, books."

"Good luck with your attitude."

She sneered again. "Good luck with whatever that dress is supposed to be."

I looked down at the bridesmaid dress I was wearing. What did she mean by that? My curves were rocking in that dress. Was I going to have to punch her in the neck? She wasn't a customer, so, technically, neck-punching wasn't against store policy.

By the time I looked up, the crew and the woman were already leaving. The front door closed, and it was just me again. Alone. Just like I would be in an hour, at my cousin's wedding.

Something made a noise at the back of the shop, and I jumped in alarm.

The cute guy came walking up, weaving his way around tall shelves crammed with books.

I held my hand to my chest, the fabric of my bridesmaid dress crinkly. "You scared me."

His voice was even deeper and sexier now. "Did you already forget about me?"

4

"I thought you left out the back. Plus I was distracted by Lady Satan, with her film crew."

He held up the book. "This is very informative. What do I owe you?"

I felt myself blushing under his sexy stare, so I started doing busy-work with my hands on the store's counter, stacking the Post-It notepads, putting away the passport stamp, and straightening the pens.

"You don't have to buy that book," I said. "Men don't even have kegel muscles."

"They don't? That's not fair."

I stared up at his beautiful green eyes, which crinkled at the sides with a smile. My own eyes are blue, and they disappear more than they crinkle. I got my blond hair and blue eyes from my mother, but neither of us is the perfect cheerleader type.

Casually, I asked, "So, are you a criminal, or a celebrity?"

"Depends on who you ask."

"You look familiar."

"So do you," he said.

His eyes traveled down my body, and I tried to suck in my middle even more, but I was already strapped into two pairs of Spanx, and my organs had nowhere left to go.

With a sexy growl to his voice, he said, "Do you always dress so fancy at work?"

"I'm going to a wedding any minute now."

"A wedding." He took two steps back and gave me an appraising look, his arms crossed.

He looked dressy himself, in sharply-creased gray trousers and a button-down shirt, rolled up at the cuffs to reveal muscular arms with a smattering of dark hairs. Even his forearms looked familiar, like I'd already spent countless hours staring at them.

He said, "That's a shame you're getting married, because I would have asked you for a date."

This caused me to laugh and gasp for air. "I'm not getting married. I'm just a bridesmaid."

"Ah." He nodded. "And this is all happening shortly, so I should be getting on my way."

I glanced at the door while mentally willing him to stay. *Stay for a few more minutes!* Just kidding. *Stay forever?*

"No rush," I said. "I'm waiting for my employee, and then I'll call for a cab."

"My driver's nearby. I could give you a lift, as a thank you for hiding me from Lady Satan."

"That reporter was nasty. I don't blame you for hiding."

My eyes were starting to hurt from looking at him. I'd probably forgotten how to blink.

I glanced down and shook the pens out of the tin can, and along with the pens, out slid an eraser, three gummy bears, and a square item that was unmistakably a condom packet.

There it was, right between us.

A condom, screaming SEX, SEX, SEX!

Naturally, I shrieked.

"Are they back?" He turned to the window, on the alert for reporters.

I snatched the condom packet and stuffed it into my purse, which was just under the counter top.

He turned back. "Nope. They're gone."

"Long gone."

He blinked at me, and I remembered how to blink.

Neither of us said anything.

We had a long, awkward pause.

I sensed this interaction was over, and it was time for him to leave, unless I did something.

"My name is Petra Monroe," I said, offering him my hand. "Everyone calls me Peaches. Peaches Monroe."

"That's the perfect name for you. I'm Dalton Deangelo."

I chuckled. "Sure, you are."

"I am."

My heart began to pound in my chest. He wasn't joking.

He was...

DALTON.

FREAKING.

DEANGELO.

We shook hands, and something strange happened.

A life flash before my eyes.

Only it wasn't *my* life.

The man standing before me was a famous actor who played a bad-boy vampire in a TV series.

Drake Cheshire, two hundred years old and forever young.

How could I be so oblivious? Why was he in Washington state?

I hadn't recognized him without the pale makeup and contact lenses that made his eyes darker, but it was him.

I was shaking hands with the man Shayla referred to as our TV boyfriend. She'd named her vibrator after his character, Drake.

"You've heard of me?" he asked.

"Kinda," I lied.

He gave me a sly, sexy smile. He knew damn well that I knew who he was.

"I play Drake Cheshire."

I frowned. "Sounds familiar."

He grinned.

Oh, that sexy grin! That face! *That body.* I couldn't see his chest and abs through his shirt, but I'd seen them on TV a hundred times. The writers always found an excuse for Drake to be shirtless and emotional.

Shirtless and emotional.

Now I was picturing him standing in the rain, water trickling down his gorgeous chest as he professed his love for...

Me. In my wildest dreams.

With an air of casual ease, he picked up our previous conversation. "You need a taxi? Why isn't your date picking you up for the wedding?"

MIMI STRONG

"I don't have a date. Or a boyfriend."

"I have an idea." He grabbed the pens strewn about the counter between us and stacked them into the pen holder. "You won't have to go alone, because I'll arrange for a date for you."

"Oh, Drake—um, Mr. Deangelo, I couldn't ask you to do that. You probably have a very busy life and lots of things to do tonight."

He raised his eyebrows, looking more like devious Drake by the minute. "Me? Oh, no. I was going to send my butler."

I crossed my arms. "Your butler?" *What the Fudgeeo cookies was this?*

He laughed. "I knew it! You're even more adorable when you're annoyed."

I scowled at him. "Thanks for the offer of your butler, but no."

"How about me? Would you be seen in public with this face? Probably not. Let me down easy."

"You're not that bad," I said, calling his bluff.

"So, it's a date."

I started laughing hysterically. How far was he going to take this joke?

Just then, the door jingled open and my employee, Amy, came running in, apologizing for being late. Without looking at Dalton, she ran around the counter and tossed her purse next to mine.

"Go," Amy said. "I slept in and—"

Amy looked up at Dalton Deangelo.

The tiniest whimper came from her mouth before she fainted into my arms. I slowly eased her down to the floor.

"I've seen this before," Dalton said.

"I'm sure you have."

"Be right back." Dalton ran to the washroom, then returned with a glass of water.

He handed me the water.

I tossed the water on Amy's face.

Amy gasped and opened her eyes.

Dalton started to laugh. "That was for her to drink."

"Well, it worked, didn't it?"

"Don't hit me, Boss," Amy said, a strand of her blue hair stuck to her wet face.

Dalton reached down and helped Amy to her feet, grinning madly. I couldn't guess what the life of a famous actor was like normally, but he seemed to be having the time of his life.

Laughing, he asked Amy, "Is your boss always so abusive?"

Her eyes bugging out, Amy gawked at Dalton, then me, then Dalton, then me again. "Is this really happening? Is Drake the vampire in our bookstore?"

"Not for long," he said. "I'm taking Peaches to the wedding. I trust you'll be able to manage without her? We straightened out all the pens in the tin can already, so you should be set."

Amy gave me a quizzical look. With one hand along the side of her dripping-wet face, she whispered to me, "Do you two know each other?"

"Not really—"

Dalton interrupted. "We're future old friends."

Amy said to me, "He's very pushy. I've read that in interviews. This is just how he is." She turned to Dalton and smiled. "I follow you online."

He pulled an old-fashioned handkerchief from his pocket and dabbed the water drops on her face.

"You follow my publicist," he said, giving her a sly wink.

Amy, who was sixteen, but texted and tweeted like she was thirteen, gasped in horror.

I said, "Ah, the sweet sound of scales falling from a young person's eyes."

Dalton tilted his head and asked me, "*Young person?* How old are you?"

"Twenty-two. But I've seen things."

"Sure you have. But have you *done* things?"

"A couple things."

"Good!" He tucked away the handkerchief and offered me his elbow. "I'm only dating girls who've done a couple things."

"Dating? I thought we were future old friends."

"This is how we get there," he said as he led me toward the front door.

I hesitated, looking back at a damp Amy, standing in my favorite comfortable spot behind the counter, near the yellow vintage phone. Behind her stood piles of special order books with customer tags sticking out like multi-colored paper tongues.

I turned my head to the left and looked over all my shelves, set far enough apart that one customer could walk past another without bumping butts, yet close enough to encourage friendly conversation.

The bookstore was my whole life. Sometimes in the evening, after we were closed, I'd stay behind and watch the traffic on the rainy street outside, as people walked back and forth, unaware of me, sitting in the dark.

Dalton pulled open the front door, and the sounds of the world came in.

How far would he take this little joke of his?

He'd probably get a phone call and make some excuse before we were half-way there. I'd had other men make big promises before, and it always started like this: the grand, spontaneous gesture. The excuses kicked in later.

We walked outside, and he said, "What is it about bridesmaids? There's something about those matching dresses you all wear that gives me ideas. Ideas about getting those dresses off."

"Wow. You don't waste any time. You just say whatever you want, don't you?"

He grinned. "And you don't?"

"My mouth does have a mind of its own."

"I like your mouth. You're not phoney."

"There are a lot of things I'm not. Not rich. Not famous. Not perfect."

He stopped walking and turned to look at me.

"Who said you're not perfect?" he asked.

For a moment, I was speechless, which isn't something that happens often.

Who said I wasn't perfect? Mostly me, actually.

But as Dalton Deangelo looked down my body with a wolfish hunger for my curves, I realized how wrong I'd been.

I was perfect.

Perfectly fine with myself, exactly how I was.

And perfectly ready for whatever happened next.

...as long as what happened next was not Dalton Deangelo kissing me. Or spending more time with me. Because that would make my entire life implode.

Plus it would be weird.

Dalton/Drake was the sexy stud I objectified on TV, with a pane of glass between us.

They say if you ever meet your idols, walk away before you're disappointed. They also say if you meet the Buddha, kill him. (I don't understand that one at all.)

I stared into Dalton Deangelo's heavenly green eyes and told myself to walk away. My body wouldn't obey. My body wanted to be back in his arms again.

We were still standing in the middle of the sidewalk. People passed by without giving us a second look.

"This is weird," I said.

"Good weird or bad weird?"

"Usually there's a plane of glass between us."

He got a crooked grin. "So, you do watch my show."

"It's the best show on TV, but I hate the cliffhangers."

"You love the cliffhangers."

"I love Drake Cheshire." *Oops.* I pressed my lips together.

He laughed. "I get that a lot."

"I bet you do."

"Peaches, you do know I'm a real person, right? I'm not an ancient vampire with a bunch of gypsy curses on me."

"Of course I know that. I'm not *completely* crazy."

His gaze slid over my curves again. "That dress is crazy. Good crazy, not bad crazy."

"Thanks. Lady Satan with the film crew didn't like it."

"She's bad crazy. Was she rude to you? I'll make her pay."

"My hero." I sighed dramatically. "Get it? That's what the little skinny blondes on your show always say when you rescue them."

He blinked and asked innocently, "There are girls on the show?"

11

I felt my cheeks redden. Oh, he was laying it on thick, but I didn't mind one bit. I had a date for my cousin's wedding. Two more points for Peaches.

Dalton kept looking over my bridesmaid gown, like he was busy formulating a plan to get it off of me.

Forget the wedding, I thought. *Unzip my dress, nibble on me, and make me call you weird names until the sun comes up.*

He smiled, just like the vampire Drake Cheshire would, if he could read my mind.

CHAPTER 2

The wedding was for my cousin Marita, age thirty-three, and her partner James, who was a whopping four days over twenty. Marita had met him at a bar, where he'd gained entry with fake ID.

They'd started dating casually, "just for fun." Neither of them had expected marriage, until suddenly it was happening. Marita had a *certain glow about her*, if you know what I mean.

His family was ultra conservative, and he had seven brothers and sisters, all of them older than him, and none of them married. I knew Marita to be a sensible, wonderful woman, but by the looks on her fiance's parents' faces, she was the she-devil who was about to ruin their youngest son's life and future.

Marita was a Monroe, after all, and our family has a bit of a reputation in Beaverdale, but that's a complicated story I'll tell you more about later.

Marita and James wore tight smiles through the brief ceremony at the chapel, but relaxed afterward, in the receiving line. *It's all done now*, their faces said.

Relief.

There's a dentist's office to one side of the bookstore, and I know post-root-canal magnitude of relief when I see it.

By contrast, I was nervous and jittery.

To my surprise, Dalton Deangelo sat patiently on his own, in the back row, through the whole ceremony. Nobody fainted, or even recognized him, I suppose because most people in attendance weren't watchers of vampire soap operas.

Dalton and I had arrived on the late side, which would have been unforgivable if I'd had any actual duties as bridesmaid, but I was simply a spare who'd been added at the last minute to balance out an extra groomsman. I stood in my place, holding my flowers, and making everyone else including the bride look slimmer by comparison for the photos.

Because there'd been no time to introduce Dalton to my family, the awkwardness with my parents was a treat to still look forward to.

The summer weather was hot, and the little chapel grew muggy with all the people inside, so I found Dalton and ducked outside to the front steps as soon as we could.

"That was a beautiful ceremony," Dalton said. "Everything happened so fast. I don't know if I've ever been to a real wedding before."

"You only go to fake weddings?"

"Yes."

I smacked my forehead. "Oh, for the show. That's right. There've been…" I counted in my head. "Four weddings."

He looked at me as if seeing me without any clothes on.

For the record, I did not hate this feeling.

"You're a fan of the show," he said.

"Don't let it go to your head, but yes, I have worshiped you for years."

He raised his eyebrows, sexy like an immortal TV vampire.

I rubbed my bare arms as a gentle summer breeze puckered the follicles on my arms and reminded me I was but a mere mortal. "I said don't let it go to your head, mister. I can stop watching any time I want."

"Our ratings say otherwise." He got an I-ate-the-whole-thing grin.

Our conversation was interrupted by my family walking up.

"What ratings?" asked my father. He squinted to protect his pale blue eyes in the bright sun, his red hair curly and golden. Before we could answer, he was onto a new topic, saying, "What they ought to have on the ceiling in there is a chain of fans. You could set them up in tandem and create a stream of air."

"You should tell them, Dad."

He ducked his head back, forming double chins of I-don't-think-so, as though the idea of telling someone something they ought to know, such as the optimal way to ventilate a building, was preposterous.

My mother, who's the same shade of blond and the same shape of voluptuous as me, couldn't take her eyes off my surprise date. She wore a blue dress that matched her eyes, tied with a red belt that matched her red shoes, her toes pointed demurely together as she gazed up at Dalton.

I introduced everyone, and it only took little Kyle all of thirty seconds to say something Kyle-like.

Kyle tilted his head up in that cute way only a seven-year-old can and said, "Are you Peepee's boyfriend?"

Dalton did a double-take. "Peepee? I don't know anyone by that name."

"Kyle!" I admonished. "Don't call me that, you little turd monkey."

"I'm a future old friend of Peepee's," Dalton said, shaking Kyle's hand.

"You're taller than my dad," Kyle said. "Can I sit on your shoulders? I want to see everything."

In response, Dalton knelt down like a trained circus horse and let Kyle climb on top his shoulders.

My mother caught my eye and loudly whispered, "He's so handsome, Peachy." (Most people call me Peaches, but Mom calls me Peachy, or Petra if she's annoyed.)

I glanced over at Dalton, running up and down the chapel steps with Kyle squealing on his shoulders.

"Is he?" I said, smirking. "I hadn't noticed, Mom. I'm not shallow like you, marrying Dad for his good looks."

At this, my father beamed, and I felt a wave of gratitude for all my riches. My family is not perfect, and we have our fights and secrets, but most of us genuinely *like* each other, and that's just as important as love.

~

I kept expecting Dalton to disappear the way a too-good dream evaporates upon waking, but he instructed his driver take us over to the dance hall where the rest of the celebration was happening. I got out of the fancy car, which wasn't quite as long as either of the two limousines in town people rent for special occasions, but it did have a glass separation between us and the driver.

I thought Dalton was stepping out to say goodbye, but he actually nodded toward the door, so we walked up together. Like he really was my date, and not the worst kind of Torture Bite.*

*When someone is eating a delicious dessert, they always try to make you take one bite, out of what? Cruelty? This is the worst of all nibbles, because if it's good (and it's always good) then you have to sit and suffer while they eat the rest. The taste is all up inside your mouth, tantalizing you with the torture of pleasure denied.

Dalton Deangelo holding me in his arms had been my tasty bite, and now I wanted more.

We walked into the dance hall and started mingling. He had his hands in the pockets of his gray slacks, and he looked as comfortable as any of the other men in attendance.

He asked me a bunch of questions, about everything from the plastic carnation decorations to the projection screen showing James and Marita's engagement photos.

"Why are they posing like depressed catalog models in front of a brick wall?" he asked.

"It's just what people in Beaverdale do."

"Why are there so many photos? Oh, here they are in a field. Okay, well, I like that one. That's a good one."

Marita was lying amongst wildflowers with her head in James's lap, gazing skyward.

"That is a good one," I agreed.

"You and she both have a woodsy look. Natural. Like you'd be right at home running naked through the woods."

"Shut up! You're making fun of me."

His handsome dark brown eyebrows rose, so thick and expressive. "Oh, am I?"

We were standing near the bar, he with a light beer and me with a glass of sparkling white wine, plus the giddy sensation one gets at her first family function where she's legally allowed to drink.

"Don't tease," I said.

"You say that now…"

I sipped my wine as he tore my dress off with his gaze. I know you're supposed to hate your bridesmaid dress and complain bitterly about having to wear it, but I liked mine. The bodice was cut to frame my chest demurely, with just a hint of naughty cleavage—or at least that's how it started out. The heat of my body had loosened up the fabric on the straps somehow, and now the front was dipping down, anything but demure.

"Stop teasing me," I said softly, almost whispering.

His eyes locked onto my cleavage. "Speaking of teasing, a guy could drink champagne from there."

I snorted and tugged the bodice up. "Don't be silly. It would drain right through."

"Only one way to find out." He turned back toward the bar and raised his fingers to call for the bartender. "Bottle of your best champ—"

I grabbed him by the arm and hauled him away from the bar before he created a huge spectacle. A few of Marita's other bridesmaids were already staring, mostly at Dalton. Correction: they were staring mostly at Dalton's ass, which was round with muscles and practically cried "grab me" in those tight gray trousers.

The Master of Ceremony tapped a microphone to get everyone's attention.

One of my uncles, not Mayor Stephen Monroe, but his brother John, was acting as the MC that night. He made a few remarks as we all found our assigned tables, and he introduced the out-of-town guests.

I thought Dalton would be bored senseless by the stories about people he'd never met until that day, but he seemed fascinated.

My stomach grumbled for dinner, my nose having caught the scent of the food in the chafing dishes being set up by the caterers.

17

Uncle John pulled something out of his pocket and said, "Twelve."

People all around us booed their disappointment, pretending to be outraged.

Dalton seemed genuinely horrified. He leaned over and asked me, "What's going on?"

The people at Table Twelve got up and made their way over to the buffet, cheering. Dalton and I were sitting at Table Seven, with a bunch of people I barely knew.

I'd been relieved of my auxiliary bridesmaid duties and shuffled to the Misfits Table, full of tipsy spinsters, people who didn't speak English, and one miserable teenaged boy, trying to sneak the adults' punch with the boozy fruit.

"Where are those people going?" Dalton asked.

"To get dinner. We'll go when our number gets called," I explained.

"Is this a religious thing?"

I laughed and put my hand on his bicep, like we were already lovers, and I just groped his *surprisingly hard* biceps all the time.

Wow. His arm felt like a really nice meatloaf, well done, and here I was touching it. Maybe it was low blood sugar, but I was feeling more comfortable around him by the minute. The glass of white wine hadn't hurt, either. I stopped laughing, shocked by how hard and big his arm felt under my fingertips. My goodness. More food comparisons came to mind. Was I more hungry or horny? I couldn't tell.

"Going up by table number is just what people do," I said. "I guess at fancy hotel weddings, the waiters bring out the food all at once. But whenever you have a buffet, people go up in tables. I can't believe you've never been to a wedding. The Monroes are a big family, as you can see, and I've probably been to twenty weddings, mostly cousins."

He grinned down at my hand, which was still groping his bicep. *Oh, you naughty hand,* I thought, but I didn't exactly stop the frisking.

"You like what you're grabbing?" he asked.

18

Emboldened by the wine, I squeezed that harder-than-aged-cheddar bicep and gave him a coy look. "Just bein' friendly," I said. "That's how we get to be future old friends."

"Keep doing that and I'll have to kiss you."

I yanked my hand back, alarmed by the intensely sexual look in his eyes.

Around us, people started tapping their cutlery on glasses and chanting, "Kiss, kiss!"

Dalton leaned in toward me.

My eyes widened, and I pulled way back. "That chanting is for the bride and groom," I said. "Another tradition."

He wiggled his shoulders as if swimming, and moved in, leaning into my space with his clean-smelling cologne, and flashing his eyes at me. Oh, those eyes. I was in danger, oh, yes, I was. Seeing him on my TV screen made my woowoo smile. Smelling him in person made my woowoo jump up and down doing a rain dance.

I leaned back so hard, I fell right out of my chair.

Lucky for me, everyone was busy tapping their glasses and paying attention to lady-cougar Marita and sweet baby James, posing for pictures as they kissed for everyone. I landed right on my ass, which didn't hurt too bad, on account of the naturally cushiony material there. My woowoo got excited, thinking this was foreplay.

Dalton held out his hand. "Sorry about that," he said. "You don't actually have to kiss me."

I got back onto my chair and looked around for the evil wedding photographer, who was obsessed with catching people in "spontaneous" moments just like this. He'd already gotten a few pictures of me stuffing enormous sushi rolls in my mouth.

Dalton's hand landed on my knee.

Hand-on-knee alert!

The hand lingered on my knee, sending delicious heat into my body, including the zesty taco zone.

"Are you okay?" he asked. "I was coming on too strong, wasn't I? I can be dramatic sometimes. Hazard of my career, I suppose. At least I'm not on a cop show, or I'd probably interrogate you or put you in handcuffs."

I swallowed hard at the idea of handcuffs. "I'm not entirely against the idea of kissing you, but if you're going to do it, just do it. Don't tell me you're going to—"

He moved swiftly, hooking one arm behind my back so I couldn't fall off my chair or get away. His lips were on my mouth, his face in my face, and the kiss felt as right as anything had ever felt right in my life.

Fireworks.

He gathered my lower lip between his and gently sucked as his breath warmed my face. People were still tapping silverware on glasses and encouraging people to kiss. The room swam around me, and it seemed like everyone was kissing, in the beautifully-decorated banquet room, with soft music playing and the scent of flowers and fresh bread in the air. How could you not kiss in a room like that?

Dalton pulled away, quickly looking down, as if embarrassed.

I looked at his hand on my knee and found my own hand on top of his, squeezing his thick fingers. I loosened my grip, and at the same time, he flipped his hand to be palm up, holding my hand tenderly.

His voice husky, he leaned in toward me and said, "Thanks for letting me tag along with you today."

"Thanks for running into my bookstore. Why were you running, anyway?"

He winced. "Stupid reporters."

"Was it just the usual Hollywood stuff, or did you do something scandalous?"

"You mean like crash someone's wedding?"

"I guess you don't have to tell me." I squeezed his hand and reached over with my free hand to take a sip from my second glass of wine. "I am a woman, though. And we're curious. Why don't you just tell me what's happening, so I don't have to sneak off to the ladies' room and scan through the gossip sources on my phone?"

He looked away, gazing at the newlyweds while displaying a breathtaking profile. Strong jawline, thick dark hair. That chin dimple was probably insured for a million bucks. Ugh. Even his ears were the cutest things ever, with all his cartilage folds being a thousand times more handsome than the ears of regular folks.

Where was that evil photographer? Why was he not getting more evidence of my once-in-a-lifetime handsome actor date?

I took a deep breath and let out an audible sigh—audible by accident.

Dalton turned to me with an intense look, the kind I'd seen him do on TV about a thousand times, right before he delivers a bombshell of a line.

Those gorgeous lips of his began to move. "Let's just be two souls tonight. Two souls who are made of stardust, and found their way back to each other, the way they were destined to."

Gulp. "And?"

"Let's wait for our table number to be called, go stand in line for roast beef, and never let each other go." He squeezed my fingers.

The way he was looking at me. The effect he was having on my whole body, from all the parts of my curvy body to my actual freakin' heart. Two souls made of stardust? I didn't know whether to laugh or cry, so I reached for my wine and tossed it back.

Nodding, I said, "Tonight, we are two souls."

To my relief, our table was called next.

Dalton jumped up and threw his hands in the air. "Table Seven gets lucky!"

The non-English-speaking gentleman at our table gave him a high five.

I turned and looked for my mother at a nearby table, and she gave me an enthusiastic thumbs up. She had her suitcase-sized purse open and was showing Aunt Gracie some pages torn from a magazine. Was she redecorating again? This did not bode well for Dad's beloved recliner.

Dalton grabbed my hand, and we got in line for the buffet.

"This is just like crafty," he said. "Craft services. That's the on-set catering. Here's a tip, in case you're ever working on a production: make friends with whoever's in charge of craft services. They'll give you advance notice when they're putting out the jelly beans, so you can get to them before the grips."

"Grips?"

"Yes. They're the biggest guys on a production, and they ransack the table like Vikings."

I handed Dalton a plate and started filling mine with salad, keenly aware that all the women at the buffet were staring at Dalton and all the men were giving him the manly version of side-eye.

Well, of course they were staring. The man was magnificent, like a racehorse, and as he loaded up his plate, I fantasized about brushing his hair. His hair wasn't very long, but it was thick and slightly wavy. The last guy I'd dated had been a balding cop with a shaved head, and I used to have these strange dreams about him suddenly sprouting long, bushy hair. I'm ashamed of how shallow that makes me sound, but it is what it is, and *I like me some thick hair to grab onto.* To run my fingers through. To...

He was staring at me. Oh crap. He knew I was fantasizing about his hair. I gave him a big smile, even as I guiltily wondered what the curly bushes around his hot dog stand felt like.

"Those bread rolls look so good," he moaned. "Oh, they're killing me. Seriously, just... Peaches, could you get between me and those rolls before I do something I regret?"

He reached for the rolls in slow motion.

"You're allergic to bread?"

Eyes wide, he said, "Slap my hand away. Do it!"

I wasn't sure what was going on, and had the suspicion he was making fun of me, but I slapped his hand anyway.

He sighed and moved down the buffet table, seemingly more relieved as we left the piles of fresh rolls and butter packets behind.

"Low-carb is tough," he said.

"Tell me about it. That's why I was up on that stool today, putting tape over the vent. We share a cooling system with the other units in the building, and I swear the bakery shoves cupcakes right into the cold air return."

Dalton laughed. "That's what you were doing?"

I rolled my eyes. "No, I was just standing on a stool, hoping some drop-dead gorgeous hunk of a man would come in and catch me in his arms."

22

He stopped laughing and smiled. "Hunk of a man?"

"That's your last compliment of the evening. I shouldn't have even..." I shook my head.

We were at the end of the line, and he tugged my elbow, steering me over to a quiet corner, away from everyone but the waitstaff.

We were both holding our plates of steaming food, but he backed me into a corner, took my free hand, and placed it on his abdomen. I felt hard bumps under my fingertips.

I breathed out a sigh. "Is that real?"

He gazed down at me, shuffling forward so that his legs were mixed with mine, one of his gorgeous, probably-muscular-as-hell legs between my own soft, plump limbs. Our lower bodies touched as my hand slid up along his gray dress shirt, over the bumps and ridges of muscle. I could feel his deep, calm breaths.

MIMI STRONG

CHAPTER 3

"Your body's amazing," I said.

"So's yours. I'm having a difficult time restraining myself, because I want to touch you all over. I want to grab your legs and bite them."

My eyebrows shot up and my breath caught in my throat. "Bite them?"

He flashed his teeth and tapped them together. "Gently. Just love bites."

I kept moving my hand up, thinking that what I was feeling couldn't get any better, but then I reached his chest. He flexed under my hand, and he was hard there, too, and now I was having very bold thoughts about visiting his hot dog stand.

I whispered, "I want to bite you right here."

He whispered back, "I'd like that. You can nibble me anywhere, any time. I work out all those hours a week for a reason, you know."

My fingers ran over his nipples, hard as buttons. "For the camera."

"For nibbles."

Oh, nibbles. So many nibbles. Our lower bodies nudged closer together, and I could feel the heat of his leg between mine. A shiver shot up my body—a shiver unlike anything I'd felt in a very long time. Forget playful words. It was the kind of shiver that gets one in trouble.

I pulled back and ducked under his arm to get out of the corner, careful not to drop my plate of food.

"Mmm, this food smells good," I said to the distant relatives who were staring at us while pretending to not be staring.

25

Dalton detoured back into the buffet line and came away grinning, two fresh dinner rolls on his plate. "To hell with low-carbs. Tonight's about fun," he said.

~

My parents came by our table with Kyle after everyone finished dinner, saying they were heading home before the Little Monster got into the spiked punch.

Kyle was having way too much fun, chocolate icing all over his face, and asked for another shoulder-ride from Dalton.

Dalton complied, and within minutes, he was the Human Bouncy Castle of the reception, with everyone's kids and babies all over him. As I watched him entertain all the little tykes, I got that overexcited-ovaries-in-squealing-mode feeling you can only get from seeing a strong, handsome man being kind to icing-crusted children.

Calm down, I silently commanded my ovaries. *He's not ours for keeps; he's just on loan from his universe tonight, taking a little holiday in Normal Life World.*

I took my purse from the table and visited the washroom, figuring it was about time, based on how much liquid I'd consumed. When I'm in my control-top gear, my muffin-top smoothes out nicely, but it's difficult to tell when my bladder is full, versus merely squashed into my spleen.

When I came out of the stall, Marita was in the ample-sized ladies' room, reclining on a wicker settee in a puddle of bridal lace, fanning herself. Marita looked like a smaller version of my mother, with her round face and sturdy frame. She and I had the same neutral, light hair, but while I streaked and lightened mine to a sunny blond, she colored hers red, and the cherry hue suited her no-nonsense personality. Marita had been my favorite babysitter growing up, and she used to dress me up in her clothes until I turned fourteen and got bigger than her, from shoe to hat and everything in between.

She used to read me bedtime stories, and get annoyed when I pointed out that she'd missed a word. One night, she said that if I was so good at reading, I ought to read her book, to her, instead of the other way around. And thus began my introduction to mushy romance novels, and a lifelong love of reading. She wouldn't let me see the folded-over pages until I was twelve. Like I said, she was the greatest babysitter, right?

"I should be doing that," I said, taking the fan from her hand. "I haven't been much of a bridesmaid to you."

"You have good reason," Marita said, pushing her red hair off her sweaty brow. "Your date is gorgeous! One of my friends asked to get the name of the big city escort agency you used."

My jaw dropped and my face-fanning faltered.

"Oh, Petra Monroe, it's a joke!" she said. "Nobody actually thinks he's a prostitute."

I glanced over my shoulder at the mirror, which was the worst thing I could have done, because the way I was leaned forward and the way the bridesmaid dress pulled across my hips, my butt looked exactly like a big, juicy peach.

"He's just a friend," I said.

"Is that code for gay? He'll make somebody a great catch. And he's so great with the kids."

"He's clearly not gay. In fact, he's been hitting on me." I shrugged. "We might end up as more than friends, perhaps."

"Really? Are you going to sleep with him?" Her grin got wide and salacious. "Tonight? Every guy dreams about bagging a bridesmaid."

My mouth opened, but then I remembered. *Eyes wide open!*

No, I couldn't pour my heart out to Marita about the thoughts I'd been having about nibbling Dalton's carbohydrate-free body. She had a big mouth, and she'd tell everyone, and soon I'd be the cousin who was having a hand-in-panties job from a gay escort.

"He's just a friend." I eyed her stomach. "How's the second trimester treating you?"

She glanced from side to side, her face turning red. "I don't know what you mean." She batted her blond eyelashes and smoothed down the waistline of her white gown. "I've been stress-eating."

"Marita, you told me last month."

She looked even more embarrassed, her eyes down. "I'm so sorry, I forgot about that. You've been nothing but supportive. I don't like lying, but James wanted to wait for the announcement until after the wedding, so his parents wouldn't be embarrassed today."

I knelt down next to her and held her hand as tears welled up in her eyes.

"Secrets are tough," I said. "Everything will be worth it in the end. You're doing the best you can, and everyone supports your decision, including me."

Her voice thick, she squeezed my hand and said, "Auxiliary bridesmaid duties accomplished. Thank you for being here with me."

"Anything for my favorite babysitter."

"Don't say that! You make me feel old, now that you're so grown up."

The door to the washroom opened, and a pile of peach-colored fabric piled in with three bridesmaids.

I gave Marita a hug. "Here's the rest of your entourage. Now kick off your shoes and dance the night away."

The other girls took over, and I excused myself to go back to my date. Marita's friends were all friendly enough, and they made me feel welcome in the group, but the band had started and I wanted to dance.

I headed for the clump of kids and found Dalton at the center. He shook off the last ankle-hugger and accompanied me to the dance floor.

He put his arms around me, and every light around us sparkled.

I guess I shouldn't have been amazed that he was an incredible dancer.

When the song changed to a waltz, he put his hand on the perfect spot on my waist, and I dare say he was a better lead than the dance instructor I'd crushed on a few years earlier.

He gazed at me, and I lifted my chin with pride as I stared into those gorgeous green eyes. The man had a perfect face, with no flaws. Even his nostrils were perfectly symmetrical.

"Is there something in my nose?" he asked.

"Sorry, I was staring. For the record, your nostrils are clear, and there's nothing in your teeth. Your lips look perfectly moisturized, and except for a streak of icing in your hair, you're camera ready."

"Icing in my hair? I blame your little brother."

I laughed, a little too loud, my chest squeezing.

He murmured, "You're a beautiful dancer. Notice how we move together as one? That doesn't happen by accident. I'm telling you, the stardust we came from has been reunited before, perhaps in previous lives."

"I took a few dance lessons. My roommate, Shayla, is always signing me up for things."

The song ended, and people were talking to the DJ, so there was a gap with no music at all. The lights dimmed down even more, and Dalton started to sway to his own music.

He grabbed me around the waist with both hands, pulled me to him, and leaned down to kiss me again.

I flushed at the naughtiness, embarrassed to be having what felt like sex, right on the dance floor in front of people.

Another song started, and people started to dance around us. Locked in his embrace, we only swayed in one spot as we kissed, and everyone moved around us like water past two stones in a creek.

The kiss traveled down from my lips, looping around my whole body, until I was glowing, alight from within.

I thought about stones in a creek, then I thought about stardust, then I thought about absolutely nothing.

~

Three things I dread:

1. Customers trying to return books because they didn't like the ending.

2. A long-overdue root canal on my lower-right premolar.

3. The last song of the evening, when everything's going so well, and you don't want the spell to break.

We've already visited the topic of me not being the fun, adventurous type. But have I mentioned how stupid I am? This girl. Petra "Peaches" Monroe.

I'm stupid in the way that only a girl with a Mensa-level IQ can be. Ask me to calculate the volume of a three-foot-tall barrel with a one-foot radius, and I'll tell you. Those questions about two trains traveling at different speeds? Love 'em. They're like Sudoku to me. I can spell *anything*, and I do the crossword in pen.

Yet when it comes to guys and dating, I'm a Capital-D Dum-dum.

29

Even though Dalton Deangelo was holding me tenderly as the last song of my cousin's wedding played, and even though he kept sneaking kisses, I didn't think he was actually interested in me. My best guess was that he was researching a role.

When he leaned down to whisper in my ear, the shadow of his end-of-day beard rasping lightly against my cheek, I stopped breathing in shock.

"What?" I hadn't understood a word he'd said.

He murmured, "Do you want to take me home?"

His words tickled in my ear and sent a tingling message straight to somewhere—and I don't mean my pancreas.

"Wow, you really go all-out when you're researching a role."

He pulled me closer, with a firm hand on my back, and led me into a turn on the mostly-empty dance floor. "You're cute, Peaches. I hope your cousin isn't mad at you for stealing focus."

"You're drunk, Mr. Dalton Deangelo."

He responded by stopping still in the middle of the dance floor and putting his hands on either side of my mouth. Squishing my lips with his hands on my cheeks, he moved my mouth in time as he said in falsetto, "Yes, you're quite drunk, Mr. Deangelo. You'd better come home with me."

I swatted his hands away. He laughed and caught me in an embrace, tighter than when we were dancing. I could feel the bumpy parts of his chest and abs right through our clothes. Whenever Shayla and I saw a hot shirtless guy, we'd giggle and say, "Ew, he's so bumpy!" Now that I was pressed up against a wall of these bumps, there was absolutely nothing funny about it.

"Yes, come home with me," I said. My heart was going pitter-patter, and I knew I was being stupid, but it felt different this time, because I knew I was being stupid and I didn't care. Maybe it was all those hours I'd watched him on TV, but I felt like I could trust Dalton. He said I was cute. I believed him.

He led me off the dance floor, I grabbed my purse, and we ducked outside to his fancy car. The driver was napping, but snapped to attention after Dalton tapped on the window.

We got in the back seat and I gave the driver my address on Lurch Street. He didn't seem to believe me that was the actual street name, but I gave him directions and assured him I knew where I lived.

Dalton waited until the privacy glass was up, then said, "If you change your mind before we get to your place, just say the word. I'll drop you off and leave you be."

"Are you playing hard to get?"

He grinned, deepening the sexy million-dollar dimple in the middle of his chin. "Is it working?"

Oh, that chin. I wanted to smack it with the back of a spoon and eat it like *crème brulee*.

"I'm glad you ran into my bookstore."

He moved into the center of the bench seat, reached over, and roughly slid me next to him. "I've had a tough week, but things are starting to look up."

He placed one hand on my thigh and caressed the outer edge of my leg as he kissed my neck.

He continued, "The press is out to make their dollar, and they don't care who gets hurt. Some people are willing to do anything to make it, except work hard."

Cautiously, I moved one of my hands up along his leg and then along his torso. His lips on my neck made my body melt, and moving my hand required conscious effort.

"You seem like a hard worker," I said.

He burst out laughing at that, grabbing my hand and holding it tight to his muscular chest. "Oh, I'm a hard worker, all right."

The heat of my face made me glad for the dim lighting in the back of the car, as I was surely tomato-red from embarrassment.

"Don't tell me that being a famous actor is already tiresome for you. What are you, twenty-eight?"

"Officially? Twenty-four."

"What does it say on your birth certificate?"

"Someone else's name." He stretched one arm behind my back and stroked my hair. "That's a secret, by the way."

"Are we telling secrets now?"

"Either that or kissing. Your choice."

31

I shook at the thought of divulging my secrets.

"Kissing."

His gaze went to my lips and he leaned forward slowly.

He murmured, his voice low and barely audible, "I'm going to give you a dramatic on-screen kiss."

I giggled in response, which normally would have made me cringe at my stupidity, but the way he was looking at me was so serious and sexy. I felt like my body was under water, with pleasant pressure pushing me together in all directions, but that at any moment, I might fly apart like so much stardust.

Dalton's expression got ultra-serious, and just like that, he turned into Drake Cheshire, the cultured vampire with a taste for big-lipped girls under one hundred pounds. He stared intensely at my eyes, my lips, my cleavage, my throat, my lips, and then up to my eyes again. I melted like a pat of butter on summer pavement.

He moved in closer, so our noses were an inch apart, and he repeated the intense look. Eyes. His, green like precious emeralds. Lips. Mine, slightly parted and trembling. Throat. Feeling very exposed. Cleavage. Mine, heaving, probably, guessing by the way I couldn't quite catch my breath.

His gaze slid back dreamily to my lips, and he tilted his head to the side, not yet touching his mouth to mine.

We held steady, the only movements our breathing and minor swaying with the motion of the vehicle. I could feel the heat from his skin against my lips. He tipped his head back and looked me in the eyes again.

Oh, the slow torture.

His hand moved from the outside of my thigh to the inside, to the hot crease where my thighs were touching. I gasped. No nylons. Bare flesh. His hand was only at the hem line of my bridesmaid dress, but the way he was looking at me, it felt much more intimate. He took one of my legs firmly in both hands and pushed it to bring space between my legs, and then his hand traveled up further.

He breathed against my lips and blinked slowly as his hand moved in, up under the peach-hued tulle skirt of my dress. His fingertips grazed the silky material of my underwear.

I arched my back as the sensation of his touch blazed through me. A tiny sigh escaped my parted lips.

He pulled his face back from mine and nodded up, as though beckoning me toward him.

With his fingers now gently pressing against my pulse point through my underwear, I found myself unable to move. I raised my eyebrows, calling him to me with my eyes.

The corner of his beautiful mouth twitched up in a grin. A pulse of adrenaline shot through me. That was the face Drake made before his fangs popped out and he bit a girl! I gasped again.

He moved quickly, and his mouth was on my neck, at my throbbing jugular vein.

I squealed in a mix of terror and delight as he pretended to bite me.

He let out a throaty growl, while at the same time he did something magical with his fingers between my legs. As he licked and kissed my neck, gently biting me, he kept exploring the elasticity of my underwear, until he had the silky material pushed aside and we were skin on skin, his fingertips on my freshly-waxed cushions of flesh.

I relaxed against the leather seat, my head back on the head rest, trying not to die from pleasure. Panties pushed aside, his strong fingertips gently stroked me. I moaned and whimpered for him to be less gentle, and he delivered a more vigorous massage. *Oh, hell yes. Just like that.*

My breathing sped up, my pulse pounding as he brought me to the precipice of coming, and then eased off, pulling his hand back to rest between my thighs.

He nibbled on my earlobe, then murmured, "Let's get naked."

"Sure," I breathed as I set to work locating the buttons of his shirt. I wanted to just rip the shirt off, but it probably cost more than my rent, so I fumbled for buttons like a good girl.

MIMI STRONG

CHAPTER 4

I'd gotten two buttons undone, which was a miracle considering the dimness of the light and the trembling of my hands, when Dalton said, "Maybe we shouldn't get naked in the car, though."

"Oh." I turned to look out the tinted window. There was my front porch, and my potted geraniums—red ones, in terra cotta pots, of course. The car wasn't moving. How long had we been parked there?

"Are you going to invite me in?"

I let out an embarrassing waterfall of giggles before I could dam up my mouth with both hands.

He gave me side-eye. "What?"

I whispered, "You asked me to invite you in. Just like Drake Cheshire does on the show."

He looked down at our laps, then back up at me with the most innocent expression, his green eyes almost sad. "Let's just be regular people tonight."

"Regular people. Sure." Now I felt bad for making him feel weird. But I was still turned on, pulsing with anticipation for nakedness, so apparently I didn't feel that bad!

I reached for the door handle, pushed it open to the cool night air, and climbed out of the car as gracefully as I could manage.

It was past midnight, but a few people were still out in the neighborhood, walking their dogs, and my cheeks flushed with embarrassment as people stared our way. Of course they were just looking at the unusual car, but the paranoid part of me was certain they'd seen in through the tinted glass and knew exactly what was going on. Someone had just had his hand in my cookie jar, and I LIKED IT A GREAT DEAL, THANK YOU.

Dalton stepped out behind me, looking left and right as he did. Something at the edge of my vision moved, and my senses buzzed that someone was watching us surreptitiously.

"Home sweet home," I said, gesturing to the old house with my chin. "It's not much to look at, but it's cheap."

When Shayla and I had moved into the old Craftsman-style home, we'd cooed over its generous porch and lovely wood columns. The house wore a dilapidated coat of peeling mint green paint, with darker, forest green trim. We'd had big plans to give the place a good scraping and re-paint it if the landlord covered the cost of materials, but we didn't get further than a fresh coat of glossy, mustard yellow paint on the front door and one horrible hour of scraping a section at the back of the house. Painting something as big as a house seems like so much fun when you see it in a movie montage, but the reality is, there's a reason even lovely old homes have peeling paint. That maintenance stuff is hard work.

"Cute house," he said.

"It's cheap."

"I'm sure it is, but it's still cute. Take a compliment, will you?"

Nodding, I fumbled around for my keys in my purse.

Dalton darted at me quickly and caught me in his arms, whispering, "There's a photographer behind that tree."

I whispered back, "What should I do?"

"Are those your geraniums?"

"Yes."

"How do you water them? Is there a hose at the front of the house?"

Still whispering, I said, "Yes. It's coiled up right behind that hedge."

"You go turn on the water, and pretend we're just admiring the garden."

I nodded my agreement to his plan, and stepped over the decorative edging along the sidewalk and onto the lawn. The in-ground sprinklers had run an hour earlier, and the wet grass tickled the sides of my feet through my sandals. With the street lamps, I had no trouble seeing where I was going.

At a regular talking volume, I said, "And this is the front lawn. We don't use any herbicides, so I'm out here on my hands and knees pulling weeds a lot."

I saw movement along the sides the tree. An elbow, and then a shadowy head and a camera. I expected to hear clicking sounds, but I guess paparazzi with digital cameras turn off the click function to be sneaky.

I bent down to turn on the water, feeling indignant that someone was taking my photo without my permission. The wedding photographer had been annoying, but this was way beyond that. I turned the metal spout, smiling as cold water surged into the hose.

Dalton already had the business end of the hose in hand, clutching the sprayer like a pistol, and he crept closer to the big tree.

"Good evening," he said to a man walking by with two sleek-bodied whippets.

"Gardening by moonlight?" the man asked as the dogs stopped for a head pat.

Dalton laughed with ease and said, "I work long days."

And then, if you can believe it, the two of them started having an actual conversation about gardening and whippets.

Meanwhile, I stood in the wet grass of my lawn feeling like I might implode. My heart was pounding, and I felt so mixed up with emotions after the events of the day, like I was a glass of water being overfilled, everything pouring over my sides. I didn't know what was going to happen next, but I wanted it to happen. Now.

The man with the sleek dogs waved goodbye and walked away. Dalton looked over at me on the front lawn, his eyes glinting in the light of the nearby street lamp. He held up the sprayer.

I gave him a nod. The water was on. *Do it.*

He fired one small shot of water at the hedge to test, then ran around to the other side of the tree, the water on full blast.

The person on the other side of the tree let out a high-pitched shriek and a series of swear words. Extraordinarily bad swear words.

Now, I'm not a big follower of celebrity gossip, but I do know most paparazzi are men. What jumped out from behind the tree,. as mad and wet as a Persian cat in a bath tub, was a woman. She looked twenty-something, with brown hair in a short pixie cut, pretty and obnoxiously tiny, like a tea cup full of buttons.

Perhaps the worst part, besides realizing I was in fact standing in the mud of the flower bed, squashing the violas, was that Dalton seemed to know this petite spy.

He stopped blasting the water and yelled, "Alexis! What the hell? Why are you following me?"

She sputtered and wiped at her face dramatically, her gaze on the sprayer in his hand.

"Don't you dare spray me again," she said.

"Or what?"

As she opened her mouth to answer, he fired off a blast of water at her midsection.

Lights flicked on in my neighbors' houses, and shadowy forms moved in windows. Mr. Galloway was probably getting a good look at this girl Alexis's lacy bra, on perfect display in her transparent, soaked shirt. Her perky bosom heaved fetchingly, and Dalton stared at her the way a lead actor does right before he passionately kisses his love interest. I kicked off my sandals and rubbed my muddy foot off in the wet grass. Was I standing in a pile of logs deposited by Mr. Galloway's cat? *Wow, when things go downhill in my life, they really pick up speed.*

Alexis swore some more, then yelled at Dalton, "You're such a child! You're a spoiled rotten baby and you don't care who gets hurt because you'll just move on to the next one, and women are in unlimited supply, aren't we? You've got your new girl here, and you probably fed her your stupid lines, didn't you?"

"Alexis! Calm down and stop acting crazy. Are you following me? Is this what you do now? You hide in bushes and take photos of people?"

Growling with sarcasm, she said, "No, I have an amazing career. Six seasons and a movie. I'm a big deal, and I just sell celebrity photos just for giggles." She raised her camera at him and said, "Huh, it still works." A red light blinked.

Dalton stepped toward her, one hand outstretched. "No. Give me that. I'm deleting these photos. You have no right."

She backed away, still taking pictures. "Work it, D-man. Gimme that Drake snarl. Oh yeah, action shot."

"Talk to me, Alexis. Do you need money? I could help you, as a friend, but you're not being very friendly."

She kept moving away from him, then abruptly changed direction and jumped over the low hedge along the front yard, running straight toward me.

I reacted the same way I would if a skunk or saber tooth tiger was running at me. I shrieked and held very still, hoping she'd lose interest.

She grabbed my forearm, her fingers cold and terrifying. "You don't know what you're getting yourself into," she snarled.

"Let go of me before I punch you some new freckles!"

She blinked, speechless. She'd probably never had anyone threaten to punch her some new freckles. In fact, it may have been the first time in human history that phrase had been uttered.

"Who are you?" she asked, her big eyes open wide.

"Just a girl named Peaches."

"You have great skin."

"Why, thank you—"

Our conversation was interrupted by a man tackling Alexis and throwing her to the ground. The man had his long hair tied back in a ponytail. The driver. Was he also a bodyguard?

Dalton came to my side, putting one arm across my shoulders.

"You're a bit late for heroics," I said as we watched the two of them tussle on the grass before us.

The driver pulled away from Alexis, camera in hand. Even though nobody was touching the girl, she continued to scream bloody blue murder with cheese on top. Now all my curious neighbors were out on their porches.

Mr. Galloway, the edges of his robe not quite covering his boxer shorts on account of how tall the senior citizen is, leaned over his railing and called down, "Peaches Monroe? Shall I call the police?"

I waved. "No, thanks! We're good here, I think."

He stayed at the railing, motionless. "Is that a bridesmaid dress you're wearing, or did someone invite you to prom?"

"Very funny. It's a bridesmaid dress. My cousin Marita got married today."

"Oh, really? Was it a big wedding?"

"Um…" (You know, some people in the city complain they don't know their neighbors. I really can't say the same. My neighbors were born to be neighborly—to spend nine out of ten Sundays digging around in the front yard for little reason other than to be available for chats. If Shayla and I go out in her Rav and don't luck into a parking spot directly in front of the house, we have to factor in an extra twenty minutes to say hello to everyone on our way to and from doing errands.) I answered Mr. Galloway, "Not too big. Maybe two hundred people."

He nodded. "Good weather for it."

The petite, muddy woman before us reached her hand up to get some help up, then yanked the driver's arm and pulled him to the ground again. Throughout all this, Dalton was dumbstruck, just watching. She was reaching for the hem of my dress just as the driver brought her under control, both of them grunting near my feet.

I felt conflicted, because this woman Alexis was the aggressor, but seeing her get held down by a man struck something in me. A deep, girl-power something. I grabbed the driver and tossed him into a hedge.

Everyone got really quiet, including Mr. Galloway on his porch.

Dalton helped extricate his driver from the hedge, Alexis got quietly to her feet, and everyone turned to stare at me.

"You are one bad ass girl," Dalton said.

"Thanks." I attempted to smooth down my hair and look demure.

The door of my house opened and my roommate and best friend, Shayla, burst out in a sleeveless T-shirt and boxer shorts. "What the hell are you all doing on my lawn?" She spotted me and her expression became more confused. "Peaches! You look so good in that dress. I don't know what those other girls were complaining about."

Cold water blasted me. I yelped and started running for cover. Everyone was yelling and colliding with me, and I basically ran blindly in a circle until somebody tackled me. We fell to the ground, and the hose-blasting stopped.

Wiping the water from my eyes, I said, "That was refreshing."

The sound of shoes slapping against the pavement echoed through the night air as Alexis made her getaway down the street.

I couldn't get up from the muddy lawn, pinned as I was by a body. At least it wasn't the driver with the ponytail, but Dalton.

I'd wanted to get him on top of me, but not like this. Not in the mud on my front lawn. Or maybe in the mud, sure, but not with all my neighbors watching.

Dalton got up and helped me to my feet. "I am so sorry about all of this. That Alexis!" He shook his head, and in the dim light, I couldn't tell if he looked guilty, or embarrassed.

Shayla stepped down from the porch and stood on the round, cement paving stones, staring at us. Unlike the older generation at the wedding, she knew exactly who Dalton Deangelo was.

I looked up at his gorgeous face. So much for sneaking him into my place, unnoticed, for the one-night tryst of a lifetime—the type you hint about to your children after a couple of drinks, much to their horror.

"I apologize for all this," he said.

"This kerfuffle?" I looked down at my muddy bridesmaid dress. "So much for wearing this dress again."

"I'll pay to have it cleaned. No, I'll buy you a new dress. Unfortunately, if you hang out with me, this is the sort of thing that happens."

"Your life must be very interesting," I said.

He pursed his lips, his eyes twinkling at me. "Let's trade lives. Give me the keys and I'll go open the bookstore tomorrow."

As I stared up at Dalton, the rest of the world disappeared. I was dimly aware of Mr. Galloway calling his cat and going back into his house, and of the driver apologizing to Shayla and explaining what was happening, but all that chaos was happening outside of a world-dampening bubble surrounding the two of us.

"You would muck everything up," I said. "In the bookstore. I have everything just how I like it."

He brushed his warm hands along my upper arms, sweeping away the beads of water on my skin. I shivered at his touch.

"Is that a metaphor?" he murmured. "Are you afraid I'm going to muck up your life?" He kept running his warm hands up and down my arms, heating me up in more ways than one. Apparently getting sprayed with a garden hose doesn't put you out of the mood for sex, which explains why it rarely works with stray cats.

He continued, "Is your life too perfect without me?"

"Thank you for being my date for the wedding, and for the ride in your car." I bit my lower lip, embarrassed at the memory of him touching me so deliciously in the back seat, just moments earlier.

"You say that like we're saying goodbye." He reached behind my back, pressing the chilly, soaked fabric of my bridesmaid dress as he pulled me to him. "If this is goodbye, give me a kiss to remember."

He didn't have to ask twice. I stood up on my tiptoes in the wet grass, mud on my feet, and kissed him with all the pent-up passion I had in me, from all the guys I should have kissed but didn't. I should have kissed tall, scrawny Adrian Storm in twelfth grade, when we were working on the yearbook together. He owned an obnoxiously loud, gas-guzzling muscle car, and we had the exact opposite taste in movies and music. We seemed to have nothing in common, but he did have a lip ring, and I had an interest in his lips.

Back then, Adrian's lip ring clicked against his teeth sometimes, and he'd flick at the metal hoop with his tongue when he was waiting for the slow computers in the library to load up photos. We had little to talk about, and he always looked bored when he talked to me, but I wanted to kiss him. I wanted to kiss him so bad, and I never did, because I wasn't the fun girl.

That night after my cousin's wedding, as I stood in the mud of my front lawn, with a sexy actor, I kissed him with all the passion my lips could handle, and then some. My hands slid up along his chest, feeling the hard muscles just beneath his shirt.

He broke away just long enough to say, "This doesn't feel like goodbye."

My hands roved down, over the ridges of his lean stomach, then around to his back so I could hold on to him for balance.

"I can't invite you in," I said. "That's my house, and my life, and —"

He stopped me with a finger to my lips, while saying, "Shh."

Was he actually shushing me?

CHAPTER 5

Dalton Deangelo seemed to be shushing me. Which I do not like, not even from someone with a face so handsome you want to crush it up and eat it.

I continued, around his fingers mashing my lips, "But thanks for the nice evening and the r—"

"Shush."

I shoved his hand away and stepped back. "Don't shush me. You're not the boss of me. Feel free to interrupt me, like a regular person, but don't you dare put your hand on my mouth."

Dalton grinned like a kid being caught with his hand up a vending machine, his fingers wrapped around a stolen chocolate bar.

"Whoops," he said.

"Uh, whoops?"

The moment of romance was gone, and my passion morphed into something else—something defensive. His arms around me no longer felt like heaven, but like a mousetrap. I shoved against his chest and wriggled myself free.

"I'm sorry you're offended," he said.

"I'm sorry you think shushing a woman is appealing in some way."

"You're cute when you're mad."

"You're not," I lied.

He stepped back, taking an audible breath. "It was nice to know you."

And then began the speedy getaway I'd been anticipating all day.

He backed away over the hedge and onto the sidewalk. The driver was already circling around to open the car door for him. I could sense Shayla's presence on the porch behind me, but she was staying quiet for now.

Something about the way Dalton was grinning and backing away from me set me off even more. He was treating me the same way he had that girl Alexis, who probably had good reason to be angry at him. *What a smarmy creepazoid!*

"Good to know you," he repeated awkwardly.

My head started to move from side to side with all the attitude that had to go somewhere. "Oh, you don't know me," I said.

Shayla chimed in, "That's right. You don't know her."

He glanced up at her and shrugged. "Your loss."

Shayla murmured behind me, "Oh, no, he didn't." Louder, she called out to him, "More like your loss."

"Yeah!" I added. "Your loss, mister. I would have rocked your world."

Dalton shot me one last smirk, then he climbed into the back of his fancy car with the tinted windows and shut the door.

Getaway complete.

As the red taillights disappeared down the street, Shayla traipsed down the front steps and slipped her arm around my back. "Let's get you out of these wet clothes and into a shot of tequila. Or wine. We don't have tequila, but we do have wine."

"Oh, Shay. What did I just do? What's wrong with me?"

"You have too much pride," she said, matter-of-factly. "You could have had your world rocked by Mr. Smoldering Eyeballs himself, but I can loan you Drake for the night if you run him through the dishwasher."

I patted her hand. "No thanks, but I appreciate the sentiment."

"He was taller than I expected. A lot of actors are quite short, you know."

I followed her into the house and back to the kitchen, where she found the big bottle of red we'd started the night before. We'd planned to make sangria, and bought the cheapest red in the store, but then we decided it was okay on its own, and nobody needs extra fruit juice calories in their drink.

We raised our glasses in a toast, standing by the fridge.

"You're perfect," Shayla said. "Guys like him think you'll be so impressed he's even talking to you, that you won't say feathers if you have a mouth full of them. But you sure showed him."

I swirled the wine and started drinking as Shayla unzipped the back of my dress and peeled the damp fabric away. I felt warmer already in just my underwear plus the wobble-taming waist shaper. I took a seat at the walnut pedestal table in the kitchen.

She'd heard a few details from the driver, and I filled her in on the rest, from our odd bookstore meeting to him accompanying me to the wedding.

Giggling, I said, "And tonight, I was going to sleep with him. Dalton Deangelo. With his penis right up in my vagina and everything."

"And you would have rocked his world. You would have spoiled him for all other women."

I finished the red wine and got my glass refilled.

"Who are we kidding? I would have turned out all the lights, then lay there with my bra still on, holding absolutely still to reduce jiggling, and faked an orgasm so it could be over."

Shayla giggled into her glass. "And you would have been so good, so convincing." She rolled her eyes up, fluttering her eyelashes. "Oh, Dalton, you're an animal! I don't know if I'll be able to walk tomorrow!"

"Gross!"

We laughed for a bit, and when the giggles died down, she said, "Too bad you didn't saddle that one up. Would have made for great stories. He's bumpy all up and down his front. They don't make 'em like that around here in Beaverdale."

"No, they do not." The wine was warming me up, and I thought about getting a robe or something to throw on over my underwear and Spanx, but my room was up the stairs, which was too far. "You know, I forgot to ask him why he was even in town."

Why had Dalton Deangelo been in little Beaverdale, Washington, population 14,041?

I guess I haven't told you much about Beaverdale, also known as The Beav or B-dale to locals. The town was incorporated in 1898, and the main street was named after the father of the town, Mr. Leonodis Veiner. In 1942, the street was accidentally renamed Leonardo Street when City Hall contracted out the new street signs to a sign maker up in Seattle. A copper-haired city clerk by the name of Donovan Monroe (my great-grandfather), rushed his paperwork that day so he could get to the pub and await the news of his first child's birth, surrounded by his friends. The pub was on the opposite side of town as the hospital, and the bartender kept the telephone line clear for the news, because that was how they did things in those days.

My grandfather, Arthur Monroe, came into the world at three in the morning on January 7, 1942, and the pub never closed that night. My great-grandfather did, however, disappear for a few hours that evening to find some trouble. The kind of trouble who hangs a red light in her window.

Nine months later, my grandfather's yet-to-be-named half-sister was born at the town's only bawdy house.

On the very same day, the sign installers got their packages and did their installation, renaming the following streets:

Leonodis Veiner Street became Leonardo Street

Orchid Drive became O Drive

Euripides Avenue became Spider Avenue

and

Larch Street became Lurch Street

People in town were cross at my great-grandfather for celebrating the birth of his first child by siring an illegitimate child with one of the town's loose women, but they were generally happy about the renamed streets, save the good people who now lived on Lurch Street.

The little brown-haired baby was left at my great-grandmother's door step. According to family stories, my great-grandmother Petra Monroe (yes, I was named after her) opened the door, took one look at the squalling infant in a basket, and shut the door again. It was October now, gray and rainy, and she shut the door.

She crossed the house to the back pantry, poured a mug full of dandelion wine, and quaffed it back in one swallow. She was unbuttoning her blouse already when she opened the door again, and a moment later she held the baby to her bare breast, heavy with milk for the baby boy asleep in the crib upstairs. The girl baby latched on even easier than the firstborn, and my grandmother cooed at her, "You're a clever baby." Their eyes met and they fell in love at first sight.

The baby was named Clever Monroe, and she grew up sharing the same classrooms and toys as my grandfather, Arthur Monroe. They were joined in 1952 by plump-cheeked Beatrice, who enjoyed being the baby of the family until 1962, when my great-grandmother gave birth to Icy, twenty years to the day after her first child, Arthur. My great-grandfather waited in the hospital for news of that delivery, because that was how things were done in Beaverdale in 1962.

They smoked five cigars, two packs of cigarettes, and one "marijuana cigarette" between him and his friends. My great-grandfather had the night of his life, and woke up in a clean hospital bed next to my great-grandmother, an ice pack between his legs from the vasectomy he didn't remember agreeing to.

~

The next morning, I did that thing where you wake up and you*know* you're awake, but you're afraid to open your eyes or do any movement beyond breathing because you're not sure exactly *how*hungover you ought to be.

Given my fuzzy recollection of the previous evening, moving my head was not advisable. Something smooth and hard was pressed under my cheek.

Dalton Deangelo? And his chiseled chest?

No.

By the feel of it, the hard thing was just my non-sexy, non-smooth-talking, un-kissable laptop. I cracked open one gummy eyelid to see a dresser, blue and yellow with a distressed paint finish, piled with books. At least I was in my bedroom and not under the garbage truck that ran me over and dropped a load in my mouth.

I rolled back and peeled myself off my computer, surprised to feel only mild nausea.

What had I gotten into the night before? The last time I really drank with Shayla, we'd had tequila shots with two of the Australians working at her restaurant. The Aussies were an engaged couple who (I thought) looked like brother and sister, both six feet tall with shaggy, shoulder-length, honey-hued hair. I started calling them The Beautifuls after the first drink, and it stuck.

Shayla's post-shift unwinding turned into a full-on party at our shared rental house, and while people set up a limbo challenge using a broomstick, and a frisbee challenge using our plastic camping plates, I retreated upstairs to my bedroom and partied down extra-hard on my laptop. That was the night I purchased an authentic German cuckoo clock via an online auction.

Since I already had a cuckoo clock, still tucked away in its shipping box and nestled in my Closet of Regret, I wondered what new thing had caught my drunken fancy the night before.

I opened my email to find a dozen confirmation messages.

Apparently, I'd joined the Dalton Deangelo fan club. An adrenaline blast of horror shot through me, making my brain throw up inside my head.

I closed the laptop to keep the awful truth quiet, and begged my fluttering heart to chill out. Dalton was a huge star, and he probably hired high-priced people to hire medium-priced people to deal with fan clubs. He was too busy running into bookstores and flirting with...

The thought of him kissing another girl sent a fireball of jealousy to my stomach. If only he hadn't shushed me with his too-perfect finger, then his bumpy chest would be snuggled into the sheets next to me.

I know some people brag about living their life without regrets. How ridiculous. We all have regrets. Some of us just deny them better than others. I keep mine in the Closet of Regret, along with the afore-mentioned cuckoo clock, a fresh fruit juicer, and a pair of pink roller skates.

Shayla opened my bedroom door and meandered in, eyes half-lidded.

"Timber," she said before falling onto the bed next to me.

"Can you be heartbroken over someone you just met? Is that even valid?"

Face-down, she muttered into my blankets, "I'll buy you a hug. Get ready." She threw one heavy arm over my body.

I groaned and patted her head, enjoying the feel of her silky, black hair. Since she turned fifteen, she's been using a shampoo for show horses. Apparently, it gives horses and humans a glossy mane and tail, and though the product never did anything for me, Shayla could be its spokesperson.

Actually, she could be the spokesperson for anything. She's absolute gorgeousness, from the nail beds of her always-pedicured toes to her full, naturally-ruby-hued lips and her golden eyes. Her skin is like chocolate milk next to mine, and her smile is dazzling, which distracts people from her secret shame, which is her unusually large feet. She claims to wear a size ten shoe, but if you catch hold of one of her new pairs, before she's filed away or peeled off the size, you'll find the number eleven.

"Shayla, I dreamed about your grandmother, Clever. She was dancing in her ruffled skirt, doing those high kicks."

She chuckled and gave me a back pat. My father and her mother are cousins, which makes us some type of cousins, though she came from the fun side of the family. She insists I got lucky on the brains side, but she's as smart as anyone I know.

"Hit the shower and I'll get the coffee on," she said. "That workshop starts in one hour and Dottie gets pissed if people come late."

What workshop? I was about to suggest that Shayla was dreaming and talking in her sleep, but I remembered glimpsing a confirmation email about a workshop.

"Noooooooooo," I cried.

Shayla rolled to her side and opened one golden eye, looking like a smug dragon. "You're more fun after a glass or two of red, and I'm rather charming, if I do say so myself."

"So, we're going to a workshop in one hour? Rolling sushi?" My mouth watered at the idea of cool cucumber slices.

Shayla laughed. Her voice flat with irony, she said, "Yeah. Rolling sushi."

"I want sushi."

"There's no sushi. We're going to learn how to be captivating, and have men wrapped around our fingers."

"I'd rather have sushi."

"Sushi doesn't give hand jobs in the back of fancy cars while a chauffeur drives you around."

I cleared my throat and pulled myself up to sit. "I guess I didn't hold back any details last night, did I? Oh, the pain of the bare-assed truth in the morning light."

She patted my knee. "Don't be so dramatic. You met a hot actor, and he turned out to be a twatwaffle, and now you'll go to this workshop and move on with your life."

"Some life."

We both glanced around my room, at the stacks of books on my dresser and on the floor.

"Peaches, are there any books left in the actual bookstore?" she teased.

"What did I pay for this non-sushi workshop?"

"It's non-refundable." She jumped up from my bed and started browsing through a stack of books. "This looks good." She flipped to the end to read the last page, as she always does. It makes me want to tackle her to the ground when she peeks at the ending, and I swear she does it half the time just to antagonize me.

I rolled out of bed and took myself to the bathroom for a hot shower and a big glass of water.

As agonizing as the workshop sounded, it was something to do, to keep my mind off Dalton Deangelo. As I washed my hair, I thought about his bumpy abdominal muscles, and how some other girl would be enjoying them. Maybe he was showering with her right now! Euch, what a pig.

I sincerely hoped that the dinner rolls he ate the night before were converting to fat at that very moment, because I'm mean like that.

~

The workshop was at the Beaverdale Community Center, and we took Shayla's little Rav. Thanks to coffee and toast, I was feeling human.

We parked the Rav in front of Black Sheep Books, and we both hissed like angry cats at the window display of our enemy as we walked by.

"They have dead flies in their front window," Shayla said.

"Figures." I narrowed my eyes at the red-painted bricks. Just as Superman has his Lex Luthor, Peachtree Books has Black Sheep Books. I have, on occasion, threatened to burn them to the ground, but they had it coming.

"Doesn't look very busy in there," Shayla said.

The little store was full of customers—at least five people—but it was good of my best friend to demonstrate her loyalty by lying.

I pushed my sunglasses up my nose, enjoying the sun on my pale skin. Catching glimpses of myself in shop windows, I liked what I saw. After I turned twenty-two, I stopped looking like a pudgy teenager and turned into a voluptuous woman. My blond hair had darkened through my teens, and I'd recently started getting highlights put in at my hairdresser's.

That morning, most of my favorite clothes were in the laundry, so I'd put on my favorite turquoise dress with a black belt. The brilliant shade of blue brought out my eyes and made me look neither tan nor pale, and the hem line ended at the exact perfect spot above my knee —the almost-skinny stretch. Around my neck, I wore chunky wood beads that tied in with my cork-soled sandals. Not bad for a hangover morning.

Shayla wore jean cutoffs and a striped shirt with a wide neck, falling off the shoulder.

A man in a city-worker reflective vest wolf-whistled at us from where he was kneeling on the sidewalk, tugging out a dandelion by its root.

"For shame, Lester," Shayla said to him. "I'm your cousin."

Lester wiped the sweat off his brow with the back of his hand, his thick bicep tanned and rippling beneath the sleeve of his tight, bright-white T-shirt.

"The whistle was for Peaches," he said, grinning. "She ain't my cousin."

I linked arms with Shayla and giggled like we were thirteen again and talking to out-of-town boys at a softball game.

After we were past hearing range of Lester, Shayla said, "They can smell it on you. One night with a man attracts more men."

I shoved her away. "Gross."

"Not literally, dumbass. You just wait, though. This is going to be your summer. Grandma Clever taught me to trust my intuition, and I can feel it in my bones." She poked me in the arm with one fingertip. "The object of your ladyboner lust will be back. Dalton Deangelo is going to call, and you should give him another chance."

I glanced back over my shoulder at Lester, who had been following my butt with his eyes and looked away quickly. He had such broad shoulders, and he was always tanned from the landscaping work he did around town. I did not care for the Birkenstock sandals he wore with wool socks, but that was just a wardrobe flaw. I'd never considered Lester Dean as a dating option before, but he was recently separated from his wife, and not that much older than me—barely thirty. An older man was certainly intriguing.

"What do you think of Lester?" I asked Shayla.

"Irrelevant. Dalton Deangelo will call."

She pulled open the glass door of the community center and we stepped into the brutally air-conditioned space, the air so cold it gave me goose bumps. My father would have freaked out over the waste of taxpayer dollars.

Shayla continued, "Once you two start dating, you can invite me along to exciting Hollywood parties."

Hollywood parties? No, I didn't think so. Meeting Dalton had been fun, but all that nonsense he'd said about us being stardust seemed ridiculous—ridiculous like the cheesy lines Drake the vampire always said to his waif-like love interest of the week.

Shayla and I travelled down a corridor and found the room of our workshop. The hand-lettered sign read:

Charm - A Workshop for Ladies!!

Your teacher: Dottie!!!

Shayla and I took two seats at the back and checked our phones for messages before the class started. People milled around us, taking their seats.

A woman's hand, short-fingered and covered in jewelry, snatched my phone from my hand. "What if I'd been a handsome fellow?" she asked.

I stared up at her, my jaw dropping open. She had pale skin, beautifully wrinkled with laugh lines, bright pink lipstick, and twinkling blue eyes. Her hair was chin-length and as pink as her lips. As pink as a Halloween wig.

She continued, her words clear and crisp with spaces between, like little bells ringing, "You. Won't. Find. Him. If. You're. Texting."

I reached for my phone. "Maybe he's texting me right now."

The women seated around us laughed.

The pink-haired lady, who looked to be around seventy, tucked my phone into the pocket of her flower-patterned dress, and strode up to the front of the meeting room.

"He's not texting you. You wouldn't be here if he was. It's Sunday, and if you had yourself a big hunky man, you'd be doing the crossword together in bed. And by crossword I mean sex stuff."

A lady near me sighed.

The pink-haired lady continued, "My name is Dottie Simpkins, I'm seventy-two, and I drive a convertible with a bumper sticker that says 'If the sun's up, the top's down.' I've been married six times, and if you take all my advice today, I guarantee you can cut that number in half, minimum." She stepped up to an easel that held a number of poster-sized cards and flipped over the front one to reveal a drawing of a mermaid. "Lesson One. Keeping your legs together."

I turned to look at Shayla, my expression asking her what she'd gotten us into. She batted her dark eyelashes at me, her gold eyes amused.

I whispered, "You're the worst."

Dottie snapped her fingers. "Young lady! You, in the turquoise. Thank you for speaking during the session and thereby volunteering to do the demonstration." She clapped her hands together. "Up, up. Up from your chair and join me here. You seem like the type who learns better by doing than by being shown."

I scowled at Shayla as I shuffled past, giving her my best you're-dead-to-me look.

Dottie pushed one strand of cotton-candy-pink hair behind her ear and stared at my legs as I walked up.

Nodding, she said, "You probably don't like the feeling of your thighs rubbing together, do you? You walk like a cowboy."

I put my hands on my hips, my face flushing hot with embarrassment. "Maybe I have dry skin and I wouldn't want to catch myself on fire."

The group of ladies seated—about two dozen, most of them well over forty—laughed at my comment. At this, Dottie seemed to relax, giving me a wink and a smile that made me feel pretty. I'd heard about the woman before, from another class Shayla had attended, and now I could see what she meant about Dottie's terrifying yet magnetic personality.

"Let's all stand for this," Dottie said.

The women set their purses on the chairs and we formed a standing circle in the open half of the room.

She continued, her words still like bells, but running together now like an entrancing melody. "Ladies, stretch your bodies up tall and shift your weight over your heels where it's supposed to be. Relax your toes and let them be light as air, light as little helium balloons. If a sheet of paper could slide under your toes, you're doing it right. Now, I want you to close your eyes and own the ground beneath you."

In the silence that followed, the chatty part of my brain started up a monologue. *This is my ground, my space. You don't shush me, Dalton Deangelo. Nobody shushes me on my ground.*

"Encourage your chattering mind to be still," Dottie said, as if she'd been reading my thoughts. "Keep standing and owning your ground. Keep your toes light and your spirit will soar. Here's another thought: Be yourself, because everyone else is taken. Fat or thin, be your wild, wonderful, unique self. Now when you're ready, I'd like you to gently open your eyes and take a look around, not at the carpet in this room or the furniture, but at what matters. Have a look at the people around you, and all of their beautiful faces. Our lives are all different, yet we share in this tapestry of life. Fate has tugged on each of our threads today, and here we are together. Why? Because it was meant to be. Now gently open your eyes and look around at the beauty and collective wisdom in this room."

I opened my eyes and beheld the woman standing across from me. She looked surprised, her eyes wide open, taking everything in as though for the very first time. Her hair was long, thick, and a mix of white and silver. She offered me a smile, and there was such kindness, it made my own eyes sting with a flush of grateful tears at the ready.

Blinking, I looked to the next woman, who was as round and short as the previous one was tall and thin. She had short, spiked hair, dyed red, and seemingly endless piercings in her earlobes, nose, lips, and eyebrows.

Dottie gently urged us to keep looking around the room, silently greeting each other. I recognized several of the women as regular customers at the bookstore, which made sense, as we do sell a number of self-help books.

The third woman I looked at was my third grade teacher, Mrs. Chan. She was a little older now, but her hair was still pure black and swept up in the bun I remembered. I enjoyed the look on her face as it scrunched up, puzzled, then relaxed into a smile as she placed where she knew me from. The woman next to her had to be her daughter, with the same round face and brown eyes.

Except for the mother and daughter duo, Dottie was certainly right about every woman in the group being completely unique.

Dottie gently called our attention back to herself and repeated, "Be yourself, because everyone else is taken. Every one of us is a role model. We just don't know yet for whom."

I was nodding before she finished her sentence.

The rest of the workshop was quite the experience, and not at all what I'd expected.

Charm, as Dottie explained it, is a combination of using your feminine charms and embracing your individuality. To draw a man to you, you stand or sit in such a way that one toe points at him. That should lure him in, bringing him over with an offer to dance or buy you a drink. Then, when you've got him near your claws (ha ha, I mean hands), you gaze up at him like he's a strawberry sundae while discreetly stroking the parts of your body you want to draw attention to.

When we got to that part of the workshop, I raised my hand and said, "What part do I rub to draw attention to my brains?"

Dottie didn't miss a beat. She said, "Honey, it's not a job interview, so I suggest you go with the boobs," and moved on to the next question.

Shayla scrunched her face at me. "Smartass."

"Hey. Smartass is who I am. I'm an original."

Dottie squealed and grabbed me in a spontaneous hug. "You're doing so well!"

Over her shoulder, I stuck my tongue out at Shayla.

She mouthed the words *teacher's pet*.

~

I left the workshop feeling more confused than ever. Three hours of being told to be yourself but also act in specific, manipulative ways will do that to you.

Shayla was trailing behind me on the walk back to her Rav.

"Hold up, I'm doing the mermaid walk," she said.

"You look ridiculous."

She was walking the way Dottie had taught us, with her upper legs close together, like she was wearing an invisible tight skirt instead of her jean cutoffs with the frayed edges.

Once she finally caught up to me, she said, "Hey, let's try out our new charms on that hottie over there." She pointed her chin to a man who was puzzling over a parking meter. "Just for practice," she said.

I would have agreed, but the very tall, very handsome Nordic-looking man with the broad shoulders and narrow waist was not suitable for *practice*. He was more like the final exam. He was the man equivalent of a PhD thesis paper.

Shayla abandoned her mermaid walk and dragged me up to Mr. Clearly Not From Around Here.

"They don't need to be fed on Sundays," she said.

"Who?"

"The parking meters, silly."

He turned to her, and I followed his gaze as it travelled from Shayla's eyes to her lips and then to her fingertips, which were rubbing back and forth along her collarbone and exposed shoulder, where her striped shirt was falling off.

Dottie had recommended wearing high-maintenance clothing that required constant adjustment. Men are attracted women who are constantly correcting their clothing, or so Dottie said. I had a little pebble in my cork-soled sandals, but I didn't think she meant I should take my shoe off my sweaty foot and shake it around to impress this guy.

"I guess I scrounged up a pocket full of change for nothing," he said. His voice was deep, but I shouldn't have been surprised, since it had so far to go, up that long neck of his. How tall was he? Six foot four? At least.

He had a good-sized shoe on him, too. My whole body experienced a naughty, tingling sensation as I drank him in with my eyes, from his hiking boots to his lightweight brown chinos and up. My gaze got stuck briefly around his zipper, pondering exactly what was causing a sizable shadow in that area. A wrinkle in the fabric? A giant python? A tree trunk for one to climb with her bare-naked vagina?

Oh dear. My cheeks flushed with heat, and my nervous hands went to my hair, twirling strands between my fingers.

That had been another one of Dottie's man-charming tricks: twirl your hair and draw a strand across your mouth, dragging your fingers across your lips to make him think about you touching his naughty business with those lips. (Okay, she didn't say that last part, but come on.)

Shayla beat me to it, already rubbing one forefinger against her lower lip as she gazed up at the stranger with her golden eyes, artfully peeking through a fringe of eyelashes.

The muscles in his cheeks moved as he clenched his handsome jaw, smooth shaven with just a few specks of his gold-hued beard hair, glowing in the afternoon sun like grains of brown sugar on a cinnamon bun. Heaven help me, but he was one beautiful man, from his dreamy blue eyes to his thick, sun-bleached hair and fair eyebrows.

I hadn't seen a man so utterly breathtaking since high school, when I'd been the President, Secretary, and only member of the Adrian Storm Appreciation Club. Adrian had been tall as well, but so scrawny that our art teacher joked that the metal lip ring was the only thing keeping him from blowing away in a stiff breeze. Adrian always wore extra-large black T-shirts for his favorite bands—shirts so big you could have fit two Adrians in them—and I'd dutifully note the names of the bands and listen to their music as though Adrian had recommended them to me personally. I didn't like the same music he did, nor his favorite movies. Our tastes were polar opposites, but I could *appreciate* the things he liked, and I thought that with enough exposure, I might also like them.

One of his favorite bands, if you believed the T-shirts, was Led Zeppelin. Which was kind of a funny coincidence, given that this handsome, muscular stranger in front of me was also wearing a Led Zeppelin shirt over his broad chest.

Hot buttered noodles, it was him. Adrian Storm.

CHAPTER 6

At the sight of Adrian Storm, my blood did that thing where it turns to iced tea. You've got warm blood in you one minute, then iced tea.

Right there, in the sexy indentation below his lower lip, was the tiniest knob of scar tissue from where the stainless steel lip ring had been. The one he'd flicked while waiting for the slow lab computers to load up yearbook photos.

"Looks like you got the wrong size shirt," he said to Shayla. "This one keeps trying to get away from you." He reached down and shifted the wide-necked striped shirt so it was centered again and not falling off Shayla's lovely chocolate milk shoulder.

"It's supposed to do that," Shayla said, pulling the shirt to the side again and sweeping her fingertips across her bare skin.

Adrian turned to me, the full force of his gorgeousness nearly knocking me down in my hungover, post-workshop, confused state. "I used to wear shirts that were way too big. Remember that, Peaches?"

"Looks like you grew into your collection, big boy," I said. "You're all bumpy now."

Shayla shot me a look of shock, but she knew as well as anyone that my mouth does not wait for my brain to send orders.

"I'd say the same about you," he said, those dazzling blue eyes roving down my body slowly, seeking every valley like a summer rainstorm.

"Adrian!" Shayla yelled, recognizing him at last.

He didn't take his eyes off me. "That dress is the perfect color for you, isn't it? Take off those sunglasses and let me see your pretty eyes."

I snatched away the sunglasses and crossed my arms over my chest. "My eyes are up here. Stop eye-groping my peaches."

Adrian chuckled, his chiseled cheeks taking on a rosy glow.

He said, "What are you up to these days? Are you just visiting, or did you never leave B-town?"

"I went away to college."

Shayla snorted. "For one and a half semesters."

I shot her a searing shut-up look. "At least mine's paid off."

"I'm a disappointment, too," Adrian said, lowering his eyes, his long, fair eyelashes nearly brushing his cheeks. "I guess I should just come right out and admit the awful truth."

Shayla was still rubbing her collarbone, angling her hips away from him but her toe pointing at him, as we'd practiced.

"You're broke," she said, leaning against the parking meter like it was a stripper pole. I wished I had Shayla's body confidence, but all mine shoots out of my mouth.

"Yes, and I'm moving back in with my parents." He put his fingers to his forehead, an embarrassed smirk on his lips. "So much for all my big city plans. I thought I had the world by the tail, but I made a few bad investments and then went double or nothing and came out with nothing. Real estate. May as well go to Vegas and play the roulette wheel."

Shayla darted forward, smacking him on the broad chest with both hands. "Snap out of it! You're the same age as us, and we're all broke. I've never been to a party that wasn't BYOB. You're so freaking handsome now, so stop complaining! You used to be skinny and weird back in high school, and nobody but Peaches took much notice of you, but now you're back, and look at you. You could be the mayor of Beaverdale, if you wanted."

"The mayor," I echoed, hoping he didn't latch onto the beans Shayla spilled about my crush.

He fixed me with his sexy gaze, silently pumping me for details. Gah! He wouldn't look away. He was smothering me.

I blurted out, "I didn't think I'd ever see you again after graduation."

He raised his eyebrows while frowning, making the isn't-that-interesting face.

"I'm back in town, so you can see a lot of me," he said. "As much as you can handle."

"You're too late!" Shayla squealed. "She's already hooked up. You had your chance and—"

I clamped my hand over her mouth. Who was the one with the big mouth now?

"Still a bit drunk from last night," I explained to Adrian.

"We should hang out," he said. "All of us. Like old times."

I gave Shayla a warning look and slowly removed my hand from her mouth.

She shook her head. "Maybe something good will happen for one of us soon, and we'll have a house party. We live up on Lurch Street now."

He licked his lips. "You both look... really good. I should have never left Beaverdale."

"Hey, remember when you took me to Dolphin Falls?" she said to Adrian. "You tried to kiss me, but I was afraid of that gross lip ring you had."

He snorted. "I didn't try to kiss you, and you're the one who wanted to go there and take yearbook photos of people in their cars."

"Right," she said sarcastically. "We only went there to—" she made air quotes "—take photos. I guess you're still a big nerd after all, even with all that body on you."

"Speaking of big nerds, whatever happened with you and Garret?"

She laughed. "Wouldn't you like to know."

This reunion was getting weird, so I stepped back, looking for an escape route. The sidewalk was all clear, so I grabbed Shayla by the arm and started dragging her away.

"See you around, Adrian!" I called over my shoulder.

"Nice to see you two!" he answered. "We should totally get together the old gang and have a five year reunion."

I turned, still moving, and walked backwards as I waved.

He looked so cute, stuffing his hands in his pockets and shrugging up his shoulders.

I wanted to say something, so I opened my mouth and did: "Hey, Adrian Storm! Led Zeppelin still sucks!"

Shayla buried her face in her hands, shaking her head. "I swear, I cannot take you anywhere."

"Sorry I dragged you away before you could throw your leg over his shoulder or whatever was next."

"What are you talking about? I wouldn't flirt with Adrian. As soon as I realized it was him, I backed way off."

"Then why were you rubbing imaginary lotion all over your neck and baring it to him, flexing your seductive neck muscles like Dottie taught us?"

We got to her Rav and she clicked open the doors. "That wasn't conscious, I swear. When I see a guy that hot, it just happens. My brain doesn't work right."

"You should look up his number and call him." I slid into the passenger seat and put my sunglasses back on. "Don't hold back on my account. He looks like he climbs mountains, with lesser men strapped to his back. He doesn't want to date a little fat girl with a big mouth."

Shayla held up one finger in warning. "Don't you dare say the f-word about my best friend."

"But I am fa—"

"Fabulous." She threw the Rav into gear and lurched out of the parking spot like a madwoman. "Hangover helper? Name your poison."

I thought for all of a full second. "It's just fruit."

"Yes, it's just fruit."

She cranked the wheel and whipped us around in a tight U-turn, so we were pointed in the direction of Chloe's Pie Shack, located at the edge of town just off the highway.

Chloe's Pie Shack had been Burt's Burger Barn until a year ago, when Burt's daughter Chloe took over and tried to class up the joint. The logo features a scrumptious slice of pie with the phrase 'It's just fruit' written in cursive around a plate.

Despite the obvious benefits of having a restaurant specializing in fresh pie made from local Washington blueberries, the people of Beaverdale hadn't taken the news well at all. They'd already lost the best Chinese food restaurant in town to a fire just months before, and they weren't giving up their burgers without a fight.

Mayor Stephen Monroe, also known as Uncle Steve to me, passed an ordinance declaring the Burger Barn a heritage site. He decreed it of utmost importance to the value of the Town of Beaverdale that burgers continue to be served from the big, red barn at the entrance to town—burgers or nothing. And the sign for Burt's Burger Barn, a neon wonder that could be seen for miles, wouldn't be touched except for the purpose of restoration.

Burt's daughter Chloe took the news in stride, thanks in no small part to the fourteen percent increase in business that came as a result of all the publicity. She added a second sign for the pies underneath the original one, expanded the barn with an all-glass addition plus a second entrance, and now we have hot burgers *and* warm pie. Who could ask for more in a town?

~

I did the sexy mermaid walk most of the way in to work Monday morning. I let my thighs rub merrily together, my knees drawn to each other like fridge magnets, my weight back over my heels so that ants could run parades under my relaxed toes.

Charm?

I checked out my reflection in store windows.

I had capital-B Booty *and* Charm.

When I walked into Java Jones, Kirsten looked up from the cafe latte she was steaming and asked me if I had a bladder infection or something.

I took a wider stance and said, "Just trying to have more charm. Probably a lost cause."

"You're brimming with charm," came a male voice from behind me. "Leave some for everyone else."

I whirled around, expecting to see another regular customer.

Dalton Deangelo sat at a round cafe table, a laptop in front of him and a foamy cappuccino next to it.

He grinned, the dimple in his chin deepening. "Wait, what were we talking about? Line?" He looked left and right playfully. "I'm lousy when I go off-script."

"What are you doing here?"

He pointed his thumb at the window behind him. "Waiting for that bookstore to open."

I swore under my breath and turned back to the counter to place my order. Maybe if I ignored him, he'd go away. *Do not think about him putting his hand in your panties*, I told myself.

For the next few minutes as Kirsten made my mocha, I could think of nothing *but* Dalton's hand in my panties, his fingers playing me like a harp. And his lips on my neck.

A flushing sensation began in my belly and seeped up to my neck, causing my skin to sweat all the way to the top of my head. I accepted my mocha, put on the lid, and attempted to get out the door without walking strangely. Unfortunately, I couldn't remember how to walk normally. Hopping on one foot would have been more natural than how I stomped out of the coffee shop.

Across the street, my hands shook as I attempted to get my key in the lock. It was like that moment in a horror movie where the idiot girl is trying to get away, but she's trembling so bad she keeps dropping the keys.

I dropped the keys.

Dalton picked up the keys and handed them to me.

"I'm in town shooting a little indie movie," he said.

I tried again with the keys, keeping my back to him. "How long?" I tried to sound casual, but it came out sounding like a squeaky gate.

Don't think about his hand in your panties.

Dropped the keys again.

"Long enough to get bored and look for trouble," he said.

"I'm sure trouble finds you easily enough on its own."

He laughed, making me feel just comfortable enough to get the door open.

We stepped inside the shop and I ran to turn off the alarm. In the silence as I flipped on the lights, I could hear him breathe in deeply.

"Can't beat that smell," he said. "Heaven is a place on earth, and it's a bookstore."

"Why are you here? Isn't shooting a movie kind of an all-day thing?"

"I'm not the only star of this one. The girl is the one with the big transformation. It's very inspiring."

I got myself behind the counter, where I felt more comfortable, half hidden.

"You're not the star? Then why are you doing it?"

"Because I get to play a really complex character, and do some serious acting. I don't mean to bite the hand that feeds me, but talking around prosthetic fangs is not the reason I… worked really hard to get into this business any way I could."

"What's the movie called?"

"The working title is *Waterfall*, but that's not going to be the final title. You've probably seen little arrow signs around town with the word *Waterfall* on them."

"Have I?" I took a sip of my mocha, thoughts swirling around my head.

"You will now, since I told you."

"Despite all the movies I've seen, I know absolutely nothing about how they get made."

"That gives us plenty to talk about." He gave me a sexy look, his eyes full of intensity. "I had a really nice day with you Saturday. And night."

I took another sip, noting how flavorless the mocha was. Stress will do that to you—suck the taste right out of your mouth. As I tried to figure out why Dalton Deangelo was in my bookstore, I felt the stress crashing down on me like angry waves decimating a sand castle.

"I'm not going to talk to any reporters, if that's what you're worried about," I said. "You don't have to pretend to be interested in me."

He leaned forward in a deliberate pose of relaxation against the counter, elbows on the countertop and chin in hand. Raising one sexy, dark eyebrow, he gazed into my eyes and said, "Tell the world."

As sweet and naive as he'd seemed on Saturday, not knowing how a wedding buffet worked, now he was radiating dark sensuality and danger.

And me? I'd never been so turned on in my life. My nipples hardened inside my bra, pulling the skin of my chest taut. My breathing quickened, and the heat sought every nook and crevice.

Never mind that he'd shushed me. He could shush me all he wanted. He could throw me onto the counter and shush me for hours. He could shush my neck, my breasts, my lower back, my…

"Dinner tonight?" he asked. "Unless you're still mad at me for shushing you." His dark eyes were hungry and wolf-like, impossible to look away from. "Shushing you is something I swear I'll never do again."

"I don't know why I got so upset. I'm certainly not perfect."

"Let's blame my stalker."

The front door jingled with customers coming in. I waved at the woman with long, white hair, realizing she'd been at Dottie's workshop the day before.

"Small world," she said to me, then started browsing in the staff picks section.

Dalton turned to wave at the woman, then returned to staring at me. "This town is incredible. You all know each other, don't you?"

"Beaverdale's not quite that small. We're not Wolfspit. That's just down the river from here. They passed a law in the fifties, that you couldn't marry within the town."

"And?"

"People just stopped getting married."

He laughed. "We love who we love, and we have little choice in the matter."

"We always have choices."

He drummed on the counter top. "Dinner tonight? Shall I swing by at closing and pick you up?"

"I don't know. Your life is not like my life. You have a stalker. It's been fun, but we had our day, and I know I'm not the girl for you."

The white-haired woman came up to the counter, no books in her hand.

"Anything I can help you find, ma'am?"

She turned to Dalton, taking a really good look at him, then turned back to me. "What would Dottie say?" she asked me.

He said, "Who's Dottie? I don't have my Beaverdale-to-English handbook."

Damn it, the woman was right. I was refusing Dalton because I worried I wasn't good enough for him. But I was the only one of me, an original, and that was way more than just good enough.

I tilted my chin, showing my sexy, vulnerable neck to Dalton. Rubbing my index finger along my lower lip, I said, "Dottie would tell me to act like I'm really busy, but offer to rearrange some things at great sacrifice so I can see you for dinner tonight. But you may not pick me up from work. I need to change into something more charming."

"I like the sound of that," he said, backing away. "Seven o'clock? I remember where you live, in that cute little house."

"Perfect."

"Perfect," the other woman repeated after me.

Dalton backed up to the door and opened it without taking his eyes off me.

"Wear something casual," he said. "Jeans or whatever."

"Casual. Okay."

He slipped out, waved through the glass door, then walked away.

I started breathing again. How long had I been holding my breath?

"Dottie would be proud," the woman said.

I didn't know whether to hug her or kick her out of the store, so I just nodded and dumped the pens and pencils out of the tin to give them a good sorting.

Eyes wide open, I told myself, though it was probably too late.

MIMI STRONG

CHAPTER 7

Here's how nervous I was about my date with Mr. Sexytrousers Dalton Deangelo: I sat in a pile of clothes, inside my walk-in closet, and bawled.

Shayla got home from an early shift at the restaurant and came running up the stairs to my room, asking, "Is somebody torturing a small mammal in here?"

"Small? No, not small." I picked up a pair of sky-blue jeans and tossed them at her. I'd sent her enough text messages that she was well-aware of my imminent date and emotional disaster. I wailed, "Why did you let me buy these? One wash and they're shrunk to hell. And the worst part is, they weren't even on sale." (More sobs, plus additional sniveling.) "Just take my credit card and freeze it in a block of ice, then grab the slipcover off the sofa and cut a neck hole in it, because that's what I'm wearing tonight."

She crossed her arms, no pity in her golden-brown eyes at all. "Poor Peaches. She has a date with a hot actor." She frowned at the bright blue jeans and picked them up. "Of course these don't fit you. They're mine. I was wondering where these were."

"Don't mess with my head! You're the one who threw out the scale, and now I've gained twenty pounds, haven't I?"

She grinned. "Wearing your fancy underwear, I see. Planning to show him your peaches up close?"

I pulled a dress off a hanger and clutched it to my chest. The pricey lingerie set had been a splurge on my last birthday, and I'd never actually worn the silky cream-colored bra and panties with the contrasting black lace. They looked and smelled lovely in my underwear drawer, but I'd finally cut off the tags that afternoon.

"A woman's fancy underwear is just for her," I said.

Shayla crouched down next to me in the jumbled closet and rubbed her palms up and down my bare shins. "This isn't this morning's shave. You're going to sleep with him tonight."

I pushed her away from me, laughing. "I'm not the fun one."

She raised one immaculately-groomed dark eyebrow as if to say, *we'll see about that*.

Shayla started looking through the clothes on the floor around me. "You know, I'll have to re-name my vibrator," she said. "Since you're dating the real Drake Cheshire, I can't be riding his choo-choo train to O-town."

"Does your sex toy really need a name?"

"What would you suggest?"

I got to my feet and dried my eyes. "How about a title? Like… The Assassin. Because he gets in and does the job."

She swatted my butt playfully. "Damn, girl. They should hire you to do their marketing."

"I'm awesome at everything but my own life."

"Let's get you dressed before the second act of your pity party."

She started rooting through my closet, setting aside things to try on.

We managed to find *my* bright blue jeans, which were a similar shade to my roommate's, but a few sizes larger. Fastening the button, I wondered if I hadn't lost a pound or two. What a good feeling it is to pull on slightly loose pants! Relaxed clothes are a gift that keeps on giving all day.*

*Sweatpants don't count.

The doorbell rang right on time, and I was surprised to find a middle-aged man with a brown mustache standing at my front door. It wasn't until I spotted the ponytail that I recognized him from two nights before.

"Vern," he said, offering his hand to shake. "I'm Dalton's driver and butler."

"Butler!" I turned and looked at Shayla, who just shrugged.

I hadn't realized butlers actually existed, outside of period dramas on BBC, but here was one in the flesh.

"Mr. Deangelo was running late with dinner preparations," Vern said. "He sent me to fetch you."

"Fetch me?" I turned and looked at Shayla, who managed another shrug.

Vern turned around and started walking back down to the car. He wore black pants and a white shirt, and from behind he looked a lot like a woman, with broad hips. Vern's body shape had absolutely nothing to do with my situation, but my mind latched onto it as relief from feeling nervous about the date. I followed him out to the car, got into the back seat, folded my hands on my lap, and thought about Vern the Butler.

Was there a Mrs. Vern who loved him exactly how he was, wide hips and all? Why did I notice other people's body shapes in a critical manner when I had such a chip on my shoulder about everyone noticing mine? Was there a school for training butlers, or some standard examination they had to pass to call themselves a butler? Could women become butlers?

Vern guided the long, black car away from the heart of town, away from the two best restaurants in town.

I looked around for the button that would lower the panel between me and Vern, but the toggle that seemed like the logical controller simply adjusted the angle of my plush leather seat.

Mystery ride, it was.

The scenery outside changed from town to fields and farmhouses, then just fields.

I sent a text message to Shayla: *If you don't hear from me in one hour, Vern the Butler has abducted me for his own nefarious purposes. We're heading north on Springer Road, so start looking for my body parts in that direction.*

Five minutes later, Shayla messaged me back: *How special! I'm glad you're wearing nice underwear!*

Me: *I hate you.*

Shayla replied with a string of emoticons implying a series of adventurous sex acts, involving vegetables.

The car bumped and jostled me as we turned onto a dirt road, and I lost my signal as we entered the dense trees.

We were headed toward Dragonfly Lake, as best I could tell. I'd been there a number of times growing up, mostly to ride full-sized horses with a friend who lived on a nearby farm. It was a pretty lake, pristine and blue, but there was nothing out there but a campground, and certainly not any restaurants.

My heart fluttered, and I regretted making those jokes about Vern murdering me, because they did not seem so funny now.

The car stopped moving, and I seized my opportunity to escape. I flung the door open and jumped out, ready to run.

My eyes were drawn by a silver cylinder glinting in the sun. An Airstream camping trailer, sleek and bullet-shaped, sat near the edge of the still lake. The trailer's silver aluminum siding acted as a funhouse mirror, reflecting the surrounding trees and blue sky.

The scent of charcoal briquettes hung in the air, and Dalton Deangelo stood over a barbecue, silver tongs in one hand and a plate of marinated, herb-flecked steaks in the other. He waved at someone —not me—and the car pulled away immediately, turning around and leaving by the road we'd just traveled in on.

A dragonfly buzzed down from the sky, zipped around my head once, and disappeared on gossamer wings. I shuddered, because dragonflies creep me out, with their enormous bodies and their crazy-ass, in-air mating rituals. Blergh.

"Do you like steaks?" Dalton asked as I approached.

"Do horses poop in parades?"

"I'm a city boy, Peaches. Is that a yes?"

He set down the plate of meat and tongs to give me a hug. "Mmm, good to see you," he said. "I'll ask you again. Do you like steaks?"

"Yes, I like steaks. I'm not that fussy."

He leaned down to kiss me, but I nervously turned my head to the side and he caught my cheek.

"Of course you're not fussy," he said. "You're here with me, aren't you?" He gave me one of his charming winks. Between his green eyes, so bright in the setting sun, plus the cute dimple in his square chin, and the washboard stomach I could feel through our clothes, I melted.

Forget dinner, I thought. *Take me now. Take me on the wildflower-strewn grass, with revolting dragonflies air-humping all around us. Put your tongue in my mouth and your hand in my...*

"Nice lake," he said.

I thought for a second he meant the lake forming in my panties, and started blushing.

"Oh, that lake," I said.

"Don't be nervous." He kissed my forehead. "You'll make me nervous, and I'll ruin this dinner and all my other plans. Fair warning, most of my plans are about getting you naked."

"Good thing I wore nice underwear."

He pulled at the top of my blouse and peeked down. "Forget dinner."

I swatted his hand away and re-fastened the top button of my pink blouse. "Mr. Grabby Hands."

He reached down my back and found plenty to grab onto. His fingers dug into the globes of my ass, gently pulling me against his body—his hard, yummy-smelling, irresistible body.

He growled near my ear, "Tell me if I'm moving too fast."

"I've been here less than a minute and you've checked out my rack and now you're frisking my body for concealed cameras. I don't know, is that too fast?"

He moved his hands to a more respectable spot on my lower back. "Noted."

"I used to ride horses around here," I said, pulling away from his embrace. With one hand still on one of his muscular arms, I rubbed my other palm against the fabric of his polo shirt. He wore jeans, but the shirt had a waffle-like texture and was the purest white. Not appropriate for camping, really.

His muscles reminded me of the horses, and now I couldn't stop thinking about the thrill of riding, and the smell of their sweat after a good run.

"Horses, you say? I can make some calls," he offered. "Vern's just over the hill in a cabin, and there's a land line there. We can rustle up some horses, if you'd like."

"Not on my account! It's nice just to be here." I looked out over the lake, at a bird with long legs stalking the shore. "Is that a heron?"

"You're the local. You tell me."

"Oh, definitely a heron." I squinted at the bird. "That's a Knock-Kneed Beige-Spotted Heron."

"I think you made that up." He took my hand in his and grinned at me. "Shall we go for a little wander before dinner? Or can you think of some other way to work up our appetite?"

I let out a nervous laugh, high and ringing, echoing over the lake.

"A wander sounds perfect."

We set off for a stroll along the lake's shoreline, stopping whenever we found round, flat stones suitable for skipping.

Dalton was really competitive about the stone-skipping, getting excited every time one of his stones went farther than mine (which was pretty much every time, given those beefcake arms of his.)

We walked past the heron, who calmly watched us, probably wondering why a couple of noisy, pink birds were walking around *his* lake and fighting each other for perfect flat stones only to throw them into the water.

We talked a bit, including me telling Dalton about the summer we came out to the lake with my family and found the water black with tadpoles. Shayla was with us at the picnic that day, and insisted that since we'd worn our swimsuits and brought blow-up toys, we absolutely had to go into the water. We'd both grimaced as we stepped into the teeming lakeside, stepping slowly so the tadpoles wouldn't be crushed under our feet.

Once I was in to my knees, my father called out asking if the water was warm from all the tadpole pee. Tadpoles, like the frogs they turn into, are amphibians and thus their pee is not warm, but on that day, the mere suggestion was enough to turn the water warm via my imagination.

Shayla was already treading water, out beyond the shore, so I had to keep going. I checked the elastic fit on the legs of my swimsuit to reassure myself that tadpoles wouldn't get in there and wiggle into the new opening I'd recently discovered, and I pushed ahead through the squirming water.

I don't know how long we were in the water that day, or what we did on our floating toys, because all that stuck in my mind was the tadpoles. Even as I stood on the shore telling Dalton, I could still feel the slippery squirming of them against my legs.

He rubbed his arms after I finished the story. "You gave me goosebumps," he said. "And the worst part is, I don't think I can go in this lake again until I get a tight-fitting Speedo to protect myself."

"I'll go shopping for Speedos with you, and you can model a few pairs for me."

He pretended to be shocked, his mouth dropping open. "You are a cheeky one. Thanks for the offer, but Vern does all my clothes shopping for me."

Now it was my turn to show shock on my face. "You don't go shopping? What's the point in being a big TV star if you don't get to shop and spend money on ridiculous things?"

"I don't know," he said, stooping down to pick up some flat stones for skipping.

He handed a stone to me and I chucked it, getting four good jumps. The sun was moving lower on the horizon, painting a gold streak across the lake.

His stone skipped so lightly, it seemed to disappear from sight without sinking.

"Crossed the lake with that one," he said, beaming.

"You are the champion."

He reached for my hand and gave it a proud squeeze, then we turned and headed back to the trailer.

"The Airstream's design is based on aircraft wings." He pointed his chin at the silver trailer, poised gracefully at the edge of the lake. "It's designed for minimal wind resistance, so it hugs the highway, which makes it more stable and also lighter on gas."

"Sounds like you're in love with that trailer. How will you ever leave it after your movie finishes?"

"No need for heartbreak. I'll take her with me."

"The trailer's yours?"

We'd just reached the barbecue, which was hot and ready to cook our steaks.

"Go ahead and have a look inside while I finish getting dinner ready." His green eyes twinkled, and by the tone of his voice, I sensed the trailer meant a lot to him.

I backed toward the trailer. "Is it really yours or are you pulling my leg?

"All mine. And in case you're wondering how big it is, I'll tell you. It's twenty-eight feet of *awesome*."

"Wow, that's big." I kept walking backwards, unable to take my eyes off Dalton, his skin looking delicious and tanned against his bright white shirt.

"Not too big, though."

"Of course." I turned away, blushing. He sure had a way of flustering me with the most innocent-sounding lines. That had to be his acting talent at work.

I opened the screen door keeping the dragonflies out of the trailer, and stepped up into the silver bullet. CREAK went the Airstream.

My heart sped up and sweat beaded on my forehead.

Great. Just great.

I imagined the trailer rocking visibly as I walked to the front and the back, the whole thing swaying under my footsteps. My next steps were careful, my breath held. The Airstream seemed solid enough, past the first awful CREAK, but I had to be cautious.

I couldn't tell how old the trailer was, but the interior looked new, custom, and expensive. To my right, the front of the trailer held a cozy seating banquette, upholstered in red fabric, and a pedestal table. The round table was already set for dinner for two, complete with fresh flowers—pink peonies the size of cabbages, not from the lakeside, but probably from a florist in town. That part of the trailer looked like a photo in a magazine, all pink and red and gorgeous. Here we were at the edge of a lake, and Dalton had asked me to dress casually, but I felt underdressed in my pink blouse and blue jeans.

Then again, maybe I was dressed perfectly. Maybe when we're in situations that make us feel underdressed, there's actually something else going on, but it's easier to blame the clothes. Hadn't Dottie said something about that at her workshop?

"Just be yourself," I whispered to myself. "Except be more charming and not weird. And stop talking to yourself."

The kitchenette looked like a regular nice kitchen with wood cabinets, but in miniature, with the cutest little round sink. Across from the counter and cupboards was more seating, and a built-in desk sized perfectly for a laptop.

Stepping carefully, so as not to rock the trailer off its axles and send myself rolling into the lake, I made my way back to peek at the tiny bathroom, which packed a lot of luxury into a gleaming white small space. In fact, if I'd been hired to write about this place for a fancy magazine, this is how I'd describe the washroom: packed with luxury, and nicer than most regular people's homes, despite being a tenth the size.

I stepped back from the washroom and peeked into the back area, which you would call a bedroom, simply because it did contain a bed. This "room" was up on a raised platform, and the only way to enter was to crawl up on the bed. The mattress, covered in luxurious red-toned linens, ended about a foot short of either side of the platform, which was a wood surface, empty except for an alarm clock and small* stack of books.

*There were twelve books, which I consider a *small* stack.

I reached out and ran my hand over the crimson bedcover, which felt silky to the touch. If I did sleep with Dalton Deangelo, it would be right here, on these red sheets. I glanced up at the coved ceiling and gasped. A mirror!

I shuddered, because seeing that mirror changed absolutely everything. No longer was the Airstream a high-end camping trailer. Thanks to that sex-mirror, it was now a bordello on wheels, and I didn't feel so great about being the next conquest.

"The mirror wasn't my idea," came a deep voice at the trailer's doorway.

I turned on my heel to find Dalton's tall, muscular frame blocking the only exit.

"What mirror?" I asked, feigning ignorance.

"Look up, over the bed. My designer came up with that. I'd been complaining that there was nowhere for a full-length mirror to check my clothes in, and she put that on the ceiling. I keep forgetting to have it taken down."

He stepped into the trailer, the whole thing rocking gently under his footsteps, and set the fragrant cooked steaks on the round table at the front.

"I guess this is the part where we eat," I said, stepping carefully over to the seating area to join him.

"You look beautiful tonight," he said. "Every time I see you, you're more luminous." His gaze moved down to my mouth. "Your lips leave me breathless."

I picked up a napkin and pretended to fan myself. "Slow down, big fella, or you'll make me too nervous to eat."

"We could skip ahead to dessert." He blinked innocently, fluttering thick, dark lashes at me.

CHAPTER 8

"Skip ahead to dessert?" I asked innocently.

"Yes. I trust you like fresh panna cotta?"

My extremely helpful brain flashed a preview image of me licking panna cotta off Dalton's chiseled chest. I crossed my legs and draped the napkin over my lap.

I hadn't eaten since lunch, and I should have been hungry, but nerves had scrunched my stomach. Dalton put greens and fixings on my plate, and we started eating.

"Why an Airstream?" I asked between bites. "Did you go on a lot of camping trips with your family?"

"Not exactly. My family wasn't the conventional type."

"Are your parents also actors?"

He made a funny expression, as though we were enjoying a private joke.

"No, I stayed in this very trailer for another film I worked on about two years ago. It was a rental, and not in the best condition. At night, you could hear the vermin moving around in their home, inside the lower pan."

I gulped and lifted my feet up reflexively, which made Dalton laugh.

"They're gone now," he said. "Along with the skeletons of the things they ate."

"Wow. Some people have skeletons in their closets."

He raised his eyebrows, grinning again. "They sure do."

My brain flashed an image of me, screaming on the tile floor of a bathroom. "Some things are best left undisturbed," I said, slicing into the seared steak. "So, you bought the trailer and restored it?"

"I had a company do the work. I wish I had the time to do things with my hands, but the show takes a lot of time and energy."

I looked down at his hands, poised over his plate. "You have nice hands," I said softly.

He set down his steak knife and reached over to wrap his hand around mine. Without looking away from my eyes, he steered my hand, along with the fork and a chunk of steak, toward his mouth. He slowly bit the meat off my tines and gave it a thoughtful chew. Still staring at me, his green eyes dark and moody, he said, "Tender enough for you?"

"Very tender," I whispered.

"Why aren't we drinking wine?"

I held still, my eyes held by his, my hand in his. "I don't know. Is there wine?"

He pulled my hand to his lips and kissed my fingers. "Red, white, or pink?"

I giggled. "Pink?"

He looked down, breaking eye contact and letting out a nervous laugh. "Just kidding about the pink, but I do have red. It's all the way over in the kitchen."

"Oh. All the way over there?" It was all of four feet away in the Airstream trailer. "Do hurry back before I get lonely."

He got up, ducking artfully to dodge the light fixture above the table.

"Do you know anything about wine?" he asked as he pulled the cork from a bottle.

"I usually just buy the mid-priced wine with the cutest animal on the label."

He turned the label my way. "This one has a koala."

"Oh, yes. That's a very good one. I've had it before."

He grinned, revealing his TV-perfect teeth and making me feel fun —more fun than I'd ever been.

"You look right at home in my Airstream." He sat back down next to me on the banquette. "I might have to keep you."

I brought the glass to my nose to smell the bouquet of the wine, rich and earthy. "You mean chain me up and keep me as your personal..." I took a sip. "Housekeeper?"

He stifled a laugh, his face red and his mouth full of wine. Fanning his face, he swallowed, then said, "I think your talents exceed mere housekeeping."

"I also play the French horn."

He snorted, his hand over his mouth. "New rule. You don't say anything scandalous while I'm taking a sip."

I batted my eyelashes. "Whatever do you mean? I really do play the French horn. It's not a euphemism."

He turned his head and gave me side-eye. "First your extensive wine knowledge, and now this. You were a band geek, weren't you?"

"Guilty as charged." We both picked up our utensils again and started eating. I'd never felt such an unusual combination of being completely at ease with someone and also utterly nervous.

"What about you?" I asked. "What were you like in high school?"

"I know all actors are supposed to say they were total dorks in high school, to make them seem relatable, but before I dropped out, I was really popular."

"No kidding. With that face? I can't believe it."

He chuckled. "Back in ninth grade, I was the most popular guy in school, and I dated the most popular girl." He looked me straight in the eyes. "And her best friend. At the same time."

I picked up my wine and swirled it around in the glass. "You cad."

"That's a good word," he said. "People don't call each other cads nearly enough."

I glanced at the door to the trailer, as did he.

"I was fifteen, and we didn't do any more than kiss," he said.

I crossed my arms and shrugged, acting cool.

"I don't know why you're telling me this."

"To be completely honest with you, because I really like you."

"I liked you a little more before I pictured you kissing two girls and breaking their hearts."

"They're fine, I'm sure."

"What about that girl who was taking our picture? Alexis?"

"I never dated her. Not even one kiss. I swear."

"Pinkie swear?"

He linked pinkie fingers with me. Even his pinkie finger was sexy. The heat from the wine spread through my belly and the rest of my body.

Keeping his finger wrapped around mine, he shifted his body closer to mine on the rounded banquette seat, so our knees and the sides of our legs were touching. The trailer felt warm. Very warm.

He murmured, "You've hardly touched your dinner. Was the marinade too salty?"

I stared at his lips, deep red from the wine and food. "Everything was perfect. I guess I wasn't that hungry."

He moved his free hand to the tops of my knees, then pushed his hand down between my legs, the heat of his palm radiating through my jeans.

My heart sped up, thrumming in my ears as he slid his hand up between my legs until he reached the center of me.

I gasped as he pressed against me through my jeans.

His voice thick with lust, he said, "I can't stop thinking about the other night in the car. I should have laid you back on the seat, put your legs up on my shoulders, and pulled off your panties with my teeth."

"Oh-my-goodness." I reached for my glass of wine and tossed the rest of it back in one shot.

He leaned in and kissed my shoulder through my blouse, then moved up to my neck. His hot lips on my skin—on my pulse points —made my body go limp and my eyelashes flutter.

He slowly made his way to my mouth, where he nibbled my lips, both of us tasting of red wine. I parted my lips as he thrust his tongue hungrily into my mouth, while his hand pressed against my swelling flesh.

Was this happening?

It felt dream-like, yet very real.

Dalton Deangelo thrust his hot tongue into my mouth and worked me through my jeans, having a powerful effect.

I wanted him. Fully. Completely. Immediately.

He sensed my desire, perhaps due to the panting or the mewling sounds I was making, and started working the button and fly on my jeans.

How was I supposed to get my jeans off, with the table right there? He undid the jeans and slid his hand down the front, making skin-on-skin contact with his fingers on my skin. I gasped and closed my eyes as his fingers slipped between those swollen furrows of flesh and nudged around.

Meanwhile, above the neck, he nuzzled my cheek with his chin and kissed my eyelid. Pulling back, he gazed at me, his eyes gentle and warm. "Like this?" Down below, he curled his fingers and stroked my silky skin.

"Yes."

"How about this?" He stroked his fingers more firmly, and pushed deeper, down where it was wetter.

"Wow."

"I'm going to pull your jeans off, turn you sideways on these cushions, and put your legs over my shoulders."

"Mmm." Waves of pleasure radiated from his nimble fingers.

"Unless you want to... go for a walk around Dragonfly Lake?"

"Mmm."

He swirled his fingertips in a circle, then up and down. For the second time, Dalton Deangelo had me wrapped around his fingers, literally.

I was breathing heavily and audibly as he withdrew his fingers, dragging the damp tips up along my lower stomach.

He suddenly grabbed hold of me by the hips and yanked my lower body along the cushioned seat. I gasped in surprise, then began to giggle as he pulled my butt down farther and my head bonked against the side of the trailer's interior.

"Oops," he said, stopping to rub my head with one hand.

Laughing, I pushed his hand out of my hair. "I'm fine. Your trailer might be twenty-eight feet long, but it's not very wide, is it?"

"Wide enough." He gave me another strong yank, so I was flat on my back on the cushions. He stood and tugged my shoes off one at a time, then removed my bright blue jeans.

I held my legs together shyly and angled my knees away from him, still with my panties on.

"Those are nice," he said.

"They're new." I glanced down at my cream-colored panties with the contrasting black lace highlights.

"I meant these." He positioned himself at my legs and kissed one knee and then the other. "Nice legs." He slid his hands up and down my thighs, making me shiver with his touch.

"Thank you," I whispered.

He pried my knees apart and started kissing my inner thighs. I arched my back and tried to quiet my thoughts. Another moan escaped my lips, and I found a place within me that was calm.

His voice husky, he said, "I'm going to pull those sweet panties off with my teeth."

He reached under me and easily hoisted my lower body so he could remove my panties. True to his promise, he used not just his hands, but his teeth to pull them off and all the way down my legs and off over my feet.

"Brr," I joked, because the trailer was quite warm. I pulled my legs back together and angled my knees away again.

"Let me see you." He stared deep into my eyes as I let my knee fall to the side, opening myself to him. His gaze moved down, his face serious, then smiling.

He whispered, "I like what I see. Let's get that shirt off."

Half the buttons had already come undone with all the excitement. I covered my chest with my hands. "Oh, now you want to see the peaches?"

He raised his dark, sexy eyebrows. "Yes, I do. Come on, Peaches, show me your... peaches." He shook his head, grinning. "I can't believe you made me say that."

"I didn't make you say anything."

"With those eyes of yours? You have all the power here."

I batted my eyelashes up at him.

He leaned over and finished unbuttoning my blouse, the pearl buttons tiny and delicate under his thick fingers. I shifted around so he could get the blouse off.

"Your bra matches your panties," he said. "Okay, I've noticed. Now take it off."

Unlatching the bra, I released my peaches. They're not the biggest fruit in the orchard, just a D-cup, and I do get self-conscious about my large hips making me look bottom-heavy, even though D-cups are a respectable size.

I held my hands over my breasts demurely.

Dalton asked, "Are we playing peek-a-boo?"

"More like strip poker, only without cards, and I'm totally losing. Are you wearing more clothes than when I got here?"

He sat up, undid the buttons at the neck of his polo shirt, and whipped it off over his head. As the shirt came off, the scent of his body, mixed with a nice cologne, reached my nose. He smelled as good as he looked, all lean and muscular, with those bumps of muscles where most guys I'd been with had love handles.

"Are you for real?" I asked, daring to press one bare foot against his stomach. Either he was naturally hairless or waxed, because his chest and stomach was completely smooth. Under my toes, his flesh was hot and firm.

His jeans were still on, but I could see evidence of his manhood, long and thick and standing at attention behind the fabric.

My foot moved down, stroking that rigid rod. *Mamma mia!* His soldier was trying to make a jail break, out the waistband.

Dalton caught my foot and brought it up to his cheek as he sat on the banquette next to my inner calf. He stroked his jaw against the sensitive inside of my foot. I'd never had a man touch me quite like that, and it felt incredibly intimate and hot.

He kissed the sole of my foot, in the arch. "You have lovely feet." He raised his dark eyelashes and gazed at me, his green eyes devilish. "You have lovely everything. Move your hands and show me the peaches."

I pulled my hands away. "They're not the biggest fruits in the orchard."

"Yum yum." He pulled away, moving his butt off the seat and kneeling next to me. My leg went over his shoulder, and he brought his face down between my legs.

Oh!

First a tentative lick, splitting the swollen flesh into two sides. Then deeper, harder. Hot and wet. Tongue on everything.

I arched my back, my breathing coming in ragged gasps.

His beautiful head was between my legs, and it felt so good.

This man had clearly been to Pleasure School. He licked, sucked, and swirled his tongue in a way I'd never imagined possible. I mean, I'd heard about such things, but never experienced them. I couldn't even tell anymore what exactly was happening. Fingers and tongue were inside me, all over me, stroking the pink satin lining and teasing.

My nub took a nibble, inflating with desire. It felt like a little fist down there, expanding and tingling with every coaxing stroke.

"Uh-oh," I said between gasps.

He murmured between my legs, his breath hot on my skin, "Uh-oh?"

"Oh! Yes?"

He growled into me, a wordless vibration that made me lose my mind. One hand kept busy betwixt my legs, and the other reached up to stroke my breast, gently pinching my nipple.

My muscles under his tongue pulsed, and a blast of goodness tore up my middle, puddling in my belly and turning my brain to soft, gooey caramel.

"Uh-oh," I said, coming.

My muscles pulsed, and I peaked quickly, coming down to earth after a few ragged breaths.

He eased back and kissed my leg. "You came already?"

"Sorry."

"Why apologize?"

I held my hand over my face, unable to meet his gaze. "I don't know. I guess it just seems rude of me to go first like that, before I did anything for you."

He took a mouthful of my thigh and gave me a gentle bite. "I enjoyed feeling you blossom like a flower. It was beautiful. Plus I am a patient boy."

"Boy?" I removed my hand from my face and propped myself up on my elbows to look Dalton in the eyes. "You're all man."

He gave me an innocent look. "When I'm with a captivating woman, I'm just a boy again."

As we stared at each other, he moved his hand back between my legs and clutched me. I shivered, feeling sensitive. He swept his thumb over the spot, and a strange sensation flooded me. My eyes hurt, like I might start to cry at any second.

I pushed his hand away and sat up. "Take off your pants," I said.

"Sure, but let's make a voyage together. About twenty-eight feet."

"To the bedroom?"

"Unless you want to try the stand-up shower?"

"Bedroom it is. You first." I waved him ahead of me.

He walked, stripped off his jeans and boxer shorts, then climbed up onto the bed platform, showing off his cute bare butt.

Seeing his rear view was a nice bonus, but the main reason I'd sent him ahead was so he didn't see my tush jiggling in front of him and then blocking the narrow doorway as I climbed onto the bed.

My body confidence is decent, but there are limits. I guarded the back-side view, so I could stay confident.

"Hurry up," he urged, patting the red sheets next to him.

"I feel like I'm getting into a big animal's mouth," I said as I climbed onto the bed. "With the red sheets, this bed is like the tongue."

Dalton laughed. "You're right." He took a long, appreciative look at me directly, and then again, using the mirror on the ceiling. "That mirror's okay after all," he said.

"Can the lights be dimmer?"

He reached for a switch and lowered the brightness of the sconces, then turned them completely off. The cave-like bedroom was still glowing with the golden rays of the sun setting over the lake, the light coming in through a sliver of a window.

When he saw me staring, he said, "Quite the view, isn't it?"

At that moment, a flock of ducks landed on the lake, next to some cattails.

I turned back and looked at the hot man waiting for my full attention. Now he seemed so relaxed, but my lust had been partially quenched, and so I was feeling nervous again. The tiny bedroom at the back of the Airstream might be described by some as cozy, but it was also freaking small.

I decided to focus on the task at hand, so I got to work on that fine-looking beast I had roused from its trouser slumber. I hardly even looked at the cyclopean creature before I popped it into my mouth.

Dalton moaned in appreciation and closed his eyes, his body both rigid and relaxed at the same time, all his fine bumps glistening with sex-sweat.

As I bobbed my head up and down, barely able to enjoy the salty taste of him, I started to freak out a little.

My brain yelled orders: Petra, slow down and be sexier! It's not a blowjob contest between you and every other girl he's been with, and even if it were, speed isn't everything! Slow down, girl, it's not a pepperoni stick!

Dalton twitched, his mouth opening a few times and some sound coming out, like he was going to say something but got distracted. *Distracted by what*, I wondered. Maybe by the lips and tongue going a hundred miles per hour up and down on his salami.

He gasped, clutching at the red blankets with both hands. *Sexy*, I thought, and he groaned and splashed in my mouth.

Mission accomplished!

Now I could go looking for my clothes, looking for my escape route. I could climb out of the mouth of this silver beast of a trailer and catch my breath.

I swallowed and treated him to one slow, languid lick as I released his meat flute, melody played.

He rolled onto his side, catching me with one arm and pulling me in to cuddle him, spoon style.

Nuzzling my hair, he said, "I had big plans, but I blew them all rather quickly."

"It was me. I blew your big plans. And also your big salami."

He chuckled and squeezed me tighter.

Now the bedroom was actually getting dark. The sun had finally set, and either the frogs around the lake got louder or my hearing got more sensitive.

Dalton's arm grew heavier, and a moment later, his breathing changed.

I gently lifted his arm off me and rolled over to face him.

"Dalton?" I whispered.

MIMI STRONG

CHAPTER 9

"Dalton?" I whispered again.

He murmured and stirred, but didn't wake up. While we'd been walking around the lake, he'd mentioned being exhausted from a long day, and he wasn't kidding.

I lay there in the dark, replaying parts of our date. Had he invited me to spend the night? I didn't want to overstay my welcome, and part of me wanted to dine and dash.

Then again, it was cozy there next to him, in the mildly claustrophobic maw of the Airstream.

My stomach grumbled.

Hungry already?

Of course I was hungry. I'd eaten one quarter of a steak, along with nothing more than green salad with a smattering of sliced strawberries and goat's cheese. The meal had been delicious, but low-carb, and now I had a carbohydrate shortfall for the day that my tummy wouldn't let me forget.

Panna cotta.

Dalton had mentioned panna cotta for dessert, so that was probably in the fridge.

I nudged him gently. "What about dessert?" I whispered.

When he didn't respond, I answered for him, "Oh, Peaches, just help yourself. It's in the fridge."

I replied to my suggestion with a convivial, "Don't mind if I do!"

Getting out of the bedroom was easier than getting in. The windows were midnight blue, and I felt exposed in the glowing light of the interior, so I tiptoed around the creaking trailer playing a game of Pick-Up Clothes.

Once fully dressed, I tidied up the plates and washed them in the tiny, round sink. Hot water came out of the tap. Where did the hot water come from? I had no idea.

I kept expecting Dalton to wake from the noises and come out, but he was completely zonked.

The panna cotta was in the under-counter refrigerator, and it was delicious—the firm custard neither too heavy nor too light.

I grabbed my phone from my purse, hoping to text Shayla, but I still had no cell service.

Fully dressed, I sat in one of the club chairs across from the kitchenette and considered my options.

After a few minutes, I decided that taking my clothes back off and climbing into that tongue of a bed was not a viable option. Sleeping here would mean using that tiny toilet, on the other side of a paper-thin wall from handsome, perfect Dalton, who probably didn't poop, what with all his perfectness. He likely had Vern, the butler, do it for him.

While we'd been on our walk, I'd spotted some of the trails I'd ridden horses along years ago. The lake wasn't that far from town, and if I took the shortcut through the trails, I'd be out to the highway in ten minutes. Fifteen minutes, tops.

From there, I'd have cellular service and be able to call Shayla, or even a taxi, for a ride.

Sure! Great idea! I'd just go crashing around through the woods in the dark at ten o'clock at night.

As I opened the trailer's screen door with a squeak and stepped out into the bracing night air, I thought I was making a logical, intelligent choice.

HAH!

The moon was three-quarters full and at my back as I set off into the dark woods surrounding Dragonfly Lake.

The trail under my feet was mostly smooth, worn flat by many hikers, but a few exposed tree roots and fallen branches threatened to trip me up and make me feel even more foolish than I already felt.

I hadn't worn a jacket, and now my bare arms were sniveling about the cold air and scratchy branches. Behind me, the trailer glowed like a space UFO. I stopped walking and stared at the rounded vessel that looked so much like an airplane minus the wings. How was it glowing? LED lights embedded along some of the aluminum seams? That had to be the answer, and not that it had come from another planet.

Dalton Deangelo was fully, completely human. So human!

I set off on the trail again, remembering the feel of his body in my hands. I'd cheated myself out of having him on top of me, thanks to my bunny rabbit blowjob. On the plus side, nobody gets pregnant from blowies. On the minus side... here I was getting lost in a dark forest, about to be taken by a sasquatch, or as the local folks call them, Forest Folk.

The term Forest Folk is misleading, making them sound like sprites or friendly spirits, but the Forest Folk in this part of the Pacific Northwest are not supernaturals you want to encounter. They're part-human, part-sasquatch cannibals. They eat the toes of children who don't clean up their bedrooms, and they have Santa Claus on speed dial. (Apparently, they have telephones.)

The best defense against Forest Folk is the same as what you learn in any self-defense course: run away. Forest Folk can regenerate missing body parts almost instantly, so even if you have an ax and chop off some limbs, they'll grow new ones and then use their bloody old arms or legs to beat you to death.

About fifteen years back, one of the town librarians gathered up all the local legends and put them in an illustrated story book for children, which she self-published. The book was almost immediately banned, which only increased demand.

As I stumbled through the dark forest, my imagination kicked into overdrive. I regretted all those nights Shayla and I pored over the Forest Folk book at her house, reading by flashlight under the covers when we were supposed to be sleeping.

My favorite tale was the one about the Forest Folk man who kidnapped a fair maiden and was transformed by her love back into a human. There was something so romantic about that story, though it had some bestiality undertones that were likely the cause of the book ban.

I tripped over a dark branch that blended with the forest floor and fell onto my hands, hard. I stumbled up and shook my hands, thanking my many days spent lugging around heavy books for strengthening my wrists and preventing worse injury.

Something rustled in the woods. I froze, my ears prickling with attention. The night music—crickets chirping across the lake and breezes tickling the leaves—rose up around me.

"Hello?" I whispered. "Dalton?"

"Grrr."

My mouth went dry and my heart tried to escape my body. "Dalton? Don't joke around. I have a heart condition." (That part was a lie; I do not have a heart condition, but the excuse does get you out of things like dodgeball and water pistol hide-n-seek.)

The growling sound came again, and this time did not sound at all like a handsome TV actor playing a prank.

Did beavers growl? I knew some were aggressive, and they could even kill a human if they got *bitey* and launched those massive sharp teeth at the femoral artery.

I listened for more noises as I pulled my phone out of my purse. There was still no reception, but the phone had a flashlight function. I turned it on, mindful of the battery drain, and slowly rotated, illuminating the trees around me.

Something that looked like a pair of eyes glinted back at me.

"Sugar!" I dropped the phone and the light turned off.

In the darkness, I heard heavy breathing. As I reached for my phone, fumbling around in the dirt and dried leaves, I swear I could also hear something slobbering and licking its lips.

I pulled my purse strap high on my shoulder and started marching with determination—the way you're supposed to move when creeps take notice of you in the city. There was no busy street to cross, or crowded restaurant to run into for help, so I stepped up to a jog.

The slobbering, heavy-breathing, eye-glinting creature padded out onto the forest path behind me.

I dared not look back, but set off at a full-on gallop. Branches smacked me in the face as I wobbled left and right on the narrow path.

"Don't run!" called out a man's voice from behind me.

Don't run? That's exactly what a Forest Folk creature would say right before he catches you!

I ran faster.

"Don't run!" he repeated.

Something was at my heels, biting my legs through my jeans and nipping my ass. A branch struck me in the face and I faltered, just as something struck my back and threw me down.

I landed hard on the ground, the breath knocked out of me. With weight on my back, I covered my neck with my hands in self-defense.

"Cujo, heel!" yelled the male voice.

With a sad-sounding yipe, the beast scrambled off my back.

I jumped up and whirled around.

"Peaches!"

"You!"

Adrian Storm stood three feet away from me, his blond hair disheveled and his face shining with sweat in the moonlight. A skinny German Shepherd sat next to him, tongue lolling out.

"Your insane dog tried to kill me," I said. "Why isn't he on a leash? And his name is Cujo? Are you kidding me?"

"He's old and toothless. His bark is much worse than his bite."

I rubbed my ass, now damp from the dog's slobber. "He shouldn't be biting people AT ALL!"

"He's retired, but the old police dog training kicks in when he sees people running."

My adrenaline was still in my blood, making my heart pound and dialing up my voice to shouting-level. "I'd be SO MAD if your dog wasn't so DAMN CUTE!"

Cujo tilted his head to the side, his big tongue dangling.

"He's my dad's dog."

Adrian's father was a police officer in town, so that actually explained a lot.

"That's NICE. How is YOUR DAD?" My adrenaline was still disrupting my volume control.

Adrian stepped closer, Cujo at his side and calm.

"Are you on drugs?"

"No."

"You seem shaken up. I can see your arms trembling, and you're yelling. Why were you running?"

I stared up at Adrian Storm's handsome Nordic face, those chiseled cheekbones fierce in the wan moonlight. Teenaged me wasn't stupid. He was a good-looking boy, scrawny or bulked up.

"I'm feeling much better now," I said.

"Why did you run?"

"I can't say, because you'll never stop laughing."

"Try me."

"I thought you were Forest Folk, coming to cannibalize me, starting with my toes."

He leaned down, bringing the tip of his nose to mine as he stared into my eyes.

"Did you eat any mushrooms? Perhaps little brown ones?"

I pushed him away, laughing. "I'm not high. I'm just... looking for higher ground to use my cell phone. And the highway. It's this direction, right?"

"This direction? No, you're headed straight for the Forest Folk lair."

I punched him in the chest right over the band logo, and he didn't flinch. It was like punching a brick wall of cuteness.

He laughed at my feeble efforts.

I yelled, "Shut the porch door, and stop telling lies!"

He licked his lips. "They start with the toes, but first they... tickle you!" He darted forward, jabbing at my sides with his fingers.

I screamed, and Cujo reacted by barking and knocking me to the ground again.

After a few choice words, Adrian got Cujo off me again and helped me to my feet.

"What are you doing out here?" he asked. "Are you stalking that actor who's staying by the lake?"

"No!" I pretended to be fascinated by the twigs nesting in my hair. "I'm out here for other, completely unrelated reasons."

Adrian grinned. Even without the lip ring, his smile brought back memories. All those long nights in the computer lab, and me being his you're-a-girl buddy, answering his many hypothetical questions about asking out Chantalle Hart.

Unlike me, Chantalle Hart was a fun girl, who had fun with all the popular boys at Beaverdale High, the only high school in our little town. Chantalle was the one who taught me how to give a blowjob— using a banana from my lunch. She oozed sex appeal. So much so, that when she did the banana demonstration, I felt a strange tingling sensation in my panties, and wondered if I was a lesbian. For about two days, I was excited about maybe being a lesbian, and getting to join the Theater Appreciation Rocking Thespians, or TARTs, who were the de facto gay and lesbian alliance.

Then I also got those same tingles the next few times I ate a banana, so I realized it was the banana part of the equation that had gotten me excited.

But I digress.

Alone in the woods with my former crush, Adrian Storm, I pulled some twigs out of my hair and lied about why I was there. "I went for a hike and lost track of the time."

"Of course. Let me walk you back to your car."

"I don't have a car, but you can walk me up to the road, if that's okay with Cujo. Or if you have your car here, you could just drop me off in town."

"I can do that." He waved me on ahead of him, along the trail. "And I do know why you're out here, but don't worry. I won't tell anyone. Your secret is safe with me."

"Okay," I said cautiously.

"But if you get a big pay check for your work, maybe throw a bit my way."

I shot him a dirty look. What exactly did he think I was doing out there? I didn't want to know.

We walked in silence up to a cleared space for parking. The only vehicle in the lot was an expensive-looking, canary yellow sports car.

"I thought you were broke," I said.

"I am. And cars like this are partly the reason why." He opened the passenger door and folded the seat forward so Cujo could amble up into the back and sit on his towel. "Get in and enjoy it with me before the repo men track me down."

I put on my seatbelt and looked around the interior of the car, admiring all the fancy dials in the dash.

Once he got in and settled, he turned to me and said, "Peaches, you're a girl."

"Yes. I am a girl." I got that deja vu feeling, because of all the times he'd said that phrase to me back in high school. What followed would be a hypothetical question about a girl, but this time I didn't mind.

As Adrian told me about this girl he'd met, who he couldn't get a clear reading on, I rubbed my index finger back and forth across my lower lip and thought about what a great kisser Dalton Deangelo was.

Adrian Storm talked most of the way back to my house, but I wasn't paying close attention. I kept thinking about Dalton, and the way his hot skin felt under my hands, and how if I got another date with him, I'd take things slower.

We pulled up in front of my house, where the lights were still on.

Adrian said, "So should I just ask her out? Actors and actresses are so weird. They're very outgoing people, and I think they have to be. To do their jobs, they have to connect with their characters and with the other actors instantly. It's, like, visceral."

"This girl is an actress?"

"Yes. That's why I feel so weird around her, like there are cameras on us when she talks to me. Everything she says to me sounds so measured and precise."

"Huh."

"It doesn't feel real to me, but I still like it. I love the attention, even if it's pretend."

"What do you mean, pretend?"

"Well, she's an actress. That makes her the world's best liar, doesn't it? Even if she's honest, how would I ever know?"

"Don't you trust your instincts?"

Cujo sneezed in the back seat and stood up, wagging his tail and bonking it against the window. He seemed like a nice enough dog when he wasn't knocking me to the ground.

"I used to trust my instincts," he said. "Then I gambled away my future."

"You could just take it one day at a time," I said to Adrian. "Whether it goes anywhere or not, it's fun while it lasts, right?"

He turned to me, his pale eyes lit by the streetlamps and suddenly looking haunted. "It's no fun to be played a fool and have your heart ripped out."

I laughed to lighten the mood. "Not even a little bit?"

He tilted his head, as though seeing me in a new light. "How about you? Are you seeing anyone?"

Ah, so clearly he thought I was *doing* something other than Dalton out at Dragonfly Lake. Perhaps taking pictures to sell to the tabloids. That added up.

"I'm seeing someone," I said. "Right now is the fun part, before my heart gets ripped out."

"Be careful. I know you're as tough as ten-dollar nails, but even a girl like you can get hurt."

"A girl like me?" What?

MIMI STRONG

CHAPTER 10

"A girl like me?" I repeated.

Adrian Storm turned to stare ahead at the clock on the dashboard, and tapped the steering wheel rhythmically. "Good seeing you, Petra."

I pushed open the car door, got out, and slammed it behind me without a word. I stomped up to the house. What the hell? *A girl like me?*

I fumbled with my keys and the lock, choking on indignation.

A girl like me. Did he mean a fat girl?

Of course he did.

That was why he used to talk so candidly to me about his girl problems. He never saw me as a viable dating option, and he still didn't.

I hoped he did date some actress and get his heart ripped out. He had it coming.

A girl like me. Hah!

He couldn't handle a girl like me. It took a real man to do that job.

I stomped up the stairs and found Shayla lounging in the clawfoot bath tub, the tea kettle on the floor next to her.

I put down the toilet seat and sat down next to her.

Her eyes widened. "You're filthy! What happened? Do you need me to call the police? Or should I put Vaseline on my face and slick my hair back so we can go kick some ass?"

"Easy there, One-Woman Army of Vengeance. Dalton was a perfect gentleman. I just took a shortcut on the way home and got treated like a training dummy by a retired, toothless police dog."

"And you say you're not the fun one. I ate a tin of Almond Roca and stalked people from high school on the computer all night."

"Freaky. It's like we're magically trading places."

I thought about telling her all about Adrian insulting me, but my mouth didn't want to make the effort. Screw him.

Shayla sunk down into the tub, opened her mouth to let water pool in, then spat it at me in a perfect arc.

I sat there and got soaked, too exhausted from my crazy night to get out of the way.

"Tell me what depraved sexual things you let Dalton Deangelo do to you," Shayla said. "Or I'll keep spraying you with water."

"Well, you know how I always say I can't see the fuss over receiving oral sex?"

Her face lit up.

"Let's just say I'm a believer," I said. "This postal outlet is now open for incoming mail of the tongue variety."

"You dirty slut!"

I got up and closed the bathroom window, because Mr. Galloway didn't need to know what a dirty slut I was, and I was about to tell Shayla every detail, even the embarrassing ones. *Especially* the embarrassing ones.

~

I woke up in my own bed, which contained only me and some fig newton cookie crumbs—a few more fig newton cookie crumbs than I would recommend for a good night's sleep.

Shayla and I had stayed up far too late discussing every word out of Dalton's mouth and what it all could mean.

She annoyed me, actually. The way she acted like what happened next was completely up to me. Garbage.

I hate when people tell you "it's all about the attitude" and "fake it 'til you make it."

You know what that advice amounts to? Kicking you when you're down. Because now it's your fault, because you didn't believe in yourself enough. You didn't clap your hands, and all the pixies died... or however that story goes. You know what I mean.

If a willingness to be confident was all it took, we'd all be confident. We'd all leave the house in one-piece rompers, ass hanging out for everyone to enjoy.

That morning, I should have been in a great mood, but I wasn't. That's the thing about moods—they're not logical. And change is stressful, even if it's good change like dating someone hot.

When you have nothing, you've got nothing to lose, but dating a hot guy meant I could potentially mess everything up with a hot guy.

Argh!

I took it out on myself by putting on a drab outfit of dark brown cords and an olive green button-down shirt. I looked like I was going off to war.

What people wouldn't know was that underneath those drab clothes, I wore a hot pink bra and panties set—another brand-new set I had been saving for a special occasion. Apparently, that occasion was today.

I ran out the door and started the walk to work with my morning Pop Tart in one hand and my phone in the other. I didn't remember giving Dalton my number, but I still had hope he would call.

Mr. Galloway, out in his front yard tending his roses, waved and said, "Sell those books at your store!"

"You know it," I replied, feeling guilty for the lie of omission.

A lot of people around town think I am the owner of Peachtree Books. Naturally, they assume the store is named after me, or vice versa. I suppose the fact I refer to it as "my" bookstore may be most of the problem, but it's so much easier to say "my bookstore" than "the bookstore I manage and work way too many hours at."

The truth is, the shop is owned by the same people who own the whole building: the Oliver family. Mr. Gordon Oliver founded the bookstore in 1982, and passed it down to his son Gordon Junior in 2003, when he retired and moved to Phoenix, Arizona. There, he lived in a trailer park half the year with his Canadian Snowbird girlfriend Ida, who, from what I hear, is a terrible cook.

Gordon Junior liked the money, but he didn't like books. For a number of years, his money-focused system worked well for Peachtree Books, and business grew. He believed in customer service, and met people's needs quite well. However, he still didn't care that much about the actual books, and when Black Sheep Books opened up across town, the customers were ripe for the poaching.

I was working there part-time, having just dropped out of college, when he started making drastic changes. Desperate changes. Like those internet coupons.

To avoid bankruptcy, we brainstormed many ideas together, along with the rest of the staff, and came up with some good ones. Our initiatives always seemed promising at first, but then Black Sheep Books would copy things like our Customer Loyalty Program and find a way to one-up us. They literally ran a sale called the One-Up Sale, where customers donated a used book for charity in exchange for a discount.

Gordon Junior knew we'd never be able to increase sales by much, so he set to work on the other side of the formula, reducing costs. Because his family owned the building, he had a lot of power.

Without consulting me, he got the necessary permits, and a construction crew showed up one day when I was receiving stock and asked where I wanted the wall.

Gordon's big plan was to put a wall right down the center of the bookstore, bisecting the place to save money. He added another door and more signs. Now the shop on one side was books, and right next door was a brand new specialty wine and beer store.

Just try and guess which business was more profitable.

As the wine business took off, and he spent more time over there (he was as passionate about wine as he was *dispassionate*about books), I took over more of the bookstore's operations. I put in the orders, then entered them in our computer. I received the stock, put it on the shelves, and hand-sold books to customers. I pretty much did everything except write the darn things, and I've half a mind to do that some day as well.

It's not so hard to write a book, I bet. You just pour yourself a tall glass of inspiration and start typing, right? I've already met a sexy, famous actor, so that's plenty of inspiration and research all rolled up in one.

I started thinking about Dalton Deangelo on the walk into work, and my vagina (I hope you're not offended by my frankness, but I'm not going to call it a funny word every time) got swollen and lubricated in a way that made walking both pleasurable and embarrassing. I tried walking like a mermaid, the way Dottie had recommended, but that felt too much like foreplay, what with all the rubbing. What had gotten into me? Not Dalton Deangelo, if you didn't count his fingers, which I didn't. Oh, but I wanted him to get into me. Big time.

By the time I opened the front door of the bookstore, my pleasure pumpkin (ha ha! I lied!) was demanding I take some "art" books into the back room for a little personal time, or "Safety Session" as my friend Ricky would call it.

Ricky was a college friend I fell out of contact with, but who will always remain in my heart. Over pizza and after tequila, he told me the most disturbing yet sweet story about watching movies with his parents. Whenever a sex scene came on the TV, his parents wouldn't ban young Ricky from the room, but simply said, "Blanket!" At that command, Ricky would cover his eyes with a blanket to avoid being exposed to on-screen sexuality at a young age. I'm sure you're snickering, thinking that *listening* to on-screen sexuality with a blanket over your eyes and your parents at your side is so much healthier!

There were a lot of things about sexuality that Ricky found confusing, perhaps due to sitting on a couch with his face under a blanket while his parents watched movie sex scenes. That could warp a person. Ricky's cousin was the one who introduced Ricky to pornography and masturbation, assuring the young boy that jerking off was not just acceptable, but healthy, because it staved off the horror of blue balls.

Ricky checked his balls every day for signs of blueness, and self-scheduled weekly Safety Sessions, usually on Sundays, as a necessity.

I learned these things about Ricky during a game of I Have Never, which is basically the greatest game ever for fun people, and just okay for people like me. Have I kissed a girl? No. I have never. No drink for me.

~

Me and my regrets reached the door of the bookstore ten minutes before opening. I had my mocha in hand, and my plan was to use the computer for nine and a half quiet minutes before opening the shop, but I was thwarted by over-eager customers who followed me in when I unlocked the door.

I turned on the lights and turned off the alarm, feeling grumpy. Who needs a book so desperately that they show up at the crack of ten in the morning, just as we're opening? People who need to tell you their whole sad story, that's who.

Trying not to think about how much I'd rather be drinking my mocha and looking over email to start my day right, I listened as the customer, a middle-aged woman with frizzy hair and terrible halitosis, told me all about her sister's daughter, whom she was hoping to induce into a lifelong love of reading.

I brought the woman over to our YA section, but she turned up her nose at the "trash" available and picked up some moldy old thing from our clearance table, whose only redeeming feature was the five-dollar price sticker.

"Good choice," I said, ringing it up. You can only offer your expert advice; you can't make them take it, especially if something else is cheaper. When I put the book into a bag, I slipped in a flyer for some better stuff, the paper discreetly folded in half.

The woman thanked me and started to leave the shop, looking very pleased with her decision. I hoped her niece would genuinely love the bargain book, which was not about cute vampires, but an English translation of a Swedish book about a young man coming to terms with degenerative eye disease; however, I had a bad feeling it was the sort of thing that scares kids away from books, much like outdated high school English curriculums and E. Annie Proulx's *The Shipping News*.

"Oo-OO-OOH!" the woman exclaimed on her way out the door. She was ooh-ing the person coming in, not me.

She held the door open for a man carrying a lavish bouquet of peonies and other pink and white flowers, blossoms and leaves hiding his face.

My heart jumped up. *It's happening*, I thought.

The flowers lowered, past dark brown hair.

This is it. We're falling in love, I thought.

The flowers lowered some more, revealing eyes a bit less twinkling-with-lust than I expected.

Nope. Not happening.

Brown mustache.

It wasn't Dalton Deangelo, but his trusty butler and driver, Vern.

With a heart full of hope, I peered behind Vern, but he was coming into the bookshop alone.

Frowning, he put the vase of flowers down on the counter between us. "You ran away last night. I was supposed to see to your safe return home."

I held out my hands. "As you can see, I'm in one piece."

"Mr. Deangelo requests your company on Friday afternoon, if you can make yourself available."

"Three days from now? What does he have in mind?"

Frowning under his bushy, ultra-serious mustache, Vern said, "That's confidential."

"Ooh. Mysterious. And so dramatic! Is Dalton always so dramatic?"

"Also confidential."

I plucked the card from within the flowers and opened it up. The note read: *Thanks for the fun.*

Thanks for the fun?

What the fudge did that mean? Was *fun* code for blowjob?

Without Dalton's gorgeous face in front of me, I felt differently about him. His charm was now coming second-hand from his butler, and Vern had a charm-dampening effect. With his grouchy face, Vern was the cold shower of charm.

Charm.

What would the pink-haired lady who gave the charm workshop advise me to do here? Dottie would want me to play hard to get.

"I'm really busy," I said, handing Vern a business card for the store. "Have Mr. Deangelo phone me when he's got the time."

Vern took the card, his face grim. "There's no need to play games," he said. "It's quite clear to me that you like Mr. Deangelo, and I'll tell him as such."

"Fine, do that."

"Why is everyone in this town... so odd?"

I put my hands on my hips. "Oh, no, you didn't. Vern, did you just insult all of Beaverdale?"

"I suppose not," he grumbled. "It's just that..."

"What?"

"I thought people in small towns were supposed to be friendly, but hardly anyone's been friendly to me."

"You can't just expect people to show up at your door with pie. You need to make the first move. Take an interest. I know you're not here very long, but check out the community cork board on our wall and find something you're interested in."

He walked over to the board and started looking, his hands folded behind his back. I let him have his moment as I cupped the beautiful flowers and fluffed up the arrangement. Flowers. From my gentleman friend! How old fashioned and wonderful.

Out of the corner of my eye, I saw Vern take down one tear-tab for a community event, and then another. This made me smile, and I was already smiling from the heavenly scent of my flowers, so my face nearly broke from smiling.

Just then, the door jingled and another person came in.

"Good day," Vern said with a curt nod, and he scurried away.

"Not a customer?" asked the man who'd just come in. He was a slim man with ginger hair—my father. "He didn't leave with a book."

"Dad! Don't worry about it. We're doing fine, and sales are steady."

He pointed to a light switch next to the front door. "Want me to turn this off?" Without waiting for a response, he flicked the switch off, which turned off the flood lights that lit up the exterior sign. We didn't need the lights on during sunny days, but they kept the store from being invisible in the evenings and through drizzling Washington winters. The owner, Gordon Junior, had been meaning to put the lights on a light-sensor switch, or a timer, but hadn't gotten around to it, what with all the wine tastings next door. We just left the lights on all the time rather than forget to turn them on when needed, but this didn't sit well with my father, who believes that a penny saved is a penny earned, and that there's no penny more shiny and proud than a penny saved on the electricity bill.

"Dad, it's pretty cloudy today. Might start raining any minute."

He leaned over to inspect the window display, then glowered up at the halogen spotlights. "If you retro-fit some compact fluorescents in there, it won't heat up and fade the book covers so much."

"Then what will be my incentive to change the window display?"

He stared at me like he couldn't believe we shared DNA.

After a moment, he tipped his head to the side. "Is that the air conditioning running? You could just open the door for a bit. Air the place out at night, get it good and cold, then pull the blinds until you get here in the morning."

"Dad, you do realize it's not *my* bookstore, right? I get paid the same no matter what the electricity bill is."

He scratched his head, looking very much the absent-minded professor. My father and his business partner run a niche business selling parts for radio-control helicopters, or as I like to call them, "flying chainsaws." They rent office space just down the street from Peachtree Books, so it wasn't unusual to have him pop in like this.

"Your mother wants you to bring your new boyfriend to dinner Friday. She hardly got to talk to him at your cousin's wedding."

"Yes, I did a good job keeping her away."

He gave me a perplexed look.

"Dalton's not my boyfriend," I said. "We've only had two dates, and that surly man who just left is his butler."

"I'd like a butler," my father said, as casually as if he'd been commenting on his desire for a grilled cheese sandwich.

I continued, "What I mean by mentioning the butler is, he's a fancy actor, and I'm a fat girl who manages a bookstore, and there's no dating book that covers this kind of a situation. I may see him again, but I shall not be referring to him as my *boyfriend*."

111

My father winced and stared up at the light fixture over the display window again. "You really should replace that whole fixture. I've got an extra one I can bring by."

It was so exactly like my father to evade a thorny question and obsess over something involving math instead.

I'd barely had a sip of my morning mocha, and was already exhausted from telling men no, so I said, "Sure. Bring the new light fixture over any time."

~

For the rest of the day, I basked in the warm glow of the pretty flower bouquet and all it implied. The arrangement came from Gabriella's, which was the most expensive florist in town. Most of our weekday customers are women, and there wasn't one who didn't close her eyes and deeply smell the flowers with a beatific smile on her face.

The phone rang a few times, but not with Dalton on the other end of the line. Closing time came and went, and I kept finding tasks to keep me there well into the evening.

Why hadn't I written my personal phone number on the business card? Because I was stupid, that's why.

I was, and continue to be, very stupid—stupid in the way that only girls who score well on academic papers can be stupid.

How stupid? When I tell you about the thing I did when I was fifteen, you may just write me off as worthless.

I can't think about that too much, though, or it makes me depressed, and not the kind of mild depressed that I can shake off with a laugh, like the way I feel when I see a wireless network named "Cankles." (I enjoy browsing around and seeing creative wireless network names like "I can hear you having sex" and "Derps" and "Click here for drug-resistant scabies," but the term "Cankles" isn't funny if you have them.)

An hour after closing time, the lights were still on and people had ceased to wander in browsing, so there was no reason for me to stick around waiting for the phone to ring.

Unless… I was changing out a light fixture.

My father had dropped a new one by, and I sent a quick text message to Gordon Junior to make sure I had his permission.

He texted back: *Knock yourself out, Petra.*

I frowned at my phone screen. Why did he sound like he was making fun of me whenever he used my name, either in conversation or in text like this? He was a nice enough guy, but he had a tendency to come off condescending.

I shrugged it off and got to work, first turning off the breaker for that strip of lights. Growing up, my father felt it was important for me to master basic home repair, so I learned from my mother how to make biscuits with bacon drippings, and learned from my father how to change a light fixture, how to snake a clogged sink, and how to hide out in the garage before dinner to avoid being asked to help make biscuits.

Instead of standing on a stool, which I'd been doing the day Dalton Deangelo literally knocked me off my feet, I used the stepladder, even though the nasty creak the aluminum thing made when you opened it caused my skin to crawl.

With my arms held high over my head, the pressure on my olive green button-down shirt caused one of my buttons to pop off. Annoyed and sweating from holding the fixture up while fiddling with the plastic connectors, I said a few choice words, then pulled shut the decorative curtain across the display window and took my shirt off completely.

As I dropped my shirt to the floor, I stared over at the yellow telephone, which was an old-fashioned, heavy thing that hung on the wall.

Ring, damn it.

As if that ever worked.

I looked down at my peaches, perkily packed into my hot pink bra. There was some serious hotness at the bookstore that evening, and a certain hunky actor was missing out on a good time.

I climbed back up the stepladder and finished installing the light fixture, then screwed in the new bulbs. My hot night was just jammed full of screwing! First all the screws, now the bulbs. I giggled at my joke, and when I flipped the breaker on the old electrical panel, I jumped up and clapped for joy that the light worked.

What I didn't know, and wouldn't find out for a few days, was that someone was watching me. Not just watching, but photographing.

In my haste and irritation, I'd neglected to close the curtain on the other window, and anyone passing by on the sidewalk would be able to see me traipsing around in my brown trousers and a hot pink bra.

When I was done tidying up, I grabbed my purse and took one last baleful look at the silent telephone. I'd stayed another half hour, sewing the button back onto my shirt using the emergency sewing kit from the office.

The yellow body of the telephone seemed a touch grimy, and I considered cleaning it.

The phone rang.

That's weird, I thought. *Now I'm having auditory hallucinations.*

It rang again, so I answered the phone, curious where this break with reality was going. By now it was half past eight, and I was so hungry, I could have eaten raw kale, no dressing.

"Good evening, Peachtree Books."

A low chuckle. "Is it a good evening?"

"That depends on who this is and why you're calling."

"You hurt poor Vern's feelings."

I smiled and wrapped the long, curly phone cord around myself as I twirled in excitement. "Poor Vern," I said.

"You hungry?"

"No." My stomach growled. "Yes."

"Is this spaghetti place any good? I'm standing out front, reading the menu. They have a Forest Folk platter that's free if you eat the whole thing, but I don't know if I'm quite that hungry."

"You're at DeNirro's?"

"You tell me."

DeNirro's was across the street from the bookstore. I twirled again to free myself from the twisty phone cord, made my way to the display window, pulled open the curtain, and peeked out. There was a handsome, dark-haired young man, standing across the street, waving at me. He almost looked like a regular person at this distance.

"Is this Robert DeNiro's restaurant?" he asked.

"No. Different spelling. Two Rs." I pointed to the logo on the sign.

"I'll have to get a photo and tell him about this place. Or maybe not. His lawyers don't have a sense of humor."

"You know Robert DeNiro?"

"Why don't you lock up that bookstore and come join me for a carb-heavy meal that my personal trainer will beat my ass for eating?"

"They have some tasty salads."

"Salads? Forget salads!" He held the phone away from himself and stare confusedly at it. Then he brought it back to his face, yelling, "Who is this? I want the bad girl. The one who's a bad influence on me."

Giggling, I said, "Give me two minutes to lock up."

"Two minutes. I'm starting the timer. If you go over, there will be Penalty Minutes."

MIMI STRONG

CHAPTER 11

"What?"

"Penalty Minutes. Tick, tick. Time's running."

"Eep!" I unwound myself from the phone cord, comically tripping repeatedly, then hung up the phone and raced around in a panic. Penalty Minutes! I didn't want to rack up Penalty Minutes, whatever they were.

My finger was shaking as I punched in the alarm code, 1225. Gordon Junior chose that number because it's the date of the only day we're closed.

I ran out the front door, then back in for my purse, then back out again, my heart pounding in a panic as the countdown on the alarm beeped down.

By the time I got outside the store, I was covered in sweat and breathing heavily. With a wicked grin on my face, I noted that if things went well, it wouldn't be the last workout that evening.

~

Penalty Minutes were most certainly accruing, and when I ran across the street to join Dalton, my face must have been bright red judging by the way it felt.

"Darling," he said in a English accent, then took my hand in his and kissed my knuckles while bowing.

"Sorry," I said breathlessly, pointing behind me like a fool. "Closing. Forgot stuff."

"You must be terribly famished," he said, still in the English accent. "You're making no sense at all. Come, now, let's get you off those running shoes. You girls and your ridiculous fashionable footwear. Why aren't you in stilettos? You'll twist a heel in those, walking with your feet in a normal human foot shape."

Why was I suddenly in the middle of an improv skit? Actors, sheesh.

I played along, saying, "Cheerio, bangers and mash."

"Darling, are you making fun of my accent? This whole time I've known you, I've put up a charade, speaking with an intolerable American accent, but I can stand it no longer! I must be me!"

He was really laying it on thick, and weirding me out more than a little, to be honest. Even his face had taken on a decidedly British look. How many faces did the guy wear?

A thirtyish couple walking out of the restaurant stopped to stare, and after a moment, the woman said, "You're him, aren't you?" To her husband, she said, "Drake. The vampire. I heard he was shooting a movie here in Beaverdale."

Dalton leaped toward the woman, also yanking me with him. He pulled me in front of him, making a horrible snarling sound and biting me on the neck. Not nibbling, but full-on biting.

"Ooh, Bitey," I said.

The woman stared with a mix of horror and adulation on her face. The husband got out his phone and asked if he could take a picture.

Dalton said yes, and what did I do? I stood there, waiting for the guy to take our photo. Because surely this stranger wanted a picture of me, right?

Nope. He wanted a photo of Dalton with his wife, without me. That was an awkward moment, as he winced and I shuffled out of the way. That moment was followed by another awkward one, where they actually asked me to take a photo of the three of them.

The man said to Dalton, "Would you mind biting my wife for one of these?"

Dalton waggled his eyebrows at the woman and said, "I'm afraid if I do, she'll never be the same."

He had his smolder turned up to eleven, and I'd by lying if I said I wasn't outrageously turned on.

The woman nearly collapsed in a heap of giggles and lust. Then he lunged at her neck anyway. She screamed. I managed to take the photo, by some miracle, because what I really wanted to do was jam the thing in her stupid mouth. Sideways. What can I say... I was an only child most of my life, and I don't like to share my toys.

After the couple finally walked away and left us alone, I said, "You seem to enjoy interacting with your fans."

He gave me a saucy look. "Jealous? Don't be. I only have eyes for one fan, and she only joined my fan club recently, but I'm very glad to have her. Her username is Peachy22, I believe?"

I jumped back like mating dragonflies were flying out of his mouth. "You know I joined your fan club? I'll just die now, excuse me."

"At least we know where your loyalties lie, and you're not Team Connor."

"Never. He's the worst."

Dalton stepped closer and seized me in his arms. "Kiss me," he said.

People were still walking around, going in and out of the theater just up the block. We were out in the open, and I felt self-conscious, so I gave him a timid peck on the lips.

"No. Kiss me like I'm dangerous," he said. "Kiss me like I'm bad for you."

His dark hair flopped around in a breeze, ruffling on his forehead above his dreamy, too-cute, green eyes.

Oh, he was dangerous. And bad for me.

I stood up on tiptoes and gave him a real kiss, my pulse racing and my whole body tingling from the sensation of his lips on mine. The smell of his skin in my nostrils. The feel of his hot hands on the small of my back. The sun setting and glinting off the windows and vehicles around us. His hands reaching down to cup my buttocks and press me against his body, the full length of both of us connecting.

Heat rushed through me like a shot of tequila followed by another shot of tequila. As we locked lips and tongues, the extremely sensitive front of me detected movement in Dalton's crotch region.

Ladies and gentlemen, we have liftoff.

I crushed my hips against his, teasing his hardness with my softness.

He pulled away, practically gasping for air. "Who's bad for whom?" he said. "I think you're the naughty one."

"I'm the girl your parents warned you about."

A look of mirth crossed his face. "If only you knew."

"So, tell me. I'm yours for the night."

He winked. "Tell me your secret, and I'll tell you mine."

I scratched my head, pretending to look innocent. "Evading each other's questions would be more fun over some food and wine."

I started for the door, but he caught me in his arm. "I'm sorry for falling asleep the other night. I didn't mean to shut you out like that."

"I'm sorry I left without leaving a note, but I didn't want to snoop around looking for stationery."

"When I woke up and you were gone, I thought maybe I'd dreamed the whole thing."

"I'm real."

"You sure are." He opened the door to DeNirro's, letting the aroma of hot bread and meat sauce waft out in the evening air.

We went in and got seated at a cute table for two at the back, on the raised platform that also doubled as a stage on nights they had live music.

"This is new," I said, running my hand over the tablecloth. DeNirro's was known for its classic red-checked tablecloths, but this table and the others were covered in mustard-hued cloths. I looked around, picking up on other changed details. The taxidermy-stuffed stag's head was no longer over the stone fireplace, and had been replaced by a wreath of branches.

"I was just in here last week," I said, feeling uneasy. "They've done a whole redecoration thing since then."

"For the movie. This is one of our shooting locations. The owner liked the changes the location manager requested, and decided to implement them permanently."

A waitress came up to drop off menus and take our drink order.

I asked her, "Are the red-checked tablecloths gone forever? Can they come out for special occasions, if we call ahead?"

"I think we have a few that we kept." She blinked at me, tilting her head to the side. "Petra? Peaches Monroe?"

"Chantalle Hart?"

She smiled, the dimples in her cheeks appearing. Had I not seen her in the five years since graduation, and did she really look even more gorgeous than ever, with her perfect tan, big brown eyes, and silky auburn hair? I still had mixed feelings about her, feelings you might describe as a girl crush. She was just one of those girls *everybody* likes.

"It's me," she said, pressing her fingertips to her eyelashes, the way I'd seen her fuss with her lashes a thousand times back in school. "You probably didn't recognize me because my eyes are puffy. Don't worry, I'm not sick. I had mono last year and I'm over it, Doctor says." She sniffed, looking pitiful. "Just been cryin' over a guy. An older man."

"So, you live here? Back in the Beav?"

"Since last month, yeah. Didn't Golden tell you?"

I glanced over to Dalton, who wasn't paying any attention at all, his gaze down on the menu in his hands. What a guy! Chantalle was a very pretty girl, and it just proved how clever Dalton was that he'd found somewhere smarter for his eyeballs to point.

"We'll hang out sometime," I said. "I'm renting a house with Shayla, up on Lurch Street. We Lurchers are a nice bunch."

Her pretty brown eyes widened, a huge smile spreading across her face. Now I could see the puffiness, the bags under her otherwise-lovely eyes.

She said, "We can invite Golden, and get the whole gang back together!"

Ugh, Golden. Also known as Little Miss Guess What. Everything was a big production, a big secret with an elaborate teaser campaign. Whenever you finally found out the big news, it was wildly disproportionate to the amount of fuss Golden put into it.

"Sounds great," I lied.

"For the record, I just want you to know that I was against the whole Least Fun category."

Dalton looked up from his menu, intrigued. "Who's-a-say-what now?"

"In high school, Peaches was voted Least Fun," Chantalle said, sucking in her cheeks and deepening her dimples. "But there were a lot worse things people could be voted."

"Yeah, but Chantalle, you were voted Biggest Dimples."

"Exactly!"

I shook my head and opened my menu.

Wow. If you don't move out of your hometown, you never really leave high school, do you?

"Did you hear Adrian Storm is back in town?" she asked, not taking a hint.

"Yes, apparently he's flat broke and living with his parents. Tragic. Utterly broke."

Just because I didn't want him didn't mean I wouldn't sabotage his chances with Chantalle, just for old times' sake.

"That's too bad," she said, jiggling and standing on one foot, kicking the other up behind her. Double-wow. I'd completely forgotten about that kick she did. Why didn't I have a signature move? I had to work on that.

She asked us if we wanted to start with some wine, and Dalton chose something from the menu. I batted my eyelashes and nodded at his excellent choice.

After Chantalle walked away, I said, "Remind me I'm a grown-up now. I don't care what other people think of me."

"Grown-ups still care."

I shook my fist in mock rage. "My parents lied!"

He pursed his lips. "All parents lie. The good ones tell comforting lies."

"Dark. Next you'll be quoting Nietzsche."

"I don't know who that is. I'm an actor. A meat puppet." He gave me a sly grin.

"I can't wait to lend you some great books."

"I can't wait to undress you. I can see your nipples through that shirt."

I fanned my face. If my nips hadn't been hard yet, they certainly were now.

He continued, "I'm going to peel your clothes off and lick your breasts like ice cream."

I took a sip of ice water, then replied, "I'm going to peel your shirt off and treat *your* nipples like they're Skittles. And I love to suck on Skittles. I can suck them all night."

"I'm going to use my mouth on your belly button like it's a single-serve pudding snack and I don't have a spoon."

I leaned across the table and whispered something almost too filthy to repeat. "Forget the belly button and try lower. It's today's special."

He raised his eyebrows and leaned back, arms crossed, considering. "Sold on the special," he said, a wicked smile crossing his gorgeous lips.

Chantalle returned with the wine, pouring it as the two of us tried to behave ourselves without success.

Dalton turned to her and said, "I'm dying for the special. I had it once before and the taste was maddening and decadent."

Chantalle scrunched her face. "We don't have a special. Do you mean spaghetti? It's our house specialty."

He rubbed his chin. "Does the sauce dribble down your face like this?"

I kicked him under the table.

"Spaghetti for me," I said.

Chantalle turned to me. "How many balls?"

My voice squeaked out, "How many balls would you recommend? Like, at one time?"

"Three is popular," she said.

I turned to Dalton, making a serious face. "Two at a time sounds about my speed, unless you'd like a nibble?"

He grinned. "I'll have the baked tortellini, and give her four meatballs with her spaghetti so I can have a taste."

"Good choice," Chantalle said with a knowing, patient smile. She could be an airhead at times, but she wasn't stupid.

After she left, I pulled out my phone and said, "I should probably give you my actual number, right? Just so you can reach me if I'm not at the bookstore."

"If you're not at the bookstore, I hope it's because you're with me." He gave me a million-dollar smile.

Another waitress came by with two long, skinny breadsticks and some butter.

I read out my cell phone number, and he punched it into his own phone. He didn't immediately give me his number, though. I sat there, aware of this, and feeling annoyed, until I got a text message from an unknown number.

He messaged: *You can gobble my breadstick. You can munch it any time, and I'll watch.*

I saved his number to my contacts, and then I nibbled the end of his breadstick in a suggestive manner.

The flirting continued through dinner, with both of us making inappropriate faces and jokes about everything going in our mouths.

As we ate dinner, he moaned and rolled his eyes up, enjoying the forbidden carbohydrates. He was a manly-looking guy, with his square chin and muscled arms, which only made it more funny that he was showing the kind of high-calorie reverence Shayla and I have for the Lemon Meringue Mile-High* at Chloe's Pie Shack.

*The meringue isn't a mile high, but it's damn close. You have to tilt your head sideways to get it in your mouth. Think about *that* lemony goodness for a minute and tell me if your mouth doesn't water.

"Did you ever work here?" Dalton asked as we were finishing up our last bites.

"No, but my best friend did for a bit. She manages a different restaurant now. Why do you ask?"

"You seemed rather attached to the old tablecloths. The red-checked ones."

I squirmed in my seat, feeling silly. "My parents took me here for my birthday dinner every year since I turned five. We sat at different tables, but the pictures always turned out the same, because of the decorations."

Dalton crossed his arms and rested his chin on one hand. "Now I've brought this movie here and turned your whole world upside-down."

"In more ways than one, yes."

"Are you afraid?"

I gave him a long look, not sure how to answer that.

He cleaned up a bit of sauce on his plate with his thumb and licked it clean.

He explained, "Most people won't admit they're scared, but with admitting something comes great peace. For example, I'm scared about the damage this movie is doing to me."

"You're doing your own stunts?"

He poured out the last bit of wine evenly between our glasses, looking very serious and sad.

"The damage is emotional, or psychological, I guess. Have you done any acting?"

"Sometimes at the bookstore, I act like I'm not bored senseless when I am."

"Imagine acting like you've just walked away from a horrific car accident, and your small children didn't survive."

I imagined Kyle being hurt, and the pain was so strong, it manifested as physical pain in my guts.

"That's horrible," I said, shaking my head. "Don't say crap like that or you'll give me nightmares."

"That's what acting is like. You can't avoid the darkness. You have to embrace it to deliver a believable appearance. If you aren't suffering, the audience won't connect."

"Can't you just say the words and pretend?"

"That's pretty much *all* you can do. Sounds simple enough, except there's a part of your brain that doesn't know it's pretend. Your ears hear the words in your voice, and you believe it. Your soul believes it."

I frowned and played around with the silverware before me.

"You seem to be having fun, though. As Drake, the vampire. You're always grinning and having a blast."

"True. But this movie I'm doing is different. It wears on me."

I glanced up, catching his gaze. "Sucky."

He blinked, and then his mouth turned up at the corners. "Sucky!" He sat up straight, looking more vital than ever. "I love how you put things in perspective. You have a real gift for stating the obvious, exactly when I need to hear it. You're right. Embracing a dark role is *sucky*. But it's also a challenge, and it's what I desperately wanted, so why am I complaining?"

I shrugged, returning his smile. "I don't know why you're so miserable. It's like all those carbohydrates sent you over the edge into a shame spiral."

"Blame it on the pasta," he said.

"Evil, evil pasta. Can you imagine if we'd ordered the deep-fried ravioli starters? They come with a sour cream dip. The mayor threatened to outlaw them."

"The horror!" He jumped up from his chair. "You wait here. I'll be back in a sec."

I sat alone at the table, carefully folding my cloth napkin into a swan shape. It's just something I like to do, whether the napkin was originally a swan or not. I find a comfort in folding napkins that doesn't translate to paper origami, though I don't know why. Perhaps a fear of paper cuts?

Dalton returned, a white box in his hand. "I got dessert to go." He stood behind my chair, leaned down, and murmured in my ear. "Actually, this is second dessert, for after the first dessert, which is —"

I twisted around and pressed my finger to his lips. "Don't say peaches."

"Are you shushing me?"

Remembering our first fight on my lawn, I yanked my hand back quickly.

"That wasn't a shush," I said, backpedaling. "I didn't say the word *shush*, so it wasn't one."

Some of the other people dining in the thinning-out restaurant were staring in our direction, with all the fuss we were making.

Dalton grabbed my hand and hauled me out of there.

Outside, I barely got one breath of cool night air before he seized me and gave me a kiss to take that breath away.

CHAPTER 12

I moaned into his lips, curving my body to nestle with his as my legs turned to something boneless, like Chicken McNuggets.

He pulled back and stared down into my eyes. "You don't want to go to my trailer," he stated.

"I don't? Is it really messy?"

He moved me, pressing my back and butt against the brick wall of DeNirro's. The brick was still radiating the day's sunshine, even though we were in darkness, lit only by streetlamps and the headlights of passing cars.

He traced a line down my cheek and the side of my neck.

"I don't think you're a big fan of the Airstream."

"Are you kidding? It combines the best parts of being abducted by aliens with the best parts of being a pioneer, taking the wagon train west and getting dysentery."

"Something tells me you don't like camping."

"I wouldn't know. I've never been."

"How about hotels?" He handed me the dessert box so he could fish something out of his pocket. He dangled a key between us.

I gasped. "Is that for the No-Tell Motel?"

He looked puzzled. "It's for the Nut Hill Motel." Pause. "Oh, okay. I hear it now. Anyway, I have a room there. With a bed. And a few dozen tiny little bottles of booze."

"We can drink from our fists and pretend we're giants."

"That's exactly how I usually drink!" He led me to the long black car with the tinted windows. I went for the back door, but he nodded for me to join him up at the front. "Vern's got the night off. He

127

found some book club thing he wanted to go to, so that means I'm driving."

"If you're driving me, does that make you *my* butler?"

We both slid into the leather seats at the front of the car.

"That depends," he said. "Does your butler do this?"

He leaned over and kissed me while cupping one of my breasts in his hand, giving it a gentle squeeze.

Even his joking gropes were sexier than other guys' concentrated foreplay efforts. Dalton had such a casual ease, like there were no wrong moves, and I wondered if the confidence came from his hotness or the other way around. Either way, my runway was wet and ready for him to land his big plane. *Woohoo, down here, Mr. Pilot! Get ready for splashdown!*

As he pulled away, I whispered, "What if I'd said no to dinner when you phoned? I'm trying to be charming, and that means I have to say no sometimes."

"You wouldn't let me down like that."

"What am I to you? Just stress relief from a busy day?"

He settled back in the driver's seat and turned the key to start the car. "I think you cause me more stress than you relieve."

That made me smile. I don't know why, but it did.

~

We drove up to Nut Hill and parked in the half-full parking lot of the motel. Dalton pulled a small overnight bag from the trunk of the car, then we held hands as we walked up the steps to the upper level and found our room.

"Woah," he said, stopping with the door open only an inch. "*Deja Vu*. I feel like we've done this before."

I glanced around nervously, worried about running into someone I knew.

"I've never done this before," I said, and it was true. I'd never been inside one of the units.

"Must have been in a previous life," he said, with a smile so charming, I couldn't tell if he was being serious or not.

I remembered the things he said to me the night we met and said, "Right. Previous life. Because we're made of stardust from the same star, and we're just being reunited again now."

"So you feel it, too. I should have never left."

He pushed the door open, then ran in and leaped on the first bed like a flying squirrel. He patted the spot next to him and waggled his eyebrows. The bedspread matched the motel room in that it was mottled, brown, and at least thirty years old.

I kept going, making my way to the bathroom.

I did a sexy striptease as I walked, dropping my clothes on the carpet, with my panties being the final item off before I reached the bathroom door.

A moment later, I was in the shower, hot water spraying down on me from a nozzle that was unlike your typical hotel shower head. I'd never been camping with my family, but we did go on many road trips, always staying in hotels and motels. One of my mother's favorite things was to write a funny review of every room's shower. She would have liked this silver beauty, because it actually found that middle ground between soft spittle and tearing your flesh off.

You'd think that a wealthy actor would stay only in the poshest of hotels, with abundant gift baskets and marble surfaces, and I'm sure Dalton Deangelo would have rented such a place if it existed, but Beaverdale was not Paris. Not Paris at all.

He tapped on the door and I invited him into the bathroom.

"Don't look," he said. A few seconds later the toilet flushed, momentarily causing a bracing cold spray from the shower head to turn my nipples into Skittles.

"Ah, so you do pee," I said through the shower curtain, which was mostly white. "You don't have your butler do that for you."

"Not yet, but I'm hoping for some advances in technology." A belt buckle dropped to the floor. "Is there room in that shower for one more?"

I hugged my soapy arms around myself, grinning madly. "Come on in. I could use someone to wash my back."

His toes entered around the edge of the shower curtain. He had adorable toes, with a few dark hairs on the knuckle of his big toe, and the nails were rounded and smooth as though pedicured.

The rest of the leg followed, and I quickly looked up to his face, so as not to make him feel like a sexy piece of meat. Poor fellow. He was so cute, girls probably objectified him all the time.

"Wash your back, hmm," he said. "I'm more interested in the front, but maybe if you show me the back, so I can make an informed decision?"

I turned around slowly, hoping the low lighting and streaming water camouflaged the cellulite situation.

I didn't expect him to grab me in one arm and pull me tight to his body, but that's what he did, my back squished to his front. He growled in my ear as his free hand roamed down my side, over my hip, across my butt cheek, and then between my cheeks.

With his lips near my ear, he murmured, "Like this?"

The back of me had never felt so good as it did pressed up against the front of Dalton's hard body.

He ran his fingers up and down, moving farther with each stroke, all the way down my coin slot and into my piggy bank.

"Mercy!" I grabbed onto the metal hand rail that had been installed for situations like this.

With hot, soapy, slippery fingers, he continued to explore my body, back and front, top to bottom. Soaking wet had never felt so good, never felt so right.

I turned to face him, and instead of kissing his awaiting lips, I stuck my tongue out and licked along his jaw, from his chin to his beautiful ear. I pulled him close and sucked on his earlobe, drinking warm shower water from his body as divine nourishment.

He gently took my hand and wrapped it around the base of his candy stick, which was upright and sandwiched between us like a third party. A very eager third party.

"Oh, you sweet thing," he said. "Your hand feels so good. I can't wait to feel your heat. And you don't need to worry about a thing, because the drawer next to the bed is loaded with supplies."

I stroked the length of his long, thick candy stick, tugging gently on the head and swirling my wet palm across the tip before sliding my fingers back down. "Mamma will take good care of you."

What? Did I really just refer to myself as Mamma?

And was it just my imagination, or did his dick harden like twenty percent more?

"You're taking all the hot water," he said, his eyes closed. "I'm very upset right now, and shivering." He had a big grin on his face, but he also did have goosebumps visible across his chest and on his arms.

We switched spots and he tipped his head back, washing his hair under the water, his hands up and all his muscles flexing and looking majestic, like a sexy shampoo commercial.

I kept tugging and simply stared in awe as the shower water dribbled down his chiseled face and his perfect chest.

And what a manhood it was, standing at attention like a fence post, and nearly as big. How had I gotten my mouth around it the night before?

(Oh, that's right. I have a big mouth.)

"I'm objectifying you," I said.

He wiped the water from his eyes and stared at me with those mesmerizing emeralds.

"Fair's fair," he said. "I've been objectifying you since the moment you fell into my arms."

I crossed my arms under my breasts, pointing the nipples up. I had fallen into his arms. And he'd acted like I weighed about half of what I did. Even though...

I bit my lip.

"And you were standing on that stool," he said, laughing.

"They wouldn't let me ride the pony," I blurted out.

"What?"

"In fourth grade. Shayla had a birthday party and all the girls were there, even Chantalle, and Golden, too. The pony's name was Lionheart, but I couldn't ride him because I was too big. The man who brought Lionheart was wearing a cowboy hat and cowboy boots, and he said if I got on the pony, even just for a minute, it could break his back."

Dalton pulled me to his chest, his arms tight around my shoulders and keeping me up. "That's awful," he said. "This cowboy, let's go find him and make him eat his teeth."

I sniffed, my nose congested. Was I crying? I couldn't tell with the shower water spraying down all around us. My eyes felt hot, and my chest was both light and heavy at the same time.

"He died," I said, sniffing. "The cowboy, not the pony. I guess he was pretty old. The next year at Shayla's birthday, Lionheart came again, but with the guy's daughter. She said I could sit on him, even though I was a year older and bigger, but I didn't trust her. I knew that if I got on that pony, I'd hear something crack and I'd never forgive myself."

Dalton pulled his hips away from me slightly, allowing some space between us. "I'm sorry to hear that. And I'm doubly sorry to be poking my boner into your belly button while you're telling me this very personal story." He frowned down at the fencepost-region. "Not cool, bro."

I wiped the water from my eyes and smiled up at his face, which was not just aesthetically perfect, but also kind and wise. "I'm embarrassed I told you that story. I don't know why I did. I'm the one who's not cool."

He held his hands on either side of my cheeks and tilted my face up. "You don't have to explain anything to me. It's all totally clear. I'm Lionheart."

"You're a little Shetland pony with black spots?"

"I'm the beast you're worried you'll break."

I shook my head, disagreeing, but he pulled me closer and kissed me so tenderly. I melted against him, meshing my body with his.

His hands cupped my buttocks as he tongued my mouth. I felt the heat growing in my shower-soaked body, and I wanted him inside me.

He reached back and turned the water handle, accidentally spraying us with ice water before getting it turned off. Still, we didn't stop kissing. I couldn't let his lips go, not when he wrapped a big towel around the both of us, and not as he walked backward out the bathroom door and toward the bed.

I finally let go of him long enough to give my hair a quick towel dry so it wouldn't drip and make me shiver. His near-black hair shone like a raven's wing with the dampness. The two lamps with their brown shades were on, dim, and the room looked more romantic now.

I tossed the towel onto a chair, pulled down the bedcovers, and climbed in. On my back, I tilted my head to one side and peered at him through my eyelashes.

He opened the drawer next to the bed and rolled a condom on quickly. Then he was kneeling between my legs, two fingers dipping into me.

I opened my mouth to say something, but only a sigh came out. Now was not the time for talking. Now was for pleasure.

His eyes took on a dark cast, lit only by the two lamps on either side of the bed. He grasped one of my legs and folded it up at the knee, opening myself to him. He glanced down briefly, then shifted his body up and fell into me, his face alongside my neck and his thickness inside me.

I gasped at the sensation of him filling me, and he heard this as encouragement, pushing further and further, thrusting until his hips ground against my body, hardness on softness.

He found a rhythm, supporting his upper body on bent arms popping with muscles. I kissed one bicep and then the other.

He eased down a ways, withdrawing partially to curl down and lick my nipple. He flicked the firm knob of flesh with his tongue, while at the same time he teased my honey out with the tip.

Sensation radiated from my breast, and I writhed on the bed, my whole body a sensitive, jiggling embodiment of desire.

He mouthed my breast hungrily, as though trying valiantly to fit the entire mound in his mouth, and then he turned his attention to the other.

His fingers crept down the hollows between us and sought the space between my legs. He stroked me up and down with his fingers, and as I arched my back, he thrust into me, sending ripples of pleasure all the way to my ears, burning with heat.

"Why don't you get on top?" he murmured.

"I like where I am." I grabbed my knee with one hand and helped pull my leg up, allowing him deeper penetration.

He groaned and closed his eyes. The moisture on his forehead wasn't from the shower, but new—sweat. His manhood was rigid, like a kinked hose under pressure, and the muscles along the side of his neck were tense and visible.

"Fill me up," I said, and he started moving again.

The thrusting was slow at first, then built up with the pressure inside me. His fingers were on me in the sweet spot, adding pressure to the friction of my skin pulled taut from the girth of him.

He rocked into me steadily, and again he implored me to roll with him and go on top for a bit. I declined, insisting he do all the work, since he was so good at it.

The movement of his fingers began distracting me rather than pleasuring me, so I pulled his hand away.

"Is that it for you?" he asked.

I nodded. "Go ahead."

He withdrew suddenly, and I instantly felt terrible, so disappointed in myself.

But he wasn't done with me.

He grabbed my legs and yanked me down on the bed, so my hips were at the foot of the bed and my feet on the carpet.

Then he balanced himself on his fists, on either side of my face, and thrust into me, high and hard. The way he rubbed against me sent new shivers of pleasure through my body. This was new. A pressure grew.

He looked me in the eyes, his forehead shining and expression intense.

He was bigger than anyone I'd been with, and I had no idea what it would feel like to have a man touch me so deep inside. As he moved through undiscovered territory, I shuddered with a pleasure that seemed to come from my tailbone. It was a different sensation than his gorgeous lips and tongue on me. Even more personal.

STARDUST – PEACHES MONROE #1

Hard and fast, gliding easily on my body's reaction, he sought me out. I had nowhere to hide, and when I closed my eyes, I saw his face. Opening. I was opening to him, and that scared me.

With each thrust, he got bigger and harder, until at last he closed his eyes, bit his lower lip, and turned his head to the side, touching his chin to his shoulder.

A small cry escaped his lips as he came, shaking inside me.

I realized my feet were no longer on the carpet, but on the bed, and I'd been lifting my lower body, raising my hips to meet him.

I eased myself back down to the bed, catching my breath. He pulsed deep inside me, holding me in the hotel room with him, nowhere to escape, not even the back corners of my mind.

He reached between us and squeezed the skin above my nub. It felt good, really good, but I wasn't going to come, so I pushed his hand away. "Maybe next time," I said.

He let out his breath all at once and collapsed down onto me, snaking his damp arms behind my back in a hug.

"You made me need another shower," he said.

His head was nestled next to my neck as I glanced over at the motel room door.

The door.

It was right there, and I could just go. Nut Hill wasn't far from my house on Lurch Street, and the walk was mostly downhill.

"How about you go hit the shower before the rematch?" I said boldly.

"How about you come join me?"

"Sure. Go get the water started."

He pulled away, though the musky smell of him remained on me, all down my front like a tattoo.

MIMI STRONG

CHAPTER 13

Once Dalton Deangelo was in the bathroom with the water on, I got dressed faster than anyone has gotten dressed in the Nut Hill Motel, and I'm sure there've been some speedy exits.

I was still buttoning up my olive green shirt when I reached for the door handle. I glanced over at the little desk in the room, next to the chair where I'd tossed the towel. There was stationery sitting out on the desk.

My heart was pounding, my nerves telling me to run, just run, so I ran to the desk and scrawled a quick note:

Thanks for the fun. Have to work early. Want to sleep in my own bed.

I could hear Dalton calling me from inside the shower, and it broke my heart to open that door and leave, but it was the right thing to do.

I had to get far away from him, and all these confusing feelings that bubbled up in me whenever he was in my arms.

My running shoes slapped against the second floor balcony outside, the impact of my footsteps ringing through the night air with a metallic clang.

CLANG CLANG CLANG.

I ran down the metal stairs and away from the motel, down the street.

Then I stopped running, because that much running when you're not used to it is going to make a girl throw up. I learned that lesson during the annual Fitness Test at high school.

I gasped over some bushes, my hands on my knees. Something moved out of the corner of my eye, and I worried it would be Dalton, running after me in a towel, or stark naked.

I peered into the darkness. Someone was definitely there, watching me. Not Dalton, but I could feel their presence.

"Hello?" I called out.

I stood in the alley that ran behind the motel, near the end of the block. To one side was the back of an office building, and to the other side was someone's back yard and garage.

As my eyes adjusted in the darkness, I could just make out shapes moving in the back yard of the house. Dogs? I squinted, willing my eyeballs to work better. Cats?

The shapes turned and looked at me with curiosity.

If there's one thing that gives me the willies even worse than dragonflies, it's raccoons.

Two of them were ambling toward me, hell-bent on giving me rabies, for sure!

I started running again, and I travelled the dozen blocks back to my house by alternating between jogging and walking quickly while wheezing.

When I got to the house and came in the front door, Shayla was sprawled on the couch watching TV. She hit pause on the remote, turned and looked at my sweaty, red face, and said, "It just gets worse every day, doesn't it? At least you're not covered in dirt this time."

"Dating a celebrity is ultra glamorous."

"Come." She pulled herself upright and patted the sofa next to her. "Chantalle phoned me tonight. She asked me how you got the job being a personal assistant for Dalton Deangelo."

I slumped into the soft cushions next to her, feeling every ounce of myself, every frizzy yellow hair on my head, and every little pimple.

"That little cunt," I said.

"Wow, Peaches. Why don't you tell us how you really feel?"

"I'm sorry. I know you always liked her, but she puts me down."

"It's your fault for being offended at her ignorance. She doesn't know what she's saying, and she doesn't mean anything by it."

"Right." I crossed my arms and turned to the frozen TV screen. "What are we watching?"

"Don't you want to tell me why you burst in here like bears were chasing you?"

I looked over at my best friend, assessing her mood. She smelled of cigarette smoke, and there was an empty cookie bag and an empty chip bag on the coffee table, as well as a half-empty bottle of Mountain Dew on the floor next to her. Oh, she was in no mood for my problems. If I had to guess, she'd had more trouble with her boss at the restaurant. He was married, and she should have known better, but apparently he was a smooth talker, and things always *just happened*.

I didn't need to hear about her frustrations, and she was likely in no mood to hear about mine. And what was my problem, anyway? A really cute guy enjoyed spending time with me and getting close to me. He made me want to tell him my secrets. I wanted to lean on him. I wanted to love him. But that would only lead to pain, because as soon as his movie ended, he'd leave town, taking the Airstream trailer and a piece of my heart. He'd probably feel good about it, too. He could draw on the experience for future acting roles.

Well, forget him.

"This looks good," I said, and I pressed the play button on the remote control. Over the audio of the reality TV show about a family bakery, I said, "Raccoons. I worked late, got some food at DeNirro's, and I ran into some raccoons on the walk home."

"They're totally adorable, with their little raccoon hands, and you're nuts."

"I agree. I am nuts."

Shayla grunted and reached for the Mountain Dew. She took a swig and handed the bottle to me.

"Thanks," I said, and we watched TV until both of us fell asleep right there on the couch.

~

Wednesday.

The flowers from the day before were opening.

139

I stared at the lush peonies and tried to escape the thought I was a flower myself, and Dalton Deangelo's attention was the sunshine trying to light my darkness.

No wonder I'd run from his motel room the night before. If I'd stayed, he would have kept at me, with his kind words and soft touch, and I would have been a blathering idiot before midnight. Telling him how stupid I can be. Having him look at me with pity... curiosity... disgust.

The flowers were heavy on one side, and as they opened, they drooped, taking up more of the limited counter space in the narrow bookstore. Their sweet perfume hung in the air, tricking me into thinking a well-dressed older lady was there with me.

One thing that always makes me smile is seeing a lady in her eighties, decked out in tons of accessories, all perfectly matched to the colors in her impeccable clothes. Our generation is just not into the matchy-matchy look.

Beaverdale attracts a number of wealthy retirees looking to soak up small town life. They're so adorable when they first arrive, the ladies clapping their hands and declaring everything "so quaint," and the men leaning in to confide to their wives, "That same exact lamp/house/pizza would cost twice as much back home."

I never understood how people from all over America would even hear about little Beaverdale, much less get the idea to retire here, until we started carrying a few magazines at Peachtree Books, and I discovered there are several periodicals dedicated to small town life.

Last summer, one of them ran a story titled *Beavers & Passports*, all about life in The Beav. They quoted a local as saying Beaverdale's "so far off the map, you need a passport."

Our mayor, Stephen Monroe (Uncle Steve to me), capitalized on this, and along with the Beaverdale Chamber of Commerce, they printed up a couple thousand fake passports and encouraged people through the Visitor Center (next to the library) to visit all the sights in town and get their passport stamped.

I designed our Peachtree Books stamp myself, and I stayed within the limitations mandated by City Hall, keeping it within one inch by one inch.

Those sneaky buggers over at Black Sheep Books made their stamp one and one-quarter inch in diameter, and argued that because it was *round*, it was taking up no more *area* than our square stamp. Never mind the fact that other businesses kept their stamps within the one inch diameter. Oh, no. The rules simply didn't apply to Black Sheep Books, because they were "creative thinkers," and perhaps the rest of the town would benefit from their many, many innovations, such as their Borrow-A-Bike program that never really took off, on account of the yellow bicycles being too attractive as souvenirs.

Not only did their stamp exceed the size limit, but Black Sheep Books didn't take care when stamping passports, and their heavy black ink often overlapped the more artistic stamps, such as our peach-hued stamp.

I'm getting myself all worked up. I'm sorry. I really shouldn't get started talking about those sheep-lovers.*

*When not in polite company, I do call them sheep-lovers. Feel free to do the same yourself, just not around children.

So, Wednesday.

I pulled a big, plump peony from the bouquet and played a very long game of He-Loves-Me-He-Loves-Me-Not with the petals.

Carter, our delivery guy, came in the door whistling. "Ten boxes!" he said to announce what he was bringing in.

"Awesomesauce."

He stopped and leaned over my pile of pink petals. "You making potpourri?"

I stared up at his big, blue eyes, framed by orange-blond, nearly-translucent lashes. "Who taught you that word, Carter?"

He put his elbows on the counter and leaned down so his eyes were at my level. I tease Carter about being a ginger, like my father, as they both have the same red hair that curls into ringlets unless it's cut short.

"Am I right? Are you making potpourri?"

He was so close, I could have counted his freckles. Was he flirting with me? I'd never seen him without his shirt on, but I imagined the freckles extended down over his broad shoulders.

Carter moved to Beaverdale about a year ago, to complete his recovery from a bad car accident. He'd been unconscious for three days, broken bones all over, and when he finally woke up, he asked the nurse for a cigarette.

His family knew something wasn't right, as he'd never smoked a day in his life—that they knew of. The truth was, he'd smoked for a few months when he was fourteen, and something about the brain injury had set him right back one entire decade, possibly to the day. There were some physical problems as well, like needing to learn how to walk without falling over once his leg was healed, but the most curious aspect was his lost memory.

He'd been a super-smart student, getting top grades in law school and being courted by top law firms in Los Angeles. But all that knowledge was gone after the coma. He couldn't take the bar, because he was fourteen inside, with a fourteen-year-old's knowledge.

Carter recovered physically, and by the time he turned sixteen for the second time, he had the mental faculties of a keenly intelligent twenty-year-old, getting smarter every day.

But this person, this new Carter, had no interest in law school. He wanted to play guitar and write music. Did the world need another lawyer, or did it need a poet? That was what he asked his parents when they delivered their ultimatum.

They felt the world needed another lawyer far more than another poet, hence the differential in potential earnings. When he wouldn't agree, they changed the locks on the guest cottage across the pool from their mansion, and he found himself homeless.

Carter packed up his car, leaving behind most of his worldly possessions, but not his three favorite guitars. He drove out of LA not sure where he was going. He stopped for gas and picked up a copy of *Small Town Life in America*. He opened the magazine to a story titled *Passports & Beavers*.

By the time he got back into the driver's seat, his mind was made up, and he programmed Beaverdale's coordinates into his car's navigation system.

"I know all about potpourri," he said, grinning and still eye-level with me. "It's petals and bark, and you girls like it. Are these flowers from some dude?"

"Yes. Some dude." I could feel my cheeks reddening, because now I was thinking about some dude. He was quite the dude, all right. My brain was traipsing around the filing cabinets full of images of Dalton with his clothes off, recalling the sensations of his soapy hands all over my body in the shower.

I continued, "Just a dude I know. We're sorta seeing each other, but he's not my boyfriend."

"I should've asked you out when I had the chance," he said.

I narrowed my eyes at Carter. Red-haired boys are always the biggest pranksters—what's that all about?

"Don't make fun," I said.

He backed away, holding his hands up. There was new ink swirling up his arm—those fancy fish people put in their ponds. Koi. Or as the local raccoons thought of them, supper.

The koi fish on Carter's arm were spotted with his freckles.

"I'm not teasing," he said. "Let me know when you get tired of this douche and I'll take you out for one of those fancy lemonades girls like."

"How do you know he's a douche?"

"I took one look at you when I came in, and you looked like you were going to cry. Usually you get real excited to see me. I like to pretend it's my good looks and tight ass, but we both know it's the new books I deliver. Today, though, your face is all droopy. So, what's the matter? What's the story, morning glory?"

I took a deep breath. I didn't want to tell him specifics, so I said, "Do you ever think other people will never understand what it feels like to be you?"

"People don't know what it feels like to truly be themselves, let alone other people."

I swept up the petals and crushed them into a ball in the palm of my hand.

"Why are you so wise?" I asked.

"Because I took a workshop from Dottie Simpkins."

"What?"

He started laughing, bending over and slapping his knee. "Just kidding. Shayla tried to get me to go for one that's just for men, but I have band practice scheduled for all the same times as the workshops." He grabbed the hand truck he'd brought some boxes in on and wheeled it to the back table where I liked to receive the stock. "Would you like your delivery here, ma'am?"

"Yes, sir."

He bent over, giving me a good view of his cute buns and muscular calves. Carter always wore shorts, even on the coldest days of winter. He claimed he "ran hot." Mm-hmm.

Carter moved quickly, tossing the boxes onto the old wood table as easy as if they were empty and not full of heavy books. He raced back out the door and returned with the other five boxes.

I grabbed my clip board with the invoice attached, plus the box cutter. Naturally, this was the cue for a rush of customers to come in the door, all needing to get recommendations. I knew that helping customers was my real job, but when you're trying to receive an order, they do feel like interruptions.

"Have fun," Carter said with a knowing look as he rolled his handcart out the door.

I got busy, unpacking boxes and helping customers until it was past lunch break. I put the "Back in Five Minutes" sign up, locked the door, and ran over to get my lunchtime mocha and my tuna sandwich from Java Jones.

Kirsten, the girl who managed the place, looked more wan and limp than usual. She was probably on another juice cleanse or three-day fast. Either way, I didn't want to know, so I didn't ask.

"What are you up to with that actor guy?" she asked as she steamed the milk for my mocha.

"Nothing. What did you hear? Who told you? Was it Chantalle Hart?"

She snorted as she finished making my drink. "Saw you with my own two eyes. In here the other day. He even asked if I knew you."

"Ah. Yes. He wanted to ask me some questions about life in a small town, as research for the movie they're shooting."

"Is he staying up at the No-Tell Motel?"

Yikes. What did Kirsten know?

I shrugged, a pitiful attempt to hide my shock. "Beats me."

Kirsten shook her brown ponytail and gave me a Like Hell look. She'd been a few years ahead of me in school, but I was well aware of her reputation. Whenever an attractive couple broke up, Kirsten would appear on the doorstep of the young man, ostensibly to cheer him up, and wearing nothing but a bit of lace under her overcoat. I heard through Shayla that she'd gone to the city for Sex Addict Rehab, but first of all, I don't think that's a real thing, and secondly, I don't think it worked.

"Who's the tiny girl with the short, brown hair?" Kirsten asked. "Do you think she's an actress? If she is, I sure haven't seen her in anything."

That sounded like a description of Alexis, the girl who'd been angry at Dalton and trying to take his picture. I was equally curious, but didn't want to let on to Kirsten how much I knew.

"Tiny girl, huh? If I see him again, I'll ask."

"That's her over there," Kirsten said, pointing to the person walking out the door of Java Jones.

The girl moved quickly, her head ducked down, and I swear she glanced over at me before she started moving faster along the sidewalk.

Oh, it was Alexis all right. What was she up to now?

We had six coffee shops in Beaverdale, five of them serving decent coffee. So why was Alexis at that particular coffee shop? The one that had a direct view in the windows of Peachtree Books?

I shuddered at the thought she might be spying on me.

Then Kirsten handed me my sandwich and I was happy again. They put diced jalapeno peppers in the tuna sandwiches, and it's to die for.

I ran across the street with my lunch and opened the door to the phone ringing.

"There you are," came a sultry male voice over the line. "The phone just rang and rang."

145

Breathlessly, I said, "Just popped out for lunch. Sorry, we don't have voice mail."

"I didn't want voice mail. I wanted you."

"You have my cell phone number."

"And have you ignore my phone call? You slipped away on me last night. Are you avoiding me? I'm beginning to think I smell bad."

I twirled in place with a big grin on my face, wrapping the long yellow cord around myself. "No, baby. You smell good."

He growled. "I like you calling me *baby*. You make me feel so good. What are you wearing?"

Some customers walked into the bookstore, the bells on the door jingling merrily.

"I'm wearing my favorite blue dress. I don't think you've seen me in it."

"I bet it would look great... on my floor."

"Ouch. That's bad."

There was a pause, and I heard voices in the background, people arguing with each other.

CHAPTER 14

Dalton sighed from his side of the phone call. "I'd better get back over there. Next time I do this, remind me that there's no such thing as a *simple* film."

"I'm glad you called."

"You know, you could call me for a change. It would go a long ways to making me feel like I don't smell like garbage."

"You smell good, trust me. I can't wait to smell you again."

"Really? Even the armpits?" He laughed.

"I hope you're not ticklish, because I plan to nuzzle your armpits."

"Forgive me for being blunt, but that sounds hot. HOT."

The customer browsing the books showed signs of interest in my conversation, so I covered the receiver with my hand and whispered, "I'm going to do bad things to you."

"Whatever you do to me, I'm going to serve you back. Double."

"In that case, there's going to be a lot of licking."

He answered with a growl.

"How's the movie shoot going?" I asked.

"Aren't you full of questions. You haven't explained why you ran out on me last night."

"I got scared."

"Scared of what? I'm not the big, bad wolf. Not unless you want me to be. Peaches Monroe, do you want me to huff and puff and blow your house down?"

I giggled in response.

There was a long pause, and I heard his muffled voice as he talked to someone else on his side.

"We're going to be filming late tonight, doing some night scenes," he said when he came back. "Actually, that's the bad news. I won't be able to see you until Saturday at the soonest."

"So, I'll see you Saturday."

"Will you call me *baby* again?"

"Saturday, baby."

He groaned. "Your voice. It's like launch control for my pants, if you know what I mean."

I cupped my hand over my mouth and the receiver again and whispered, "Am I making you hard, baby? Do you want me to ride your pony?"

He chuckled. "You can ride my pony any time, but you need to get on top."

"I don't know," I whispered.

"You will ride me, and you'll call me Lionheart. I want to feel your fingernails digging into my chest as you throw your head back and ride me senseless, crying out, 'Faster, Lionheart, you little stud-pony, faster!'"

I fanned my face with my hand. He sure could paint a vivid scene.

A white-curled lady with a coral necklace and matching sunglasses approached the counter with her romance novels. She coughed politely to get my attention.

"Thank you, sir, for the special order," I said with a professional tone into the mouthpiece. "We'll have that particular item ready for you Saturday. What time will you be by?"

"I'll come to your house in the morning. Is ten too early?"

"Not at all," I breathed. "I look forward to it."

Someone hip-checked me, nearly knocking me over, wrapped up in the phone cord as I was.

Amy, my employee, was there for her shift, and she'd simply shoved me out of the way so she could ring up the coral-necklace-wearing customer expediently.

After the lady paid and left with her smutty novels, Amy turned to me and asked, "Who were you talking to?"

I'd already hung up the phone, and struggled to come up with a cover story. I couldn't just tell people I was dating Dalton Deangelo, because then they'd demand updates and ask questions I didn't have the answers to, such as *why*? Why was a famous actor whose nude torso appeared on television weekly dating Peaches Monroe? And *how*? And then, once more because it begged to be asked again, *why*?

"None of your beeswax," I said. "Grownup stuff."

Amy snorted. She was sixteen, and even though I was barely six years older than her, she liked to act like there was a giant generation gap between us, implying I was closer in age to her parents than to her. She had blue hair. When I was in high school, only the skanky girls (like Kirsten) colored their hair, but it seems these days they're all experimenting, with streaks at minimum, but frequently the whole head. So, maybe Amy and I were from a different generation after all.

"Boring," she said of my vague non-answer. Her face brightened as she spotted the boxes on the back table. "NEWNESS!" she cried out, racing toward the boxes.

Together, we made short work of receiving the order and rearranging the displays to set everything out. Dalton's name sat on the tip of my tongue. My tongue. His name sat there, and I'd had a dozen other parts of Mr. Deangelo on, under, and all over that same tongue. Oh, I wanted to share the news with Amy and revisit those pleasant memories. I wanted to impress her, because so few things I said to her about my life ever did.

But I didn't say a word, because telling Amy would amount to telling her two hundred closest internet friends, and I did not need that kind of heat. Too much heat. Thinking about the things he might do to me on Saturday was already causing my temperature to rise.

"Have you seen Drake since Saturday?" she asked as we were breaking down the cardboard boxes for recycling.

"Who?" Oh, I was a terrible actress. "Right, you mean that actor who plays Drake. I've seen him around. I guess he's in town for some movie."

"I heard he's dating someone right here in Beaverdale."

We were near the counter, and I leaned down to take a deep sniff of the beautiful bouquet, fondling one heavy peony with my hand. I could feel the dumb smile on my face, too—a smile that meant, deep down, I wanted to be found out.

Amy continued, "Probably a publicity stunt. They totally do that to get free press for whatever project they're doing." She blew a wisp of blue hair off her face. "Question everything, man."

"Question everything?" I gave her side-eye.

"Yeah, like authority and stuff. Don't believe a word they tell you. Mortgage is just another word for ownership of your soul. And don't eat genetically-modified corn syrup, because your guts will turn to cement." She looked around, making sure we were alone in the bookstore, which we were. "I think the new bakery next door might be putting something addictive in their stuff, because I can't stop thinking about those cupcakes. I swear I can smell them right now."

I pointed to the vent on the ceiling—the one I'd attempted to seal up with packing tape on Saturday. "The smell keeps coming through. It's not just you, Amy."

"Are you sure? Maybe we have that thing where two people share the same crazy. Like how our periods went on the same cycle when I started working here."

"Amy, do you ever think about the things you're going to say before they pop out of your mouth?"

"No." She pulled her head back, giving herself multiple double chins, even though she was a skinny girl. "Do you think before you talk?"

"Of course not." I glanced up at the tape on the ceiling. The corner had pulled away, and the scent of vanilla buttercream frosting was wafting into the bookstore like the devil himself.

Amy and I both turned to look at the calendar. It had been twelve days since the last Cupcake Cave-in. Now I had all these emotions roiling and boiling inside me, and I wasn't going to see Dalton for three days, and what were we doing anyway? Dating? Hooking up?

He'd awoken something inside me. Now, correct me if I am wrong, but I believe the scientific term is *vagina*. Let's call her Miss Kitty. Ever since the phone call, and all the talk about armpit

150

nuzzling and pony riding, Miss Kitty had been meowing and drooling for dinner—a dinner that wouldn't be coming for another three days.

In the meantime, Miss Kitty was going to howl and scratch at the doors, driving me crazy.

I reached for my purse as Amy watched.

"It's time," I said.

She nodded.

I shook my fist at the evil ceiling vent. "Damn you, evil cupcakes!"

"You give 'em hell," she said. "I say we start with the coconut ones. They are the most evil, and must be taught a lesson."

"We'll line the others up and make them watch," I said, laughing maliciously.

"A lesson will be taught today."

"They'll be sorry."

Together, we howled, "They'll all be soooorrrry!"

Then I handed her some money, and she went next door to do the deed.

~

The rest of Wednesday, and Thursday too, was normal enough, though at times I got a weird out-of-body sensation, like I was observing my own life as a stranger might.

On Friday morning, Mr. Galloway was out puttering in his flowers as I walked by on my way to work.

He pushed his wire-rimmed glasses up his thin, sun-burnt nose and said, "I'm sorry to trouble you, Petra, but a rat has moved into my house. Mr. Whiskers brought him in through the cat door, I suspect."

"Sucky. Should I pick up a mousetrap for you on my way home?"

"That's kind of you to offer, but I think he's a big fella, and he'd just wear one of those little mousetraps as a hat."

"Won't Mr. Whiskers catch him?"

Mr. Galloway leaned his long, beanpole body against the pergola, making himself comfortable for a long chat. "I believe they are new friends. I came out last night to find Mr. Whiskers watching as the rat dined on his kitty food."

"Cute!"

"His little droppings aren't so cute. And I haven't been able to sleep through the night, because I hear him skittering around. Cats and rats should not be friends."

I put my hand over my mouth and laughed. "You know, I think we have a children's book by that very title. *Cats and Rats Should Not Be Friends*."

"Some things just aren't natural," Mr. Galloway said. "The universe has an order. Now, you know I'm not the religious type, but there is a design, and it's beautiful and true. Sometimes the sign comes to you as a number, or sometimes it's a color."

Mr. Galloway wasn't usually so new-age-y, and I wondered if the lack of sleep was making him a touch loopy.

He continued, "The stars are not just in the sky, but in everything, and they do align."

"What does the universe think about two people with very different backgrounds dating?"

"You mean a cat and a rat?" He narrowed his eyes, like he suspected me of making fun of him.

"Never mind."

"Watch for a sign," he said. "And don't let *anyone* eat from your food dish."

"Good advice," I said, nodding.

"Did I ever tell you how I met the late Mrs. Galloway?"

I pulled my phone from my pocket and glanced at the time to drop a hint. "I'd love to hear about it some time."

"It's an amazing story." He had that misty, far-away look on his face.

I knew, however, from working a few years in a bookstore, that the personal anecdotes people billed as amazing rarely were. Something about being around all those stories, though, made them want to share their own, amazing or not.

"I should let you get back to your weeding," I said, backing away while waving. "Off to work!"

He held his gloved hand, complete with garden spade, up in a salute, and then returned to crouching over his perennials.

The rest of the day, I couldn't stop thinking about what he'd said. I located the children's book I'd mentioned, and found the title was actually *Cat and Rat, Best Friends Forever*. Goes to show you how your memory shifts the pieces around to suit the situation.

I looked at the illustrated images of the cat and the rat. The cat was built for comfort, not for speed, and the rat was devilishly handsome. Plus he was a real smooth talker. The rat got the cat to close her eyes for a kiss, and while she had her eyes closed and her little kitty-cat lips puckered, he snuck all his rat friends into the house. He even gave the cat very strong perfume to wear so she wouldn't be able to sniff the rats, and then a beautiful collar, covered in bells.

The stupid cat was so lonely and desperate for love, she didn't suspect a thing.

Suffice it to say, I couldn't read to the end of the book. I put it back on the shelf, near tears. Children's picture books frequently have this effect on me. There's something about raw emotions stated plainly that breaks through all my defenses. Maybe it's knowing the truth when I see it.

~

Friday night, I went for dinner at my family's house.

My mother had been decorating again, and this time she'd gone too far. My father's reclining arm chair had been relegated to the attic, so he had retaliated by relegating the television, a mini fridge, and himself to the attic as well.

My mother grabbed me by the arm as we walked into her gleaming white kitchen. "There's no bathroom up there," she whispered.

"And…?"

"I think your father is urinating in a bucket and throwing it out the window, like we're in medieval Europe."

"Mom! No, he isn't."

She took me to the window and pointed to the hedge along the house, to a spot that seemed absolutely no different from the rest of the hedge.

153

"Look. It's wilting," she said. "I'm worried Kyle is going to pick up on it and start doing the same."

I put my hand over my mouth to stifle a laugh. When he was younger, Kyle certainly did enjoy running around the front and back yard with no pants on, widdling on everything with unfettered joy. *Boys*.

That evening, the house was quiet, with just the three of us adult Monroes there, and Dad upstairs. Mom had some jazz playing on the stereo in the living room. She didn't like jazz, but said it put her in the right frame of mind for entertaining.

Kyle was sleeping over at his best friend's house, two blocks away, so we were having an all-grown-ups dinner.

"You could just move the recliner back downstairs," I said.

My mother shook her head, her plump cheeks flushed with frustration at both of us. "I should have known you'd take his side."

I leaned back on the kitchen island, enjoying the cool white marble on the small of my back. "I'm actually on the side of the poor bushes," I said.

"Well, ha ha, aren't you funny tonight. I'm glad you're in fine form, because the Storms are joining us for dinner."

My palms started to sweat. Adrian's parents. What if they knew about Adrian finding me traipsing through the bushes at Dragonfly Lake, and brought it up over dinner? I'd been telling too many fibs, and the idea of lying to my mother's face gave me a stomach ache.

"Mom, I have to tell you something. That cute guy who came to the wedding with me last weekend is actually a famous actor."

"Dalton Deangelo. Yes, I figured that out, no thanks to you. I had to google it on my phone, just to set to rest those family rumors he was your hired escort."

I smacked my hand to my face. "I don't know whether to laugh or cry," I said. "Is it so unbelievable that a guy like Dalton would actually date me?"

She gave me a pitying look that only made me feel worse, and the too-long pause before she said, "Of course not!" didn't help either.

I went to the fridge and started rooting around for booze. Jackpot. I poured a vodka and soda, mostly vodka, and chugged it while Mom's back was turned so I could refill with another.

She said, "Don't tell people, but when I was your age, I had an affair with someone quite famous."

"Shut up!" I pulled up a bar stool to the counter and got comfortable, my elbows on the marble. Now we were talking!

She came over to my side and whispered his name in my ear like it was a state secret. I can't repeat who it was, but let's just say if I'd been conceived a few years earlier, I would've won the genetic lottery. Not that I'm not absolutely, positively, mostly happy with myself exactly how I am, but... you know.

My mother told me the story of how she'd been working in New York, back when she did art restoration, straight out of college. I knew that part, but not the next. She dealt directly with many wealthy clients, and one night a distraught man came in, devastated that his wife had taken a razor blade to several of his paintings.

My mother wondered what the man, an up-and-coming actor, had done to deserve such wrath, and then she found out for herself. He seduced her in about twenty minutes flat, *taking her* right there on the workshop table, amidst the restoration supplies.

As she was telling me the story, I didn't know whether to cover my ears or beg to hear more. I mean, she's my mother!

The affair continued for three weeks, the duration of time it took for my mother to complete the restoration and repair the paintings.

When the job was complete, he paid the invoice in full, and also wrote her a second check, for ten times the amount.

I was on the edge of my bar stool. "What? Holy balls, Mom. Did you cash the check?"

"Where do you think your father and I got the down payment for this nice house you grew up in?"

"I thought you got an inheritance from some great-aunt who lived in Texas?"

"That's what we told the neighbors," she said, a sly grin on her face.

I looked down at my now-empty glass, the kitchen around me already taking on a pleasantly fuzzy feeling. "I'm going to need another drink to clear my mind of this picture of you getting rogered on a workshop table."

She got the vodka and soda from the fridge, her cheeks rosy with the memory. "Oh, Petra, he didn't *roger* me. People didn't do that back in those days."

"Pour, woman, and please stop talking." Exactly what did she think *rogering* meant? I had a pretty good idea, but didn't want to find out.

She topped up my glass. "I'm so glad we can be girlfriends now that you're older."

"I had sex with Dalton Deangelo."

She frowned. "Did he roger you?"

"Yes, but you do know that just means regular sex, right? Anyway, we have another date for tomorrow."

"You do know how babies are made."

"Mom, would you say that to one of your girlfriends?"

"Probably. I have no filter."

"That just makes you better."

She took a seat next to me, and we were both sitting quietly, looking out the window over the sink into the back yard, when a bucket's worth of *something* rained down on the bushes.

"I knew it!" she yelled, slamming her hand down on the counter.

By now, I had more vodka than blood in my veins, so I said, "Chill out, he's just marking his territory."

"I'm going to glue that mother-flipping attic window shut, that's what I'll do."

Mother-flipping? I snickered.

"With crazy glue!" she yelled at the ceiling.

"The front room looks really good, by the way. I can see how Dad's recliner would ruin the aesthetic."

"That fucking chair is an atrocity."

I busted a gut laughing, because she rarely swore, and seeing her this upset was like visiting the zoo at the exact right moment, when something cool was happening, like animals escaping their pens and running amok.

A few words about my mother's decorating:

The woman karate-chops her throw pillows. She buys new wooden things and puts an antique paint-chipped finish on them, while simultaneously buying paint-chipped things and refinishing them to a glossy newness. She knows the names of interior decorators who appear in magazines, and refers to them by first name: "*Stephen and Chris said that foxes are the new owls.*"

It's a wonder my father's beloved La-Z-Boy made it this long, albeit periodically covered in doilies and slipcovers that restricted its natural movement.

The doorbell rang. The Storms were at the door! Could the evening get any better?

Yes, yes, it could. They brought Adrian.

He walked in behind them, tall, blond, and muscular, looking like coming there that night was punishment.

"You're here," he said when he spotted me.

"Get used to it," I said, still feeling sore from his comment about *girls like me*, whatever that meant. "I'm all over this town. *I am this town.*"

Adrian jerked his head and commanded, "Cujo! Take her down!"

I screamed and ran for cover in the dining room, where the table was already set for dinner.

The four of them came into the dining room a moment later, laughing merrily. Apparently they hadn't brought Cujo, and it was all a joke.

My father came down from the attic and joined us, no mention of the chair or things that may or may not have been tossed out of the attic window. My parents were on their very best, most charming behavior. We were, after all, entertaining company. Jazz was playing on the stereo.

Maybe it was the fact my entire mouth was numb from the drinks, but I didn't feel compelled to talk about anything at all that night. I just sat there and listened to Adrian's mother talk about her orchids (she and my mother headed up the Beaverdale Orchid and Dandelion

Wine Society), and nodded along as my father talked about how amazed he was more people didn't lose their limbs in radio-control helicopter accidents.

Mr. Storm Senior sat through dinner quietly frowning under his copper-and-white mustache. If you ignored the mustache and the ugly plaid short-sleeve shirt, he was actually a handsome man, which was why the Beaverdale Fire Department had borrowed him from the police station to pose shirtless for their fundraising calendar project the last five years.

Now, if Adrian had been on the calendar, I would have bought a box of copies. I gazed across the table at him, admiring those cheekbones and feeling like I was seventeen all over again.

I thought I was being stealthy in my eyeball tour of Adrian, but when I was washing up the dishes in the kitchen so my mother could continue visiting, Adrian came in and said, "What's your beef with me?"

"No beef." I turned on the tap and started filling the sink with hot water to clean the serving bowls.

I started to feel very funny, being alone in a room with my former crush. Not funny in the ha-ha way, either.

CHAPTER 15

Adrian Storm grabbed a dishtowel from the stove. "I'll dry," he said. "Hey, remember when we used to use Photoshop to mess around with portraits for the yearbook? Remember how you changed my hair to black and gave me a matching goatee?"

I turned and stared up at him, the world still pleasantly soft and squishy around the edges from good food and booze.

"I completely forgot about that. You have a good memory."

"Sure do. And I remember how you used to love bubble gum. Either strawberry or watermelon. I still think of you any time I smell either flavor." He picked up the serving plate I'd just rinsed in the second sink and started wiping it dry, the towel squeaking on the ceramic surface. "Simpler times. Do you ever wish you could go back and do things differently?"

"Like not make bad real estate deals like you did?"

"Well, that. But I mean further back. Remember when we went to Toby's party? We were all about fifteen, I guess. And remember when we played that game?"

"Yes." How could I forget?

"I wish I'd fought for you."

I swallowed hard, my throat full of something buzzing like a hive of bees.

He continued, "Who knows what would have happened, but I always regretted being such a wuss."

"We're too young to have regrets."

"We're too young to have much of anything."

I stopped washing bowls and turned to him.

Adrian's gaze moved from my eyes, down to my lips.

I tilted up my chin, and he leaned down. The floor beneath our feet squeaked as our weight and our bodies shifted toward each other.

Oh, no! Adrian Storm is going to kiss me, I thought.

Only he didn't, because his mother walked into the kitchen, calling back over her shoulder to the others, "We can't break with tradition! Two members are present, so there *must* be dandelion wine!"

"Mom!" Adrian said, sounding exactly like his fifteen-year-old self and making my insides get squishy. "You're such a lush."

Mrs. Storm pulled a bottle of hand-labelled wine from the cupboard. "I'm not a lush, I'm lush-scious." She wiggled her ample butt.

Adrian looked like he was going to die right there in my parents' kitchen, yellow dishtowel in his hand.

After she left, I said, "Two members of the Beaverdale Orchid and Dandelion Wine Society *are* present tonight, so she's not wrong." I got back to washing the dishes, head down to avoid any awkward kiss-like movements. "I like your mom. She's cool."

"Um. Yeah! She's only the best mom ever, except for maybe your mom." He took a platter from my hands, careful not to touch me, and wiped away at the platter fastidiously. "So, are you curious about that movie they're shooting here? Is that why you were out in the bushes at Dragonfly Lake that night?"

My cheeks grew warm with fury. I wanted to tell him everything, just to crack that look on his face.

"Well?" he asked.

"If you must know, I was having sex with Dalton Deangelo. Me and him. Bigtime. Naked and everything, stuffing body parts in each other's faces."

"Sorry I asked. No need to be sarcastic."

"He's coming to my house tomorrow so I can ride him like a pony."

Adrian chuckled, still not believing me. "So I guess you're not available to go for a bike ride with me?"

"You could check back Sunday, but I'll probably be too sore from all the hot movie star sex."

Adrian stared down at me in amusement.

I added, "In the vagina area."

"Yes, I'm familiar with the concept. Are you flirting with me?"

"Never." I shook my head. "That's something fun girls do."

Adrian kept staring down at me. He really was tall. From that distance, did I look smaller to him than to other not-so-tall guys?

"I thought I knew you," he said.

"And?"

He shrugged and reached into the soapy water, moving in on my washing job. "Maybe the truth is nobody knew you, because you always had your nose in a book."

"And you always had your nose up Chantalle Hart's perfect heart-shaped ass."

He grinned, and the little scar below his lower lip where his piercing had once been glinted and caught the light of the fixture over the kitchen sink.

"You still love her," I said.

"I wouldn't call it love. Just a silly infatuation. It's better to want something you can't have, because human beings are never satisfied. The wanting is better than the having."

I gave him a little hip-check to jostle his mood, which was taking a turn for the goth. "Serious much?"

"You should have seen the house I had, at the peak of my business. Four thousand square feet. A clover-shaped pool in the back yard, as blue as a tropical sky. And I still wasn't satisfied. You'll never be as lonely as you are in four thousand square feet of dissatisfaction and envy."

"Who were you envious of?"

"The neighbors had better parties."

"You always were moody. You probably need more sunshine, Mr. Pale."

"You sound like my mother."

"That's okay. If I start to sound like *my* mother, just smother me with a pillow."

161

He laughed and gave me a sidelong look, his pale blue eyes looking down his aquiline nose at me. Adrian Storm had been cute in high school, but now that he'd filled out and wasn't so scrawny, he was breaking my brain. He looked like a cologne ad in a magazine. Was that a fold line running up along his chiseled cheekbone? Could I just peel it back and inhale the scent sample?

"What are you smiling about?" he asked.

"I could never tell you, because you wouldn't stop laughing."

He pulled out the sprayer wand from the edge of the sink and aimed it at my midsection. "Tell me or you get the hose."

"Hmmph."

He blasted me with lukewarm water—one short burst that rendered my pale blue T-shirt translucent across my lacy D-cups.

"Tell me what's so funny," he repeated.

"You look like a cologne model," I said, holding up my hands to protect me from another blast.

He raised his eyebrows, salaciously looking at my damp peaches. "And you look like the winner of a wet T-shirt contest."

I crossed my arms over my wet chest. "Gross."

"Wow. That shirt is really see-through when it's wet."

"If you keep looking, I'll have to send you an invoice for the peep show."

"You know I'm broke, right?"

"I'm sure you've got some assets hidden somewhere." I moved my gaze down his chin, then down his chest. He wore a green T-shirt, and the effect of the cotton fabric on his lean, wide chest was that of an inviting grassy park. The kind you want to roll around on. My gaze moved further down, to his jeans, and that enticing, mysterious area around his fly. Oh, goodness me, it was a button fly. Perhaps it was the extra layer of thick denim, plus the bulk of the buttons themselves, but something about a button fly on a hot guy made my mouth water.

From his muscles to whatever was behind those buttons, Adrian wasn't *without assets* at all.

While I was distracted, Adrian pulled his phone from his pocket and got ready to take a picture of me. "For later," he said.

I leaned forward like a pin-up girl, pushing my cleavage together with the tops of my arms.

The phone's tiny flash went off.

I gasped. "No you did not! Delete that right now."

"You can hardly see anything," he said, laughing and holding the phone up out of my reach. "I swear, it's mostly your face."

I gave up on trying to get the phone from him, since his reach was twice the length of mine. We stared at each other, both of us grinning stupidly.

He nodded in the direction of the dining room. "I should get back in there. Unless you want to show me your old bedroom."

"It's a guest room now, but my old bed is still in there."

He gave me a wolfish look. "Pink? Four poster, with one of those frilly pink canopies?"

"Every little girl's fantasy."

"Every big boy's fantasy."

I bit my lip. Something was definitely happening in my body. The return of a kittenish, youthful lust. Miss Kitty was wide awake and feeling awfully curious.

I was still pissed at him for whatever he'd implied the night he drove me home, about how a "girl like me" could still get hurt. Whatever that meant.

He started toward the back stairs, the second set that ran up to the second floor from the kitchen. My parents had debated for years removing them and gaining extra pantry space, but my mother hadn't gotten her way just yet.

Adrian disappeared, his footfalls quick on the carpeted stairs. I couldn't just let him go up there unattended, so I patted my front quickly with a dishtowel and followed him.

When I got to the second floor hallway, I couldn't hear or see him.

"Adrian?"

I sniffed the air, surprised to find I did detect his scent. He was wearing cologne, plus he had a musky Adrian smell. I crossed the hall to the front stairs and sniffed again. No, he didn't seem to have run back down again.

I called out, "Are you hiding?"

No answer.

My heart started to pound. Hide-n-seek always made me so nervous. The anticipation of someone jumping out of a closet at you was so much worse than the actual event.

The door to Kyle's room was closed. I turned the handle and pushed it open slowly. This was the smallest of the upstairs rooms, and had been his nursery as a baby. My parents had always planned to move him into my old room when he got older, but whenever they broached the topic, he'd get upset. He and I went for a long walk one night to talk about it, and he told me that if he moved out of the baby room, a new baby would come. He had no reason to worry, I said, but he started to cry. That was when I delicately tried to explain what a hysterectomy was, and accidentally got myself into explaining Where Babies Come From.

The floor creaked. Was someone behind me?

"Adrian?" My voice sounded small and scared, which triggered my irritation. "Don't you dare jump out and scare me. You do not want a big girl punching you in the face."

Silence.

Pulse racing, palms damp, I whipped open the bifold doors of Kyle's closet.

Nothing but a row of little shirts and a row of little jeans. My heart briefly squeezed at the cuteness of all his plaid button-down shirts in a row. They dressed him like a mini version of my father.

I turned around, checked under the bed, and stepped softly out of Kyle's bedroom.

I was able to check the main bathroom from the doorway, then I paused at the door to my parents' room. There was something sacred about the room where someone's parents made love, and Adrian wouldn't violate that by hiding in there, would he? He wasn't a bad boy, was he? My soaking-wet chest said otherwise. Adrian was not the good boy he once was.

I stepped into my parents' room carefully, moving from hardwood to plush carpet. The master bedroom was the only carpeted room in the house—a low-pile pale mushroom carpet, two shades lighter than the brown paint on the walls. The king-sized bed was covered in twenty-six pillows of various sizes and fabrics. My father had grumbled about the pillows for a while, until my mother explained there was one for every year of marriage. Then he decided it was romantic and awesome, and he helped her pick out a new one the next year for their anniversary.

The floor nearby creaked again.

I froze in place, staring at the doors of my parents' walk-in closet. Was the sound behind me or inside the room?

I reached for the doorknob, my hand shaking.

What was that sound? Was that my heavy breathing, or someone else's?

My fingertips touched the doorknob, slippery with perspiration. I flung open the doors, expecting to see Adrian's lanky body amidst my mother's dresses and my father's full-size plaid shirts.

For a second, he was there, right in front of me, but it was just my mind playing tricks on me, using a pair of my father's loafers at the floor of the closet plus a shadow to create an Adrian-like form.

So, he was in my old room.

"You bugger," I muttered.

And then he grabbed me. From behind. His long arms wrapping around me like boa constrictors.

Screaming hadn't occurred to me—not until a big hand landed over my mouth.

As he held me tight, I struggled against my muscled restraints and did the only thing I could. I bit his fingers.

Adrian released me immediately, chuckling and shaking his hand. "I win this round," he said.

"I'm going to kick your ass!"

I came at him, fists flailing at his chest area. My boy cousins used to terrorize me and Shayla all the time, and beating them up for it seemed more logical than stopping playing with them entirely.

He backpedaled, and I kept coming at him, until he reached the foot of my parents' bed and fell backward, but not before hooking me around the back and toppling me down on top of him.

Pillows of various sizes flew everywhere in the kerfuffle.

165

I struggled to get away, but Adrian wrapped his arms and legs around me, laughing.

"Lemme go, spider legs!" I yelled.

"I've got you in my web." His blue eyes shone fiercely bright as he grinned up at me.

His body was solid beneath me, and all the squirming was exciting something not just in me, but in him, by the feel of it. A long, thick something. Miss Kitty got very interested.

I stopped struggling and rested with my forearms against Adrian Storm's chest, so broad like a pleasant lawn in his green T-shirt. His hands moved up my back to my shoulders, then slid down to my buttocks.

And then, for the first time in my life, I did something daring and fun with Adrian Storm.

I said, "Kiss me like I'm dangerous. Kiss me like I'm bad for you."

He moved his hands up from my ass, to either side of my face, and pulled me down to him.

My lips got closer and closer to his. The heat between our bodies grew stronger, like a campfire between gusts of wind. His lips parted, and his eyelids fluttered closed.

I didn't just want to kiss Adrian Storm. I wanted to grind my hips against his, and feel his lips, his tongue, his teeth on my flesh. I wanted to reach down into his jeans and grab hold of the beast hardening beneath my thigh.

One of the turquoise pillows near my face caught my attention and broke the spell. I was on my parents' bed. And why was I about to kiss Adrian Storm when I was already involved with someone?

CHAPTER 16

Lying on top of Adrian Storm's sexy body, on my parents' bed, I came to my senses. We couldn't kiss. That would be the worst thing for us to do.

I changed trajectory, stuck my tongue out, and licked the tip of Adrian's fine nose.

Pulling back, I said, "Say uncle."

"Uncle?"

I rolled to the side, off his hot body. "I guess I win this round, after all."

He sat up, shaking his head and looking around as if just awoken from a dream.

"You win," he said.

"For once."

"We should go back downstairs before my parents get worried."

I slapped him on the thigh. "Worried I'll get their son pregnant?"

He caught my hand and held it in his. "Petra."

"I was just kidding about you kissing me. I'm actually seeing someone right now. A guy. So obviously that was just a joke."

"Who?"

I pulled my hand away, got off the bed, and started gathering the tossed pillows. There was obviously no point in saying who, because he wouldn't believe me anyway.

"Nobody you'd know," I said.

"I haven't been out of town that long. Is it that delivery guy? The red-haired coma guy?"

"Carter is a talented singer-songwriter. He's more than just a coma guy."

"I guess he's okay." Adrian got up and walked to the door. "Yeah, he's okay."

I stared after him, my mouth slightly ajar. "He's okay, you guess? Wow, Adrian, you sure wanted me bad. I feel so desired right now. Thanks. Thanks a lot for reminding me of old times."

He backed away, his head down and gaze on the floor. "Whatever I said or did, I'm sorry. For the record, I think you're a really cool chick, and I hoped we could be friends again, like how we used to be."

"There's no reason now. No yearbook." My words hung in the air for a moment. "Chantalle Hart is working at DeNirro's. She asked about you. I think you should go for it."

He backed away a few more steps, until he was just out of sight, in the hallway. He called out, "I'm just going to go home now, before I make things worse."

At that moment, his mother called for him. "Adri-aaaaaan? We're ready to go, dear!"

"Thanks for the fun," I said.

He muttered something I couldn't discern, and then I heard his footfalls on the front stairs, the wood ones.

I went into my parents' en-suite bathroom and shut the door to bide my time until the Storms left.

Looking at myself in the mirror, I said, "Girl, what's gotten into you?"

That's when I noticed the big, green chunk of spinach covering most of my eye tooth. I quickly picked it out, silently cursing stupid Adrian Storm. Imagine what would have happened if we'd kissed! A partially-chewed chunk of my salad would have transferred from my mouth to his.

Ugh.

The thought of it nearly made me hurl.

The door downstairs slammed, and I heard a car drive away. I waited a full minute, ran some water, and ventured back downstairs.

I found my mother sitting amidst her coordinated throw pillows on the new flower-patterned sofa in the front room.

"Tummy beans?" she asked.

I rubbed my stomach and grimaced. "Yeah. That spinach goes right through me."

She nodded, giving me a knowing look. "I suppose it hit Adrian at the same exact time, which is why you two were upstairs together."

I flopped down on the couch next to her, then scooched over so I could lie there with my head on her lap.

"Mom, he tried to kiss me. In between insulting me."

She patted my hair. "What would your movie star boyfriend say?"

"Something utterly charming that turns my insides to goo. And he's not my boyfriend."

"They're not like us, are they? These actors. They're like the sun, and we all revolve around them."

"What am I doing with Dalton? Am I crazy? Should I just keep hanging in there hoping he'll break my heart then write me a big check so I can put a down payment on a house?"

My mother silently stroked my hair for a moment, then said, "Jewelry is less vulgar than straight cash."

I covered the side of my face with one hand so she couldn't see my wide-eyed expression.

"Sheesh. My own mother is prostituting me," I said. "What next?"

"Now, now. What you meant to say is, 'My own mother is *pimping* me.' One can only prostitute oneself."

"And the hits just keep on coming."

She patted my shoulder. "You do know I'm joking, right? You're young, brilliant, and adorable. You're practically a clone of your dear mother. Any man would be lucky to catch your eye."

"Okay."

She kept patting my shoulder. "I know your birthday is a ways off, but he doesn't know that. You could make up a date, drop a few hints, perhaps walk him by Topaz Jewelry and stop to admire the window display, or—"

I sat up and gave her my most disapproving look.

Her eyebrows pulled together. "I'm being inappropriate, aren't I?"

"Very. And a little ruthless."

"That dandelion wine," she said, shaking her head. "It makes people do the silliest things."

I rolled my eyes as I got up from the couch and started gathering my things to leave. Dandelion wine, my ass.

My father came into the room with perfect timing to volunteer as my taxi ride home. I would have considered just staying there and getting a lift home in the morning, but I had a date with Dalton in the morning.

The whole ride home, I was quiet, silently sorting through whether or not I'd done anything improper with Adrian Storm.

He was the one who'd grabbed me and pulled me onto the bed, on top of his very hard body that felt way too good underneath mine.

I was the one who dared him to kiss me, though. And using the same words Dalton had said to me outside DeNirro's. I was kind of a skank! The idea put a smile on my face.

I hugged my dad goodnight and ran into the house, eager to tell Shayla everything. She was out, though, with Golden and Chantalle, according to the note on the fridge.

I frowned at the felt-pen-scrawled words for several minutes. They all went somewhere to hang out without me? How rude was that? Very rude.

I opened the fridge and drank some of Shayla's precious fresh mango juice, right from the bottle, no glass.

~

Saturday morning, I woke up three hours before Dalton Deangelo was due at my house. It still wasn't enough time for me to sort out what to wear.

I pulled on the blue dress I'd mentioned on the phone—the one he said would look good on his floor. The color did bring out my eyes, and the shirring above the waistband did wonders to hide my recent cupcake incidents. Then again, I remembered from Dottie's workshop that red clothing made a stronger impression on the male mind, so I was rooting around for something else when the doorbell rang.

Shayla was silent in her bedroom, still crashed from returning late the night before.

I opened her door and said, "Get up if you want to meet Dalton Deangelo properly." She'd given him heck on our front lawn that first night, but hadn't talked to him since.

She stirred, moving just enough to pull the top cover over her head. "Merff," she said, which was more of a sound than a word.

"You guys really tied one on last night, didn't you?"

She waved one limp hand. "Go 'way. Your voice. Ugh."

"Nice. So, you don't want to meet him?"

"Merff."

"Your loss." I started down the stairs.

Shayla and I lived in a delicate balance, and her recent grouchiness shouldn't have been surprising. She *claimed* to be happy for me, but whenever something good happened in my life, it took her some time to get used to the idea. Either that, or by wild coincidence the universe would make something bad happen to her to keep us in balance.

I pulled open the front door to find Dalton lurking a few feet off to the side of the porch, his arms crossed and his head nodded down.

The red geraniums in the terra cotta pots sat unharmed on the porch and front stairs, so he wasn't looking guilty due to kicking one of them over (which happened a few times every summer when friends came over).

"What's up?" I asked.

He turned a little to the side, taking on an even more lurking pose.

"Are you bailing on me today?" I asked. "Do you have to go back to shooting right now?"

He shook his head, no, but still didn't say anything.

Now I was starting to get worried. "Something worse?"

He nodded, yes.

I knew, immediately, that he was dumping me. Without a doubt.

So I said, "You're a douche," and slammed the door shut.

The doorbell rang again. I didn't want his stupid explanation, but I opened it anyway.

"Invite me in," he muttered, standing closer to the door but still keeping his distance.

"Fine. Come in."

He stepped in with a flourish, his face lighting up with maniacal glee. His mouth opened wide in a snarl, revealing giant scary vampire teeth.

I shrieked, like any normal person would, given the situation.

He was already laughing, bent forward with his hand on one knee. Waving his hand breathlessly, he said, "The look on your face!"

Holding my hand to my hammering heart, I said, "What's with all you guys trying to terrify me?"

"What guys?" he said, sputtering around the prosthetic vampire teeth.

"Nobody." The memory of me squirming on top of Adrian Storm's body returned with clarity, and I plunged into a deep well of guilt.

Dalton adjusted one of the top teeth, which looked really sharp and dangerous. "Sh-h-ould I wear d-f-ese all day?"

"I don't know. Definitely keep them on until you officially meet my roommate." I glanced up the stairs for signs of life. "Unfortunately, she's impersonating a person in a coma."

My face twitched as I realized I'd made a coma joke. Once you actually know someone who's been in a coma (my delivery guy, Carter), you either make twice as many inappropriate coma jokes, or just become aware of the ones you do. And the *brain damage* jokes are nearly as prevalent. I guess that, like *cankles*, some things just aren't as funny when they're personal.

"Does she sleep in the nude?" Dalton slurped around his vampire teeth.

"Nope."

He was already moving past me, up the stairs. I followed him up, my hand clapped over my mouth to keep myself quiet.

He opened the door to her room and crept in, the old wood floors squeaking under his feet.

From within her covers, Shayla muttered something about coffee.

Dalton climbed right up onto the bed, his knees and hands on either side of Shayla's form. I frowned, not pleased to see *my* vampire boy being so comfortable with another girl. But that was so… just… like Dalton, wasn't it? For him to instantly feel comfortable and at home wherever he was, to not have any fears about being close to another person. It had to be an actor thing, as I'd never known anyone who acted like that.

He opened his mouth, raised his eyebrows, and pulled his lips back in a crazed expression that showed off the pointy teeth.

He nodded to me, so I said, "Shayla. Wake up. I've made a huge mistake."

She grumbled and wiggled around.

I continued, "I've let a vampire into the house."

The blankets peeled down, and she pushed her long, dark hair out of her eyes.

Dalton—no, Drake Cheshire—stared down at her silently, his fanged mouth wide open.

Time seemed to stop momentarily as she stared up into his eyes. The silence was broken by a high-pitched squeal and then hysterical giggling.

"That's it?" he sputtered around the teeth. "No begging for mercy?"

She pushed his face away with one limp hand. "Bad kitty."

He jumped up from the bed and started popping the prosthetic teeth off. Shrugging, he said to me, "Not the impression I wanted to make, but an impression all the same."

"At least you scared me."

"I sure did. Let's see your room now. I bet it's a girlie room with a pink canopy bed."

His guess was so eerily similar to what Adrian had said the night before, I had to wonder if the two of them had been comparing notes.

"Right this way, sir." I led him out of Shayla's room and across the hallway to mine.

"I see you like books. And country furniture." He picked up a handful of paperbacks from my yellow-and-blue antiqued dresser.

That particular piece of furniture was actually a contemporary piece, from a cheap chain store. My mother had done her magic on it, painstakingly sanding the surface, applying one paint color, then the other, and finally battering the poor thing with a variety of implements.

He set down the books and wandered over to my walk-in closet. "Not bad storage you have here," he said.

"Yeah, right. Back in LA, you probably have closets bigger than my whole room."

"That, I do. Big rooms and huge closets. I have a wine cellar with sort of an art gallery in it."

"Art gallery?"

"More of a shrine. To the balls-out crazy former homeowner."

"Sounds cool."

He turned away from my closet and crawled up onto my bed without being invited. "Mm, nice bed."

I remembered what Adrian had said the night before about his huge house making him feel bad.

"Do you think a person gets more lonely in a big house?" I asked.

He kicked off his shoes and got comfortable on my bed, lying on his back with his head on my favorite pillow.

"Why do you ask? Are you offering to stow away in my trailer and come home with me?"

"Not at all. I was just curious. I've never lived without family or roommates, and usually in places that are cheap, which always means small."

He patted the bed next to him. "Come here and let's share the story of our first apartments away from home."

I climbed up and arranged myself next to Dalton, my cheek resting on his outstretched arm.

"You first," he said. "Did you go away to college?"

"I did. I rented a place sight-unseen, with Shayla."

"Brave."

"You have no idea. It wasn't completely sight-unseen, because we talked to the landlord by email and got some photos, but I think they must have been standing on ladders outside the rooms to take the pictures, to trick you into thinking the rooms were big."

I was lying on my side, fiddling with the fabric of my dress over the curve of my hip, and Dalton rolled in to face me, one hand landing confidently atop mine, on my hip.

"Did you have vermin?" he asked, which sounded surprisingly sexy coming from his handsome mouth.

I whispered, "Funny you should ask. Our third roommate was rather cockroach-like. We hardly ever saw her, and she wouldn't venture into a room with the lights on."

He squeezed my hand and smiled at me, that cute chin-dimple of his begging to be bitten. It seemed a little odd to be *starting* a date with pillow talk, but nothing about our relationship so far had been conventional.

"What about your first place?" I asked.

"Bath tub in the kitchen."

"New York?"

"Where else?" He chuckled as his hand wandered down my hip, along my leg past the hem of my dress, and then back up again under my dress, along the top side of my bare leg. I shivered from his touch, even though the room was warm and full of morning sunshine.

"Something lived in the walls," he said. "I don't know what, but it skittered around at night."

Something about his expression gave me another chill.

I whispered, "Were you scared?"

"Scared of being evicted, and of catching something in the damp air and not being able to afford a doctor."

"Did you have roommates? Other actors?"

"A few." His expression grew complicated, and he didn't offer more.

"Was your next apartment better?"

He brightened. "Much better. I booked some jobs, things started happening, and within a few years I was out in LA, shopping for mansions like they were cars, and shopping for cars like they were tennis shoes."

"That sounds like fun."

"You like shopping?"

"I like to sign up for accounts and shop online, and then I mostly make lists and look at all the things I could buy. I click them into a shopping basket and imagine them showing up at my door, but then I don't ever finish the purchase. Well, not unless I've been drinking wine, and then I buy the dumbest things, like a cuckoo clock."

His hand was heavy on my leg, and he slid it down to my knees, then brought it back up, between my thighs. My breath caught in my throat, and he stopped his hand just inches from my panties. Something about the way he gazed into my eyes made my breasts heavy, aching to be touched.

"Um." I was having a difficult time staying on topic with our pillow talk.

"Is that dress what you're wearing out today?" he asked.

"Why? Is there something wrong with it? Don't tell me you want to go hiking. I don't mind a walk in the woods, but I don't own proper hiking boots, or the appropriate hiking body."

"I can see why that dress is your favorite," he murmured, his voice low and seductive. "The blue matches your beautiful eyes."

I broke his gaze long enough to peer over his shoulder at my door. It was nearly closed, but not clicked shut. Shayla was probably going to sleep for a few more hours, but the things I wanted to do with Dalton were closed-door things.

He continued, "If you want to wear that dress today, you should take it off right now."

"Off?"

"Yes. It's probably getting all wrinkled right now with you laying on it."

He inched his hand up to a more sensitive location. Tingling sensations radiated through my lower body, focusing mainly in the area I sometimes jokingly refer to as Brazil.*

*A leg wax is for removing hair from your leg; therefore, a Brazilian is for removing the hair around Brazil.**

**With apologies to my friends from Brazil, who are probably dismayed by the whole thing. On behalf of every waxing salon who understandably doesn't want to write the words "pudenda waxing" on their sandwich boards, I apologize.

"What about your shirt?" I whispered. "You're getting all disheveled right now."

"You think?"

"Your shirt would look great tossed over a stack of books."

"I like the way you think."

CHAPTER 17

"So, about that shirt," I said.

"Your desire is my pleasure," Dalton Deangelo replied.

As he spoke, he gently pinched the rolling hills of Brazil and probed for a hot spring.

I moaned, helpless with pleasure and urgency, limp from his touch and his warm breath on my face.

He leaned closer and caught my lips in his, stealing my breath and making me quiver for him. His tongue danced with mine, and in an instant we were rolling together, entwined and struggling to free ourselves from our clothes.

I got his shirt off and immediately got to work kissing his tanned, muscle-bound chest. He lay back, and as I licked around his nipple and gave him a sidelong look, he gestured up with his chin in a go-for-it move.

"Suck my nipples like they're Skittles," he said.

"You remembered."

I had difficulty forming suction between his flesh and my mouth, because I couldn't stop laughing over the Skittles comment.

Finally I latched on like a clever baby, and he groaned with pleasure as his manly nip hardened in my mouth. I was on my knees at the side of his torso, folded down with my butt on my heels. I walked my free hand down his bare torso and on to his belt. My fingers traipsed down over the buckle and across the denim plains, stopping over a swelling feature. I gave his hardening mountain a squeeze.

With his eyes closed, he whispered, "You do everything just right, don't you?"

I let go of his nipple and licked the cut line between his pectoral muscles. Salty. I licked my lips, then went in for more, licking all the way up his neck and over his Adam's apple.

"Perfect," he whispered.

Carefully, I looked down at my body and raised one leg so I could straddle him. With my knee down on the other side, his body felt solid and good between my legs. I leaned in again and kissed the side of his neck, where it was smooth shaven but the stubble could be felt just under the surface using my tongue. His pulse ebbed under my lips, and I found myself sucking hungrily on his flesh.

He groaned. "You're going to give me a hicky."

"No, don't be silly." I flicked my tongue against his pulse point and went in for another bite and suck. His neck was yummy.

As I enjoyed his neck, he raised his hips beneath me, grinding against my growing-damp panties.

I moved from his neck to his lips, kissing him eagerly, as he matched my every greedy move. Our bodies moved, and we were grinding together like teenagers, him rock-hard and still in his jeans and me in my underwear and dress.

He grabbed hold of my dress and pulled it up over my head, then tossed it aside without pause or ceremony.

In my underwear only now, I pressed my palms into his chest and arched my body, throwing my head back and exposing my neck.

He curled up, his abdominal muscles rippling, and kissed my neck as he pulled me back down with him. I felt his tongue, his lips, and even the bright pain of sharp teeth, the pleasure like the setting sun flashing through trees while you're driving fast on the highway.

With one hand, I blindly reached for the drawer next to the bed and grabbed one of the packets.

He clutched my hips and pulled me up long enough to unfasten his belt and wriggle his jeans and boxers down.

I eased back down, his bare flesh hot against my inner thigh, now slick with perspiration. We slipped back and forth, rocking with him nestled in my hipbone, and my nub grinding down against his pubic bone.

"C'mere," he said, calling me to his lips with a tilt of the chin.

I cinched up and kissed him, leaning forward enough for his fingers to get to me, pressing at first and then pulling the thin cotton thong I was wearing to the side. His fingers stroked my wetness, making me quiver again. He thrust his tongue inside my mouth, and I could barely think, barely breathe, barely do anything but exist with his beautiful body under mine.

Something round nudged against me, and I ground down eagerly. He felt so good sliding inside me, that first smooth stroke.

It only lasted an instant, though, because my eyes flew open. Eyes open! Eyes open, Petra!

Panting, I looked down between my legs, relieved to see that the condom was already in place. With a contented sigh, I slipped back down again, engulfing him hungrily.

"Yes," he said, raising his hips as I lowered mine, filling me with his length, his width, his desire.

With my palms on his chest, I adjusted my body position, distributing my weight on my knees so I could move freely.

"Yes," he repeated, his eyes closed.

I was on top.

My body took over, moving with its own mind. My gaze roved over the beautiful body beneath me, and mine, catching sight of the tops of my breasts, milky white in the morning light next to Dalton's tanned body. If I didn't have my pretty bra on, holding the girls at attention, there was no way I would have moved as freely as this.

I didn't have time to think about that, though. Or anything. My orgasm was coming, and it was my master. I rocked my hips obediently, my insides gripping tightly.

"Call me Braveheart," Dalton urged.

"You mean Lionheart. So help me, do not make me think about Mel Gibson when I'm in this state," I breathed.

"I am your pony. I am Lionheart. Ride me hard."

I whispered, "Lionheart."

A feeling zapped through me, like I was doing something very naughty.

"Lionheart," I growled, letting myself land a little harder.

"You're so beautiful right now. You're my princess. You're my girl, now ride me. Ride me all the way home."

I growled again.

"Call my name," he said.

His chest glistened with sweat, and I could feel his pulse against mine, his skin sticking then sliding against mine.

My butt started to slap against his skin on each down-thrust, a naughty, spanking sound.

My toes curled and my heart jumped up as I started to climax. "Lionheart," I said.

"Yes."

"Lionheart!" I dug my fingertips into his chest.

"Yes!" He was already coming himself, shaking and pulsating inside me.

"Oh, Lionheart!"

I fell apart, my orgasm blossoming everywhere at once, from my bones to my skin, especially my skin.

My hands slipped on his chest, sliding off the sides and to the bed below as my arms weakened and collapsed with sweet relief.

He thrust once more, his body strong and compact beneath me. Dalton Deangelo was no pony; he was a stallion.

I whimpered as a second, smaller detonation leveled me completely. My head found a resting spot on his shoulder, my lips nearly touching his neck.

We both stopped moving, and I stared at his ear with newfound curiosity.

He had the handsomest ears. The way the cartilage curled around, it was like that Golden Mean perfect swirl thing you can find in all the most famous works of art.

My bra was soaked through, and our chests were stuck together as readily as two sides of a licked envelope. I didn't dare move and feel the grossness. Normally, I wouldn't have rested my body weight on top of a guy, but this time, it was the furthest thing from my mind. I just stared at the swirling contours of his ear, my mind blank.

His chest rose with a deeper breath, and then rumbled with the tremor of his voice as he said, "What are you thinking about?"

"You have a really cute ear."

Without missing a beat, he said, "Yes, that's my good ear. The other one isn't quite as nice."

I started to chuckle, which made him gasp and groan, because a certain part of his anatomy was losing its rigid structure and being squeezed out of a very satisfied Miss Kitty.

He rolled us to the side and I pulled away, the room's air cool on my glistening front. The sensation of the side of my stomach touching the sheets made me aware of my floppiness, so I kept rolling, onto my back. With my bra on, my breasts weren't headed for my armpits, so this was the most flattering pose.

Even though I was still self-conscious, I felt more comfortable in the nude around Dalton than I ever had with another guy. Not that there had been many guys, but I'd done a thing or two, some of them with ice cream.

He grabbed my robe and excused himself to the washroom for a moment, then came back and stretched out alongside me. His panther-like body made everything he was touching look better. Even me.

He took my hand in his and raised it to kiss my knuckles, a sweet smile on his face. He tugged me toward him, and I rolled back onto my side, floppiness be damned.

This is what mornings are like in heaven, I thought.

"This is nice," I said.

"I feel so relaxed, but I don't dare fall asleep or you'll make like Cinderella and disappear on me."

"This is my house. Where would I go?"

I reached over and traced the contours of his hipbone with my fingertip. He twitched, like he couldn't decide if he was ticklish in that spot or not. I kept tracing along the hollow, then looped up around his navel. His skin was so smooth and firm, his body breathtaking in its beauty.

As I was admiring him, he reached around my shoulder and unhooked my bra, then pulled it away. My girls slipped down without the support. Usually, being naked with a guy in a room full of sunshine, I would have reached for a sheet to provide some cover, but this time I didn't.

He reached over and palmed the bottom of one breast, lifting as though curious about the heft. My nipple hardened at his touch, sending a pulse of desire down the core of me.

"You're so feminine," he whispered. "Like the pure embodiment of femininity."

I ran my finger up the valley of his chest, enjoying how perfectly suited to my fingertip the shape was.

"And you're so masculine," I said.

"Thanks, but I wasn't fishing for a compliment. I meant what I said."

His words gave me one of those smiles you feel all the way to the back of your head, like an ultra-tight bun.

Maybe his god-like body was why I didn't feel more self-conscious. Even if he slept with really attractive women, if they were mere mortals, they couldn't compare to Dalton's beauty. So what if my thigh was the same circumference as his waist? He and I were simply not in competition with each other. We were in beautiful contrast.

~

We lay in bed together for a while, neither asleep nor awake, but somewhere in the middle.

I woke up with a start when the bathroom door slammed and the shower turned on. Shayla was awake. It was still Saturday, right?

A handsome man was snuggled up next to me, a streak of sunshine across his muscular calf, turning the dark brown hair golden. It was nearly one o'clock.

He stirred next to me and groggily threw one tanned arm over me.

I whispered, "You can stay sleeping for a bit, but I'm going to get started making some lunch."

He grumbled, "Breakfast."

"It's after one."

"Scrambled eggs and ketchup?"

I told him I would do my best, though I suspected we had neither item in the kitchen. Had he asked for tofu hot dogs and chipotle-infused mayonnaise, that I could have provided. I quickly pulled on my clothes and headed downstairs.

Nope, no eggs in the kitchen.*

*Except for chocolate ones.

Off I went on a quick jaunt to the corner store, three blocks away, on Spider Avenue.

On my way into Moody's News & Milk, I spotted a headline on a copy of *The Beaver Daily* that caught my eye: *Hollywood Loots Local Treasures.*

A lady with a toddler was coming in behind me, so I held the door open for her. She thanked me, and scooped the one and only copy of *The Beaver Daily* left on the newsstand. I quickly assessed my need for local news and decided not to fight her for it, since I had my own inside scoop, naked in my bed.

The woman gasped audibly.

I turned to see what the fuss was about. "What does it say?"

She covered her mouth with her hand and laughed, the newspaper shaking in her hand. Her toddler wandered off to rearrange the gum and candy on the toddler-height shelf near the checkout.

"I get it now," she said. "Beaver-Daily. Not Beaverdale Daily. It's like Beaverdale-y."

Ah, so she was just cottoning onto the pun-like name of our local paper.

"All part of the charm. We're a charming town. Chock full of charm," I said.

"I've lived here for five years. I even wrote a big article about the town a year ago for *Small Town Life in America*, but I missed that detail."

I nodded politely and went off to locate the items I'd come there for: ketchup and farm-fresh local eggs. Even though Dalton would probably frown at the carbohydrates, I picked up a loaf of bread as well.

As I paid for my things, I got the sense the woman was peeking at me over the newspaper she was reading. Her kid was running amok, two fists full of candy. I paid for my stuff and got out of there, eager to share my first breakfast with a certain sexy actor.

The woman watched me all the way to the door, and I didn't think much of it, until...

... I turned the last corner before my house and nearly ran into a film crew, swarming around a big-haired woman with too much makeup.

With horror, I realized the woman with the snooty expression was the same one who had chased Dalton into Peachtree Books exactly one week earlier. *We. Hate. Her.*

Something crashed and there was the sound of terra cotta breaking. My geraniums.

I wasn't wearing any sleeves, but I pushed them up anyway and prepared to kick some serious ass.

"This is private property!" I yelled into the teeming mass of them.

Nobody paid me any attention.

I cleared my throat, set down my grocery bag, and yelled, "GET OFF MY LAWN!"

A couple heads turned, but nobody got off my lawn. The guy with the camera who was standing on my steps took another step up and rang the doorbell. *My doorbell.*

Well, I sure showed them, because I wasn't in my house. Hah!

I picked up my grocery bag and was about to back away and sneak around to the alley, to go in the back door, when I realized the door of my house was opening.

It opened slowly. So slowly.

My eyes widened and my mouth dropped.

Shayla stood in the doorway, wearing the tiniest little tank top, and the pair of men's boxer shorts she usually slept in.

OH MY GOD we're doing a Notting Hill.

The crewmen who were back by the van, close to me, let out some appreciative chuckles and other noises at the sight of Shayla, generally giving their approval.

Shayla didn't back away from the open door, but stood her ground. She also raised one toned arm and ran it back through her raven-black hair like a professional swimsuit model on a cover shoot.

The big-haired reporter woman jumped up the steps and stood next to her, a microphone held between them.

The woman said, "How long have you been dating Dalton Deangelo?"

Shayla gave the woman a coy look. "Who?"

"He's here right now, isn't he?"

Shayla looked down over the crew and made eye contact with me. I shook my head, no. He'd been trying to avoid them for a reason. Furthermore, and I cannot stress this too much, *we hate that reporter woman*. Hate her!

"Nope, he's not here," Shayla said.

Now, if you play poker, you know many people have a tell, a physical sign that reveals they're bluffing. Some people rub their nose, while others might give too much eye contact, giggle, or sweat. Shayla does all of the aforementioned things.

Sweating profusely, she giggled and made aggressive eye contact with the reporter, then stared blankly at the camera.

Spoiler alert: the reporter lady didn't believe a word.

"Would you say you're friends?" the woman asked.

"I don't know."

"Keeping things casual?"

"Um…" Shayla's forehead glistened as she rubbed her nose, coughed, and gave me a wild-eyed, pleading look.

I elbowed my way through the crowd, saying, "Shay, get in the house and put a shirt on."

The reporter turned and stopped me on my own steps, microphone waggling in my face and tapping against my lips and chin in her excitement.

I shoved the microphone to the side with one hand and said, "Jeez, buy a girl dinner first."

"And are you the mother?" the reporter asked.

The nerve! Something shifted in the universe, and everything took on a red tinge. Was I the mother? As in Shayla's mother? Oh, hell, no. In the words of an eloquent comic book hero, HULK SMASH!

"Of course not," I snapped. "I'm the sassy best friend with the good advice and a soft shoulder to cry on. Now get off my porch before I break my foot off in your ass."

She stepped back, looking genuinely frightened, but now she was blocking my front door. She was also reading something from her cell phone, and holding one palm up at me, like she was the traffic cop of my damn porch.

"Seriously, lady?"

"Two questions," she said.

I looked to Shayla for advice, but she'd already disappeared into the house, much to the disappointment of the leering film crew.

"Sure," I said. "Go ahead and ask."

She tucked the phone away, a devious look on her face. "First, isn't this gorgeous weather we're having today?"

I slowly turned to the side, looking beyond the camera shoved in my face, at the blue sky. "Yes," I said. "It's very nice, if you like that sort of thing."

"Second," she said, sucking up air with a deep breath. "I understand you're sleeping with Dalton Deangelo. How would you describe sex with him?"

I dropped my grocery bag on the porch and raced away from her, down the porch stairs. I knew how to deal with people like this, thanks to Dalton.

I jumped over the flowers, cranked the brass tap connected to the house's water to fill the hose, then grabbed the hose by the sprayer and sent an arc of water right into the chest of the nearest guy. He had been taking still photos with a camera, but now he held his arms high over his head, yelling, "Not the camera, not the camera!"

"How about the face?"

"Huh?"

I blasted him in the face with the water, then turned on the rest of the crew.

The big-haired woman was not my favorite person at the moment, but I'll say this: the broad could run and dodge a good hosing. She moved like a movie action hero evading slow-motion bullets.

Within seconds, the lot of them were packed up in their nearby van. I kept the water trained on the vehicle until they pulled away. And then, since I was already in a watering mood, I took care of the potted red geraniums that hadn't yet been destroyed.

After a little spontaneous gardening, I went inside the house and said, "Who wants scrambled eggs?"

Dalton was walking down the stairs, fully dressed but with scruffy bedhead hair.

MIMI STRONG

CHAPTER 18

Dalton said, "Did that just happen, or was I having a vivid dream about you threatening Brooke Summer with foot-related violence?"

Shayla, who was leaning against the back of our front room sofa, said, "Oh! Brooke Summer. Yeah. I knew I recognized her. Didn't she leave that one show to have her own show, where she visits celebrities at home unexpectedly?"

Dalton ran his fingers through his dark hair, looking all cute and sleepy and handsome. "I thought her show was all fake, but I guess if today is any indication, she really does ambush people." He frowned, looking concerned. "Shayla, I'm sorry you got caught up in this. Just pray the producers and editors find the footage of you in your underwear boring and don't run it."

She crossed her arms over her chest and started edging around us, toward the stairs. "They can't do that. I never signed a release."

"It doesn't work like that," Dalton said. "They do whatever they want. You can go ahead and sue them, but it'll be after the fact. They'll run the footage and photos of you, unless they get something juicier this week."

Shayla swore as she ran up the stairs to her room then shut the door behind her.

Dalton took the bag of groceries from my hand and headed toward the back of the house. "The kitchen's this way, I assume? I guess I'd better get to work, since these nice eggs you bought aren't going to scramble themselves."

I followed him back. "Did you happen to tell anyone about us?" I asked. "I only told Shayla, and my mother."

"My private life is nobody's business but mine." He kissed me on the forehead, right above my eye. "And your business too, now."

"That reporter woman, Brooke Summer, she asked if I was sleeping with you, and she acted like she knew something."

"Probably just fishing. Does it matter? Don't tell me you're embarrassed to be linked with me?" He grabbed me suddenly and lifted me up to sit on the countertop. I hadn't been picked up like that since I was a kid, and the good feeling it gave surprised me.

With his hands gripping me around my hips, he kissed me hard, pushing me back until my head tapped the upper cupboards.

I had been so fuming mad from that horrible woman, and all those people tramping on my lawn, not to mention stomping all over my geraniums. Now, though, alone with Dalton, my anger dissipated.

"I'm not embarrassed," I said. "But aren't you? Like, to be seen with me? I'm not exactly Hollywood starlet material."

He kissed me again, sucking my lower lip into his mouth briefly, then offering me his tongue. He must have brushed his teeth, because he tasted minty. *Mmm, refreshing.* I wanted more.

Pulling away, he wiped a strand of my blond hair back behind my ear. "*Nobody* is Hollywood starlet material. Nobody. They'd have to build one from robot parts to get what they want. You do know there are entire industries devoted to the illusion, from hair and makeup people to digital retouchers?"

"Do you think that reporter knows you're in my house right this minute? Getting your package groped by me?" I reached down and made my statement true. He had nice balls that really filled out the package area.

He bounced his eyebrows. "They'll never catch me."

"So what if they do? They'd just take your picture and ask you stupid questions. Isn't it good for you to get more publicity?"

"The way to get good publicity is to pretend you want your privacy."

"Interesting." I kept fondling his package through his jeans, enjoying guessing what was sausage and what was beans.

He winced, and the package in my hands grew in size.

"Careful what you start," he said.

I pulled my hands away and put them behind my back. "Sorry! I have no control over my mouth, or my hands."

"One of the many things I love about you."

I snorted in surprise. He said the word *love*.

"Breakfast," I said, eager to change the topic.

"Right." He held one hand up, motioning for me to stay seated on the counter. He got the eggs out of the grocery bag and started hunting for a frying pan.

"Right here, sexy." I parted my legs so he could access the cupboard beneath me. I was wearing the blue dress again, and pretty sure he'd get a view of my panties.

He crouched down to get the frying pan, but couldn't resist taking a nibble on my bare calf. My panty zone pulsed with heat. Oh, the way he touched me—like I was a fancy android-sex-bot and every square inch of me was a turn-on panel. Oh, my circuits! He licked and nibbled my calf and then my bare knee.

In a robotic voice, I said, "I am your sex-bot. How may I pleasure you?"

He stood up slowly, giving me a sly look. "Nobody's ever asked me that before. Not in that exact way, at least."

"I am the Peach Three Thousand. Your pleasure is my top priority."

He reached into the cupboard behind my head for a bowl, pausing to drink in more kisses. I was so hot, my baby oven felt like an incinerator. Which was weird. But not entirely unpleasant.

His voice throaty and thick, Dalton growled near my ear, "I'm going to wear out your warranty."

I would have reached down and tried to pull his clothes off right there in my kitchen, but he moved away and danced over to the stove. I sat and watched as he made breakfast for us, to eat for lunch. There's no lunch quite like breakfast, when you missed the latter because you were making love and napping.

"C'mere, sex-bot," he said once our meal was ready.

I sat across from him at the walnut pedestal table in the corner of our eat-in kitchen. The table was a "loaner" from my mother. She'd found it a few years earlier at a garage sale, covered in decades of layered paint and marked up from love and abuse. She'd painstakingly stripped off all the layers of paint in our garage, using a heat gun and finally a chemical stripper to get into the carved detailing. The wood was still scarred, its giant ruts filled with walnut-stained compound, but that was what she called "character."

There are two kinds of people who love antique furniture. The first kind appreciate character in all its many flavors, meaning flaws and quirks in everything, from people to towns and objects. The second kind is those who think everything made today is crap. I'm glad my mother is the first.

As we ate our scrambled eggs and bread (I had three slices of toast while Dalton begrudgingly had one that he savored), we talked about antiques and furniture restoration. I wasn't that surprised when Dalton told me he liked mid-century modern pieces with teak wood and clean lines. Considering the guy was staying in a silver bullet Airstream trailer, it made sense he couldn't just like normal furniture from IKEA, or whatever the rich-person equivalent of IKEA is.*

*Now that I think about it, there probably is no rich-person equivalent of IKEA, no more than there's a rich-person version of marble cheese, Pabst Blue Ribbon, or beans and wieners.

He talked some more about his house in LA, and as he did, there was an awkwardness in the air. He shifted back and forth between explaining his home to me like I would never see it myself, and then changing tone and saying things like, "But of course, you'll see for yourself that the swimming pool isn't garish at all. Make sure you bring your sunscreen, though, because your pale Washington skin is unaccustomed to so much sunshine."

"I could tan if I wanted. Just six to eight weeks of blisters and peeling skin, and I'm as brown as my cousin, Shayla."

He pointed to the ceiling, as she was still upstairs. "Your roommate's also your cousin? Wow, I really am in a small town."

"Don't say it like that. We're not *all* related."

"Are you related to the Weston family?"

I gave him a sidelong look. How did he know about the Weston family? They'd lived in Beaverdale for generations, but their descendants never married anyone from the town. Spouses were always met elsewhere, then imported. They didn't even have their weddings in Beaverdale, but you couldn't fault them too much, because through their lumber mill they did employ a good portion of the town. They also sunk money back into the community, sponsoring local sports teams, and paying for improvements to the recreation center. I'd certainly enjoyed the new tennis courts countless times. Not playing tennis, but walking by and enjoying the fit young men sweating and chasing the yellow ball.

"Nobody's related to the Westons except the Westons," I said. "How do you know about them?"

"I have my ways. Do you know about their hot spring?"

"That's a rural legend. Um… the small-town equivalent of an urban legend. The hot spring isn't real."

He looked down at his cleaned-off plate, his smile smug. "Interesting you believe that."

"Doesn't matter. Even if the hot spring is real, nobody's allowed on the estate who isn't family, which rules out all of town."

"I hear the spring has magical restorative powers."

"Oh yeah?" I said. "I hear Old Man Weston has quite the shotgun collection, and doesn't take kindly to people trespassing on his land."

"Are you sure you're not related? He sounds a lot like you, when reporters show up on your front porch."

"You just *had* to bring that up. Now I'm getting mad all over again. I should send them a bill for my plant pot. Do you think I could sue the crew for something?"

He laughed. "Let's go skinny dipping in the Weston hot spring. I think it's the perfect thing for us to do today."

I jumped up with a start. "Poor Vern! Has he been waiting in the car this whole time?"

Dalton pulled a set of keys from his pocket. "I told him to take the day off. Someone recommended the tennis courts, so I believe he's starting there, taking a tennis lesson."

"Careful about that," I said, grinning. "He's going to get too comfortable here in the Beav and you'll find yourself without a butler."

"We'll see about that." He nodded for me to follow along as he walked toward the front door. "Just me and you. Let's have an adventure. Put on your adventure boots."

"Sure, but they don't go with this dress." I ran up the stairs to my room and got changed into my Disco Duck T-shirt, plus sweatshirt layers in drab colors, plus a pair of dark, lightweight cords with some stretch. I didn't own a pair of hiking boots, but I had some year-old, unused tennis shoes that could use some breaking in.

I popped my head into Shayla's room and told her we were heading out.

She looked up from her computer and gave me a worried look. "Be careful."

"How do you know what we're doing?" I looked down at my outfit. "Is it that obvious I'm dressed for trespassing on the Weston estate?"

"Oh." She scrunched her lips from side to side thoughtfully. "I just meant be careful in general. He's so charming, just like his vampire character. But you wouldn't trust Drake Cheshire with your heart."

"He's not Drake. That's just a character, and Dalton's not a character."

More lip scrunching, plus wincing.

"Funny you should mention that," Shayla said. "You say Dalton's not a character, but what if he is? This whole super-playful personality thing he has going on... insisting on going to the wedding of a complete stranger, with a stranger. It's messed up."

"Maybe that's just how he is. Some people are impulsive. Fun. I hope he rubs off on me."

"He's going to fill your head with promises and leave you broken hearted."

Now, I love Shayla like a sister. Or, based on the siblings I know, *better* than a sister. I knew she meant well with the warning, but her condescending tone was not helping her message get through.

I stepped into her room, pulled the door shut behind me, and whisper-yelled, "He's going to fill me up and leave me satisfied. You're not the exciting one now. Get over it."

Before she could retort, I quickly exited the room, shutting her door firmly behind me.

With a deep breath, I put a smile on my face to lift the weight in my chest, and I ran down to join Dalton on an adventure.

~

We drove toward the Weston Estate, which is on the opposite side of town as Dragonfly Lake.

With Dalton at the wheel of the sleek black car, and me beside him on the passenger side, we drove past the Burger Barn and Chloe's Pie Shack, both of which seemed busy with the Saturday afternoon crowd. Through the large windows, I spotted a table full of boys in baseball uniforms, trying to get the attention of a table full of girls with their hair up in buns from the afternoon's ballet classes.

Dalton had slowed down to a crawl to catch a good look as well, and said, "It's like a Norman Rockwell painting in there."

"You should buy a house in town if you like it here so much."

He didn't respond, just smiled and tapped the steering wheel, staring straight ahead at the road.

Now it was my turn to feel awkward about touching on that forbidden topic of The Future. When you're dating someone, you need to have intercourse at least ten times before you start talking about The Future.

(That's not one of Dottie's rules, just one of my own. I probably got it from my mother's trashy magazines that she hides under a stack of decorating and craft magazines in her impeccable, non-trashy living room.)

To date, I'd never talked about The Future with a man.

I'd made The Beast with Two Backs more than ten times, but never ten times consecutively with the same person. I made the mistake of trying to talk about Two Weeks From Now with a guy I'd had intercourse with three and a half times, and he'd claimed I was suffocating him. Ironically enough, he liked being suffocated, and had asked me to smother his face with my breasts. Because I am a lady, I refused.

Just kidding. I totally smothered him as requested, but the whole thing was weird and I think I did it wrong, because we didn't work out a safe word or signal, and he kept begging me to stop, so I stopped, but then he got annoyed and said the begging was part of it. We tried again, but by this point I was about as excited as a school janitor after a cafeteria food fight. We finished the smothering, and I was on the bottom as he wiggled his wormy dick around, and the whole thing just felt so wormy that I awkwardly began to make small talk to cover up his weird grunting. I mentioned a family barbecue planned for the upcoming holiday weekend.

"You're smothering me!" he cried as he spurted out his hand lotion in or near my leg crease.

I'd held out hope he would change his mind, and even bought a big package of tofu hot dogs just for him. The wieners had been more expensive than regular meat wieners, which seemed all kinds of wrong to me, so I'd thrown them in the freezer so as not to waste the money. A year later, I'd found no takers for the tofu hot dogs, and as I sat in the car next to sexy Dalton Deangelo, I thought about those hot dogs. I wasn't going to repeat the mistake of buying fake meat products or trying to talk about The Future before it was time.

The landscape on either side of the road grew more lush and green.

We reached the turn-off for the Weston Estate, and Dalton turned onto the road, completely ignoring the multiple posted signs forbidding trespassing.

A chill passed over me, giving me goosebumps as we moved through the shadow of the trees, bumping as trespassers along the narrow dirt road.

We passed a sign that read: *You're not lost. You're trespassing. Turn around now and go back the way you came.*

Dalton found the sign rather amusing, even slowing to snap a photo of it with his phone.

"You got your souvenir photo," I said. "Now let's turn around and do something legal. Do you like five-pin bowling? It's like ten-pin bowling, but not as good. You know, bowling is funny. I think people enjoy the idea of bowling a lot more than actually doing it. Have you ever turned around and looked at all the faces of people in a bowling alley? Except for maybe one table of extremely smashed guys, who could be just as happy in the drunk tank, everyone has this serious look on their faces. And they're always shaking their head, saying, 'You got robbed. Robbed. That pin must be glued there. Oh, the humanity.'"

Dalton slammed on the brakes, put the car in reverse, then took a quick left turn, onto what looked like anything but a road.

I squealed and held on tight to the dashboard as the car bounced and rocked over the rutted terrain.

"Your poor car!" I warbled, my voice broken up by the bouncing.

"I suppose my four-wheel-drive truck might have been a better option."

"You have a truck?"

"For towing the trailer."

"Of course." I looked back over my shoulder at the path through which we'd come. If you really looked, you could just barely make out what could be mistaken for a road.

"Almost there," he said.

"How would you know? This path is completely overgrown. Nobody's driven this way in months."

"Easy. I saw the hot spring from the helicopter."

"How? Was it with one of the Westons?"

"Nope. I don't know them."

"What? You aren't friends with the Westons? We really are trespassing?" I'd been hoping he had permission and was just pulling a prank on me.

He turned and gave me a mischievous look. "Trespassing? Hmm. I'm certainly no lawyer, so I couldn't say exactly what we're doing. Maybe we're lost. I don't see any signs along here telling us otherwise."

I looked around. He was right about there being no more of the threatening signs. And that probably meant we were heading straight for the hot spring, and the lack of signs was their attempt to thwart trespassers.

Trespassers!

This was exactly the kind of thing my boy cousins would want to do when we were all kids, and me being me, I'd cross my arms and stomp my foot and tell them we weren't allowed.

Now I was older, and apparently I did things like cowgirl-style sex with a handsome actor, with the lights on.

We bumped along for a few more minutes through the bushes, low-hanging branches whacking the windshield. I worried for the car's suspension, but it just kept on going.

"Hmm," Dalton said as we lurched to a stop.

"Did we blow a tire?"

"Don't be a worry wart."

"Too late. I am what I am. Dalton, I might have a big mouth and way more attitude than necessary, but I'm not a law breaker. I'm not a trespasser."

"Bulldoodles."

I laughed, hard. "Bulldoodles? You crack me up."

He winked. "Something my mother used to say."

I stared at his gorgeous profile, wondering for a moment what his parents looked like. They likely had dark hair like him, and surely his father was handsome, but I couldn't imagine a mother.

"What does your mother look like? You don't talk about your family much."

He turned off the engine and opened the car door.

"All shall be revealed once we locate the hot spring."

I stayed seated in the car. "We should probably turn around and go back to town. I'll take you to Chloe's Pie Shack for a Lemon Meringue Mile High. My treat."

Standing next to the car, he stretched his perfect arms over his head, then whipped off his shirt. He stretched again, his muscles rippling in the dappled light come through the trees.

Think what you want about your own willpower, but mine is in limited supply, and a good portion is expended daily resisting cupcakes. If you were in my shoes, you'd see why he broke my resolve. When a man that hot and charming *ripples* for you, you go with him.

I muttered some choice words under my breath as I got out of the car. Dalton Deangelo's job was to appear shirtless and boost ratings. No sense trying to deny the desires of my flesh. He was like the Pied Piper of modern day, his voice the enchanting music that lured the youth away from the small village, and his flute was… well… sort of flute-shaped, depending on how you looked at it.

Ugh. I needed to stop thinking about his flute, and start using my head. *Eyes open, Peaches. Eyes wide open.*

When I caught up to him, he slipped one bare arm around my shoulder. My arm went to his waist, and I tucked my hand into the back pocket of his jeans.

"This is nice," he said, and he kissed my forehead as we kept walking, moving now through a narrow path.

We walked for a while, enjoying the woodsy sounds of birds around us. I was about to suggest we turn around when I noticed a change in the air. Moisture. I checked the sky for signs of rainclouds, but it was all blue showing between the leaves.

We stepped into a clearing dotted with a few boulders. Up ahead, near a rock outcropping, was a plume of steam.

"Holy porkchops, the hot springs are real," I said as I ran toward the pool of water. I would have screamed, but we *were* trespassing, after all.

MIMI STRONG

CHAPTER 19

Dalton raced ahead of me. He pulled off his shoes and jeans, then stood near the edge of the water on the rocks, his socks getting wet. Or, I assume his socks were getting wet. I was looking at his perfect ass, filling out his boxer shorts so nicely.

"Be careful," I called out. "Check the temperature that it isn't boiling hot."

He pulled off his socks, yanked down his boxer shorts, and slapped one of his butt cheeks. "Check this temperature, cutie." And then he just jumped in.

His naked body and dark hair disappeared beneath the water line, and I was all alone in the silence. The songbirds in the nearby branches sang their tattle-tale songs. Trespassers! Naughty, naked trespassers! Playing the meat flute!

Dalton shot up from the water like a majestic merman, tossing his head back in a spray of water.

"You look pink," I said. "Is it boiling hot?"

"Jump in and find out!"

I sat near the edge and took off my shoes and socks, then dipped a few toes in cautiously.

He dipped down for a mouthful of water, then spat it at me in an arc.

I stepped back. "Don't drink that filth. Isn't warm water basically party town for bacteria? Like a petri dish?"

Dalton wiped water from his grinning face. "I wasn't so great at science, but this isn't agar."

"Agar!" I stepped back closer to kick water at his face. "Sounds like you know plenty about science."

"I'm not as dumb as I look."

"Who said you look dumb?"

He fixed me with a serious gaze, his dark green eyes never looking more enticing than now, surrounded by wild grasses and flowers in a natural hot spring.

"Take off your clothes and get in here with me," he commanded.

"Pass." Something flitted at the edge of my vision, and I turned around expecting to see Old Man Weston with a shotgun.

Only it wasn't him. Or any human.

A deer stepped quietly out of the trees and walked around me, to the river of water running away from the pool. With her big eyes watching me warily, she lowered her head and took a tentative drink. And then, just as calmly as she'd arrived, she gave a flick of her tail and disappeared back into the woods.

"That was a sign," Dalton said. "From the universe, straight to Peaches Monroe. Now take off your clothes and get in here with me before I climb out of here like an angry sea monster and drag you in."

I pulled the gray sweatshirt off over my head.

"Nice T-shirt. Is that Disco Duck?"

"Don't watch," I said, but of course that only made him watch me more intently.

There was certainly no changing room out here. If this was *my* hot spring, a cute little cabana would be the first thing I'd add.

I could feel the heat of his gaze on me.

"Dalton! Stop watching."

He whistled. "Take it off!"

I undid my brown cords and shimmied them down, still facing him rather than offering a side or back view.

"Careful," I said. "You should avert your eyes or you'll be blinded by the sun reflecting off all my pale flesh."

He waded to the near side of the rocky pool and rested his elbows on the edge, his chin in his hands.

"I could watch you undress all day. All those curves are so much fun to ogle. Hey, there's a great word. *Ogle*. I'm ogling you like an ogre."

I pulled off my T-shirt and stood for a moment in my underwear, debating leaving my bra and panties on.

He held up his hands with his thumbs and fingers forming a square between us.

"I'm framing you," he said. "For future reference."

Bathed in his generous praise, I found the courage to unfasten my boulder-holder and drop it to the ground along with my panties.

Ladies, you'll never feel as naked as when you're trespassing on private property and standing in front of a handsome guy, without so much as a g-string along your crack.

I hurried around to one side of the steaming pool, where it had some stone steps leading down. The water was surprisingly hot, about as warm as a freshly-drawn bath (assuming your hot water tank is bigger than the one in my house and you don't have to supplement with the boiling tea kettle).

Once I was all the way in, I found that I could stand at one side with the water just above my waist. At the deeper side, the rocky bottom could just barely be grazed by my toes while I held my head about the water.

"How can this be?" I asked. "How is this pond so perfect?"

"How are *you* so perfect?" He drew me in for a kiss, his lips warm and wet from the water.

I pulled away, distracted by the mysterious stones all around us— not too rough and not too smooth. The pond was kidney-shaped, and big enough to fit ten people comfortably. There was even a stone bench along one side.

"Is this real?" I asked.

He dipped down and drank some water. "Tastes real."

"But the hot spring didn't just form in this perfect shape, did it? Someone must have moved around the rocks and improved upon nature."

Dalton seemed annoyed by my questions. "If it's good, isn't that enough for you? Does it matter how real it is?"

I looked down at my peaches, which looked really good floating in the warm, pristine water.

"But why is the water so clear? Shouldn't it be a little muddy?"

Dalton sighed. "This spring has likely been here thousands of years. Millennia, even. All the mud washed away long ago, before Beaverdale even existed. Maybe there was a time dinosaurs came here to take a little skinny dip."

"Millennia." I would have shivered, if I wasn't so warm.

"Enjoy it while you can. These hot springs open up and can disappear after earthquakes. They're not forever."

"Nothing is forever," I said.

He pulled me back into his arms, locking his hands together against my lower back.

"Stardust is forever," he said. "The form changes, that's all."

I gazed up into his gentle green eyes. "Don't talk like that. You make me feel serious, and I don't like being serious."

He took a gasp of breath and submerged, his dark hair disappearing under the water. Strong hands grabbed my legs and pulled them apart, and an instant later, his mouth was on me, deep below the water line. As his tongue darted between my twin pillows of flesh, a plume of bubbles rose from below, tickling as they fought their way up and between my breasts.

He rose for a quick breath and disappeared again. Tongue and fingers and bubbles. Tongue. Fingers. Bubbles.

When he came up for air again, he was surprised to find me gasping as well.

"That feels crazy good," I said, then I took a deep breath and went down myself. I've always been comfortable in water, though I would never have done something like this in a real hot tub, not with all the chlorine in the water.

This natural spring, though, was heaven. My eyes didn't sting at all when I opened them to get my bearings.

I found the sea cucumber, no problem, but sucking it while holding my breath was a challenge. I could do the task, somewhat, but suspected by the degree of *bonership* that I wasn't doing a great job.

Surfacing, I sputtered, "Lemme try again."

He kissed me tenderly, then hopped up out of the water and took a seat at the edge of the pool, his legs still in the water from the lower knee down.

"Look at you bobbing around. You're a true mermaid," he said. "I've always wanted to know the pleasure of a mermaid."

I rolled back on the water, taking a deep breath for buoyancy and floating on my back for him. He grabbed my hand as I swirled by and tugged me toward him.

Upright again with my toes on the stony floor, I waded toward him and nestled between his legs.

He gazed down with a big grin as I wrapped my arms around him and squeezed the tops of his buttocks. His sea cucumber filled up quickly, straining to reach my lips. With a nod down, I had the head in my mouth, and I pulsed down on the shaft with a quick swirl of my tongue.

On the third bob, he caught my head in his hands.

"Slow down," he said, panting. "Not so fast, baby."

I pulled away, apologizing.

He caught me under the chin with his fingers and tilted my head up to face his. With the sun high overhead and nothing but trees above him, he was so beautiful, he took my breath away.

"No need to apologize," he said. "I'm the one who can't control himself when I'm around you. Your mouth feels so good. So does everything else. I'm addicted to all your pink bits."

I covered my face with one hand, feeling shy.

He laughed. "It's just you and me and the trees. Let's enjoy ourselves."

Nodding, I moved back into position and gently took him into my mouth, slower this time.

I sensed his body shift, as he leaned back with weight on his hands behind him, just enough to lift his hips toward me.

"Mmm," he moaned. "I'm being blown by a beautiful mermaid. I should talk to the writers about doing something like this for Drake."

I pulled away, making a lollipop-pop sound with my lips. "What?"

"Well, not for this movie, but for my TV series. We have so many supernatural creatures involved in the season arcs already—werewolves, succubi, and of course, vampires. Why not mermaids? It's fresh, original, and... what are you doing? Why'd you stop?"

"You can't tell the writers about this."

"I can't tell them about the ethereal creature who seduced me with her eyes the moment we met? How she jumped into my arms and made me feel like a hero?" He reached down and adjusted his sack, grimacing. "How she gave me a tragic case of blue balls?"

I floated back on the water, feeling the warmth of the dappled sun on my front and the hot water at my back.

Closing my eyes, I said, "This moment is private. Don't talk about me. I don't like being talked about."

"Then you shouldn't have an actor as a boyfriend."

I went tense and started to sink. Boyfriend?

Upright again, my toes on the stone bottom, I squinted up at Dalton's perfect face. "You're my boyfriend?"

He shrugged, his face neutral and unreadable. "Unless you want me to be your vampire lover. Do you want me to be Drake for you?"

I gave him side-eye.

With grit in his voice, he said, "Petra! I command you to come to me, at once."

My brain did a little double-hop of confusion, because he'd changed. Dalton Deangelo was gone, and Drake Cheshire sat naked at the edge of the hot spring.

My breathing sped up, and I could feel myself swelling with excitement. Oh, no. Drake Cheshire. Oh, screw me three times and don't call me in the morning, I was about to blow the world's hottest vampire.

"Come here, now," he commanded. "It isn't going to suck itself, so put your pretty lips around it and blow."

"Blow it yourself! Nobody talks to me like that."

Still staring intensely at me, he held out one arm and beckoned me to him with a finger. I'd seen him—Drake, the vampire—do this to his girls. He could be sweet at times, but he still had that evil vampire side. That beckoning gesture made me yell at the TV screen, but it also made me put my hand down my pants. So conflicting.

Still playing Drake, he said, "Come here and do as you're told."

I paddled my way to him, still feeling conflicted. And very swollen.

With a subservient whimper, I nudged my way between his legs.

"Lick it."

I ran my tongue along the midline, from the base to the gleaming bead on the tip.

"Good girl," he said, his tone still stern. "I will allow you to pleasure me, but only if you sound grateful. Can you sound grateful?"

My whimper turned into a moan, and I took a full mouth and throat full of his engorged yumminess, around the most grateful sounds I could manage.

His manhood really was hard, too—nearly as hard as the stone under my toes. The more I moaned about how grateful I was, the more I felt grateful. My own body was roaring for attention, so I slipped one hand down in the warm water, but he grabbed my arm and pulled it back up.

"Bad girl," he said. "Don't you lose focus on me by pleasuring yourself."

"I'm a bad girl," I sputtered around his meat flute.

"Yes, you are. You're a trespasser, and an exhibitionist. Suck a little harder. Mmm, that's good. Slower. Yes, I need this. Oh, Petra, I needed you so bad, and I didn't even know."

Was he still playing Drake, or was this Dalton?

I didn't know, and I didn't care.

Something buzzed nearby. Just one loud pulse. I paused, but not for long, because he was thick and urgent, ready to blow.

The buzz happened again.

"Damn it!" he said. "What the hell is that?"

I pulled my mouth away, blinking and looking around. The spell was broken. We were no longer a sexy vampire and a slutty mermaid, but two trespassers, naked and engaged in a sex act on private property.

The buzz sound happened a third time, and then speakers crackled to life with what seemed to be a pre-recorded message: "Attention trespassers. Motion sensors have detected unauthorized activity. A security team is on its way to this site. Please vacate the premises immediately."

Dalton was already pulling his legs out of the hot spring and getting to his feet.

"Come on, let's run," he said.

I splashed over to the side with the rock steps and climbed out, feeling very big and conspicuous. Motion sensors? Were there cameras out here?

I reached my clothes and started looking for my underwear.

The recording was repeating itself, "... security team is on its way to this site. Please vacate the premises immediately."

Dalton grabbed my clothes and bundled them in his arms along with his clothes. He'd slipped on his shoes, but not tied the laces. He nodded down at my shoes, for me to do the same.

"But I can't get my pants on over my shoes!"

"No time," he said. "Shoes, and then we run."

I let out a streak of swear words.

By some miracle, I got my wet, sandy feet into my sneakers, and then the two of us were off and running through the forest trail. Naked.

"Faster," he urged.

My boobs were flying everywhere, threatening to knock me out, so I clamped down on them with folded arms.

As we ran through the bushes, with evil whipping branches whacking me on all my sensitive areas, I continued my panicked refrain of every swear word I knew, mashed together.

Dalton interrupted, saying, "Just breathe. Swearing doesn't make you run faster, but breathing does."

I wanted to punch him in the face so bad.

Instead, I wheezed out, "Motion sensors? Why? How? Who? Why?"

"They're probably bluffing. I bet there's no security team coming, just—"

Over the sounds of our footfalls was another noise. A dog barking, and a man yelling excitedly. Then, what sounded like a gunshot.

I began swearing again, because contrary to what Dalton said, it *did* make me run faster.

"Shortcut," he panted, and hauled me sharply to the side, off the very rough trail and onto what wasn't even a trail at all.

Now the tree branches and bushes really started slapping my bare flesh. I guess some people are into that sort of thing, and it certainly was exhilarating, but I wouldn't recommend it. I was moving fast, but soon my lungs were on fire, so that slowed me down.

"We're almost there," Dalton panted.

I stopped and leaned against a tree to catch my breath. "Go on. Save yourself. Leave me here. I'll take the rap for both of us."

"I could carry you?"

He was strong and probably could, but how far? The horror of him attempting to do that prompted me to get moving again, my arms still acting as the worst sports bra ever.

We trudged on, still naked, the barking dog still behind us.

Was that a glint of metal up ahead?

Never before have I been so happy to see a car as when we emerged from the bushes and found the black car waiting for us.

We yanked the doors open and jumped into the seats, our naked, damp bodies making rude noises on the leather.

Dalton started the car and began doing a ten-point turn to get us headed in the right direction. Just as we took off down the trail again, he turned to me, his eyes wide, and started howling with laughter.

"What's so funny?"

We bounced up and down as the car dove over bumps and ruts on the rough trail.

"Look at yourself," he said.

I looked down at my body, surprised to find I wasn't exactly as naked as I'd thought. I had a smattering of green leaves and flower petals all down the front of me. Dalton wore the same decoration, all down his chest and on his arms and legs.

"We have matching tattoos," he said.

211

"Very funny." I reached down to the floor, to where he'd tossed the ball of our clothes, and fished out my sweatshirt. I had a short coughing fit, from all the phlegm brought up by the running, and when that calmed down, I pulled on the sweatshirt.

"That was so worth it," he said. "Remember when the deer came to say hello?"

He was clearly amused with the whole adventure, but I was not. I just wanted to get dropped off at home, where I could shower off the leaves, then get dressed and never be naked again.

We bumped along the rough trail in silence.

A few minutes later, he pulled the car out onto the access road, and it wasn't long until we were outside the private property again.

I thought I'd be relieved, but I just felt more anxious.

When we got to the turn-off to head back into Beaverdale, he turned the car in the opposite direction.

"Next adventure," he said.

"Seriously? No. How about you just take me home. I think we've had enough fun for one day."

"You're mad because I channelled Drake Cheshire for you."

"No."

"You're mad because I made you go trespassing."

"I'm not mad. Just tired." We drove for a moment in silence, then I said, "I'm not really that out of shape. I go to the gym sometimes, and I walk absolutely everywhere, but I don't do much cardio. Obviously."

"Oh." He nodded slowly, his gaze still on the road ahead.

"I've had a lot of fun with you, but I think I've reached my limit. It's time for me to get back to my regular life." I looked down at my naked lower body. I was sitting in a car with no pants or underwear on. "This is *so* not my regular life."

"Mine neither." He reached over and squeezed my greenery-dotted bare leg right above my knee. "I think that's why I feel happier than I've ever been. I'm alive, and it's all because of you."

I squirmed in my seat and turned to the window.

"Great, now you're making me feel bad."

He kept his hand on my leg.

"That wasn't my intent," he said. "Hey, have you ever noticed how much easier it is to tell secrets when you're driving somewhere?"

"I guess." I pinched my lips shut, unwilling to tell secrets.

After a moment, he said, "Why is that?"

I sighed. "I think the road makes you feel safe. The repeating pattern of movement. It's like staring at a river, or a crackling fire."

He pointed to a turnoff sign up ahead. "What's that? Is it really a waterfall?"

"Dolphin Falls? It is a waterfall."

"How about we go check it out? Two water features in one day? Like a double feature. Then I'll take you home."

"Sure." I could feel myself falling under his spell again, willing to do anything Dalton Deangelo suggested. I didn't want to fall, but even with my eyes wide open, it was unavoidable.

We turned off and drove along the access road until we got to the small parking lot. We were the only vehicle there, which didn't surprise me, as it was around dinner time. The place was more popular at night, as a makeout spot.

When I was in high school, there was this trend of parents all trying to act like they were the most progressive parents in town, so much cooler than everyone else. Most of the kids in my class could have just hooked up with anyone they wanted, at home, right under their parents' noses.*

*With the bedroom door respectfully closed, of course.

A few of Beaverdale's more progressive mothers even kept their bathroom cabinets stocked with a no-questions-asked supply of condoms. They felt teen sex was inevitable, and they did what they had to, to prevent having to feed, clothe and raise any little mistakes.

Perhaps this parental acceptance was exactly why rebellious kids continued to drive out to Dolphin Falls and have unprotected sex in the back seats of cars rather than parent-sanctified sex in beds, with parent-purchased condoms.

My own personal path was neither of those two, so my heart skipped a little, knowing I was in the Dolphin Falls parking lot, with a cute guy, for the very first time.

We parked at the edge of the lot, where we had a clear view of the falls.

"Is there more?" Dalton asked. "Should we put some clothes on and get out of the car?"

"Nope. That's pretty much it. People mostly come here to hook up in cars."

He leaned over to my side of the car and kissed me without warning. With just the touch of his lips on mine, I was under his spell instantly.

"Mercy," I murmured as he kissed me deeply, his hands slipping up underneath my sweatshirt to lift and palm my breasts. My nipples firmed, and all my skin rippled to attention, tighter now and wanting to be touched.

"I'm going to take you now." He pulled the sweatshirt off over my head, and we were both naked again. "I'm going to take you like this." He reached down roughly between my legs and thrust two fingers inside me. I whimpered and spread my legs wider for him. "Then I'm going to flip you over and do it some more."

I whispered, "Okay."

He kept up the thrusting with his fingers, pushing me to dizzying heights. "Tell me you want me, need me, and you deserve me," he said.

"I want you."

"And?"

I whispered, "I need you. And I deserve you."

He pulled his hand away quickly. "Now get out of this car. Open the door and step out."

CHAPTER 20

My voice shaking, I said, "Get out of the car?"

"Yes. And get into the back seat, where I have a little more room to do a decent job."

Oh, of course. Why did I think he was planning to abandon me there, naked? Apparently, I had some trust issues.

I opened the door and stepped out, then climbed in the back. My shoes didn't go with my nudity, so I removed them. I still had bits of green leaves all over my skin.

He came around the other side, kicked off his shoes, and started kissing me. I was about to ask about protection when I saw he'd already donned a sheath.

"Spread your legs," he said.

I lay back in the center of the bench seat, sliding down so my hips were at the edge.

"Good girl," he said, sliding his fingers back inside me.

I moaned and closed my eyes, embarrassed by how quickly he made me wet.

"Now get on your knees," he said.

Shuffling around, I got on my knees, praying he wouldn't be turned off by the view from that direction.

He entered in one smooth thrust.

I gasped and got a tighter grip on the back of the seat.

Oh, the angle and the depth, it was exactly what I needed. My anger flared up as he filled me and left me no place to hide.

"You're the worst!" I moaned.

He grunted, plunging deeper and shaking my whole body. "You don't mean that."

I clutched the seat. "You're a bad influence!"

"I'll show you a bad influence."

What happened next was what I would call a Good Rogering. Flesh-slapping, grunting, sweaty grasping, and even (bless his heart) a courteous reach-around.

In the midst of the Rogering, with his fingers on me, I came, crying out and biting the back of the leather seat I was hanging onto for dear life.

By the time he finished, with a triumphant moan, my hair was stuck in strands to my face, and I was as damp as when we'd fled the hot spring.

As he withdrew, he gave my butt one hard slap. The crack sound startled me, and my flesh stung.

I turned around quickly, giving him a hurt and confused look. "What was that all about?"

He shook his head, like he was the confused one. "Sort of a high five?"

"You're kind of a dick sometimes."

He raised his eyebrows in a bitches-be-crazy-sometimes kind of look—the exact look that actually makes us crazy.

"I didn't mean anything by it," he said.

As I stared at his face, an anger simmered inside me. My orgasm had been deep, but also unsettling, as if the tremors and the rough physicality of what we'd just done had shaken something loose in me.

"You're a lot more like Drake Cheshire than you let on."

Smirking, he wiped a strand of damp hair from my cheek. "You love it. You love it. You can't wait to get reamed again."

I shoved him away from me. "Gross. Get up front and drive me home right now."

He made a pouty face. "But I've got the whole day off."

I reached past him and grabbed the door handle to pop the door open. The summer breeze freshened the air in the back of the car and brought everything into focus.

I had the strangest out-of-body experience, where I was myself, but also outside of myself, seeing this chubby, naked girl, sweaty and used, in the back of a car. I didn't like what I saw when I opened my eyes like that.

"We've had our fun," I said. And there was that word. Fun. Was I having fun? I was uncomfortable and emotional.

"I've pushed you too far." He shook his head, leaning toward the open car door, but not getting out. "I don't have normal boundaries. It's all my mother's fault."

Sarcastically, I said, "Oh, of course. Blame the mother. Don't take responsibility for yourself."

He stepped out of the car and closed the door gently.

My words hung in the air, and I shook my head with my face in my hands. I was doing it again. Pushing someone away. And I was glad that soon it would be over—albeit a little sad it was always so easy like this. Guys never fought for me. I wasn't the kind of girl they fought to keep. Friday night booty call, yes. Grand romantic gesture, no.

The tinted glass separating the front and back rolled down enough for him to politely hand me back my clothes. Shockingly, everything except one sock was there.

In a minute, the car started moving, and I was finished getting dressed before we turned back onto the main road back to town.

"I know I shouldn't blame my mother," came Dalton's voice. The glass divider was already rolled up again, so it had to be coming from a speaker.

"Hello?"

"Are you talking? I can't hear you unless you push that green button on the ceiling."

I looked up and spotted the button. Of course! Now that I saw the button, I couldn't believe I hadn't been able to find it when Vern was driving me out to Dragonfly Lake.

"You don't have to talk," Dalton said.

I pressed the button. "This is weird."

His laugh crackled over the speakers. "It might be easier to tell you this way."

"What?" A dozen horrible thoughts raced through my head, including but not limited to the following:

He was married.

He was dying of an incurable illness.

He was leaving town tonight.

He never wanted to see me again, *but thanks for the fun.*

"I was born into an adult film star family," he said. "Also known as porn stars."

I had no response for that at first, but after a moment, I pressed the green button and said, "Congratulations?"

"My mother, my father, and their girlfriend were all porn actors. Correction. Some of them *continue to currently be* porn actors."

I stared at the tinted glass on the driver's side, where the outline of his head was barely visible.

"And that's my big secret."

I pressed the green button. "I didn't know that about you."

"Nobody does, except my attorney. When I was sixteen, I ran away from home with a... family friend. That was when I moved to New York and lived in that awful apartment I told you about. It was really stupid of me to trust someone who was barely more than a kid herself, mentally. I had no idea how dangerous it was."

"I understand. I did some dangerous things when I was about that age."

We continued to drive along the road into town, the trees outside the windows being interspersed with farmhouses and lawns. Who was this family friend he'd run away with? I didn't feel jealous, so much as fiercely protective of a young and naive Dalton Deangelo.

He wasn't talking, so I pressed the green button again. "So, I'm guessing Dalton isn't your real name?"

"Do you hate me for lying to you?"

"I don't hate you. And you lied to the whole world, so I know I'm not that special."

"Ouch."

I sat back in the seat and crossed my arms.

He continued, "Everything else I told you is true. My family members were fine with keeping the secret. As long as the checks kept coming. I'm always looking over my shoulder, though. That reporter, Brooke Summer, has a major hard-on for getting some dirt on me."

I leaned forward and jabbed the green button. "She's a phony baloney."

"And a lousy lay."

I sat back, crossing my arms again. I couldn't see his face, so I had no idea if he was joking or not.

Dalton continued, "Full disclosure. I slept with Brooke once, after an awards function. It was the kind of dirty sex you regret while you're still doing it. I took off right after and didn't give her the intimate interview she'd been after, and then I refused to take her calls."

Ugh. The image of Dalton and that woman. Together. I felt sick, a gritty nausea deep in my stomach. And his parents were in porno movies? I liked to think of myself as being open-minded and progressive, but I'd seen enough reality shows about the adult film business to know it had a real seedy side. And he'd been raised around all those people. What would that even do to a kid? I couldn't imagine.

I pressed the intercom button. "Is that everything?"

"Yes, Peaches. That's everything. I'm an open book to you. I hope you won't tell anyone, but maybe it wouldn't be so bad if my secret got out. I was only in a few adult films myself, and it was credited to other fake names."

I pressed my fingers to my lips, horrified. He'd been in a few adult films? How many? Not that it mattered. Even one was too many.

He continued, "Okay, now that's everything. I was underage when I did those films, so if word gets out it's me, they'll have to pull them. They won't be able to profit. Of course, it will get leaked, and the gossip sites will run screencaps, and I'll be a laughingstock with limited career options when my show inevitably ends, but I won't die. You can't die of shame, can you?"

The tinted screen was still up between us, and I was glad he couldn't see the horrified look on my face. I'd just had sex with a former porn star—a former underage porn star who was himself the offspring of porn stars. My emotions were truly split. I was both horrified and also insanely proud, like that one time I drank vodka shots too quickly and threw up a little in my mouth.

I had sex with a porn star.

Maybe I was a fun girl, after all.

"Peaches?"

"I'm still here. And no, I don't think a person can die of shame." I licked my lips, choosing my words carefully. "It's very brave of you to bare yourself to me. It takes great strength to be vulnerable."

"That's really nice to hear. You're a sweet girl, do you know that? I'm always slobbering over your hot body like a damn fool, but you're the real deal. The whole package. You're a triple threat: cute, smart, funny."

The car came to a stop, and I blinked at the tinted window, surprised to see the front lawn of my house.

I turned and looked up at the green button on the ceiling. I could just press it and tell him my secret, too. My heart sped up at the thought, my cheeks flushing.

Instead, I pushed the car door open, jumped out, and ran all the way to my house without saying goodbye.

Trespassing? A sordid porn star past? It was all too much. Way too much.

~

When I ran from Dalton's car into my house, part of me expected him to chase me. Not a big part of me—because I've never been the type of girl guys fight for—but a small, hopeful, pathetic part of me.

The car sat in front of the house for a long time. Maybe fifteen minutes. From my bedroom on the upper floor, I watched the darkened windows for some sign. And then he just drove away.

Some sign.

Shayla wasn't around, so I phoned my mother, just to hear a friendly voice.

"Oh, good. A sane person," she said. "How are you, sweetie?"

That's when I started bawling.

With patience, she eventually talked me down, and I explained to her a bit about what had happened that day. I left out the cowgirl-style sex from that morning, and the trespassing, as well as the car sex, and the porn-past revelations. So, basically, I told her almost nothing.

"Let's see if I've got this straight," she said. "He came over and you ate scrambled eggs. Then Shayla got weird and jealous, and said he was fake. You and the hunk went for a drive to Dolphin Falls, and then things got real when you had sex in his fancy car."

"Mother!"

"Petra. I may be twice your age, but I know what goes on at Dolphin Falls.

"I feel like I'm being really stupid. He can't possibly like me as much as he says he does, can he?"

"Why wouldn't he?"

"Because I'm a regular person, and he's Dalton Deangelo."

"He's still human." There was a paused as she talked to Kyle for a minute.

"I should let you go," I said. "Maybe I'm over-thinking this."

"Is the problem that you still have feelings for Adrian Storm?"

"Hah! Not in a million years."

"Mm-hmm. That's not what I heard from his mother. From what I understand, you were flirting with him, inviting him upstairs to see your old bedroom."

"Gross! Mother!"

"Then go for the TV fellow. At least he's not bankrupt. Apparently Adrian had his fancy sports car taken away, so now he's got nothing."

"Don't sound so disgusted. I've got the same amount of *nothing* as Adrian. I work at a bookstore for what amounts to minimum wage based on the number of hours, and I'm still paying off my credit card for a cuckoo clock I bought three months ago in an online auction."

"We all live in houses of our own construction."

"You live in a house bought by… some movie star who rogered you."

"Exactly," she said.

I howled in exasperation. I hated it when she got philosophical, but more than that, I hated it when she was right.

221

My phone beeped with a dying battery. "Running out of juice, Mom. I should let you go."

"Date this movie star for a while," she said. "And then when Adrian is on the upswing, maybe give him a shot. There's no rush. You're only twenty-two. Have some fun, will you?"

We said goodbye and I ended the call, feeling a tiny bit more normal after a typical conversation with my mother.

For the rest of the night, I vegged on the couch, alternating between TV and books. I forgot to plug my phone in, so it sat mutely on my bed while all my friends sent me text messages and left voicemails I didn't know about.

I ate dinner in blissful ignorance as my mailbox filled up.

I went to bed, feeling confused and ambivalent about seeing Dalton again, but I slept soundly, still ignorant of what awaited me the next day.

~

On Sunday morning, Shayla tapped timidly at my bedroom door.

With my face still in my pillow, I waved in the general direction of my closet. "Help yourself. Wear whatever you want."

Sounding really concerned, she said, "How are you feeling, really?"

I sat up, on high alert. "What did you hear?"

She gave me a patronizing look. "Everything."

"You talked to my mother?"

"Not yet. Should I?"

My skin felt clammy. Something really bad had happened, and Shayla knew, but I didn't. I reached for my cell phone, but it was cold and dead.

She said, "How are you? Really?"

"Shayla, my phone's kaput. I don't know what it is I'm supposed to be upset about right now. Would you please break it to me gently?"

"There are half-naked photos of you all over the internet."

Every sweat gland in my body pumped its guts out. The world went dark, pulling into a pinhole of light. My mouth watered. The sweet relief of passing out, however, did not come. I was still sitting in my bed, in drenched pajamas, my roommate giving me her best concerned look, mixed with a touch of her I-told-you-so look.

"Show me," I said.

She pulled up something on her phone and handed it to me. I fully expected to see hidden-camera images of me trespassing in the hot spring, or even images of me transferring naked to the back seat of Dalton's car.

Instead, there was a video clip of big-haired Brooke Summer interviewing me on my front steps. I had to watch it three times to figure out what the hell I was seeing.

Brooke: "I understand you're sleeping with Dalton Deangelo. How would you describe sex with him?"

Cut to me, with my blond hair mussed up from recent sex: "Yes. It's very nice, if you like that sort of thing."

My reaction to this video clip was complicated. I was angry at that c-word for tricking me, but I was also pleased to be getting a few minutes of fame for something other than running a successful pledge drive for the local library.

Again, the universe was hinting that I might actually be a wild and crazy girl.

"Whatever," I said to Shayla. "That's not too bad."

She shook her head. "There's more."

My stomach dove into my other organs. Now here would come the nude photos in the hot spring.

Shayla fiddled with her phone for a second, then handed it back, sucking in air between her gritted teeth.

"Um, this could be worse," she said. "You look cute."

On her phone, I found photos of a girl in brown trousers and a lacy bra, no shirt, standing on a stepladder and installing a light fixture. It took several views of the same images for me to reconcile that it was me, inside the bookstore.

"Cute, right?" she said.

"This is it?" The text that accompanied the photos said I was *linked to* Dalton Deangelo, but didn't even say I was dating him. "This is nothing," I said.

"That's the spirit!" Shayla said. "Sticks and stones may break our bones, but nasty words will never hurt us."

Words? I hadn't read any nasty words. I'd just been scanning in a panic, then relieved by how tame the photos were, compared to the eyeful they could have gotten.

I shouldn't have read the text below. I should have stopped after one cruel nickname, but I didn't.

Horrible internet comments.

About me.

One of the posts had a whole list of awful names for me, as well as a poll. People were voting on a nickname for me.

In third place was Porky Peaches.

Second-most popular was Peachalicious.

And leading the polls was... Peaches by the Pounds.

I'd been called names before, and while most of these were new ones, the feeling in my heart wasn't a unique experience. I'd been to this heartbreak rodeo before.

I was used to some people being disgusted with me. I knew that if I wore a short skirt, some wretched buttmunch would sneer at me like I'd ruined their appetite with my dimpled thighs.

What I wasn't accustomed to, as I'd never been *linked to* a popular movie star, was the raw anger.

As I read through the anonymous internet comments, a part of me died. Perhaps it was the last shreds of my youthful naivete. Or my faith in humanity. Either way, it died.

I fell back on the bed. If this had been a comedic moment in my always-wacky life, I would have tugged one of my pillows across my face and growled into it hysterically.

Instead, I stared at the ceiling and silently began to weep. Not just about this time, but every time people had been cruel. Despite the wet tears, my eyes felt hot and dry. When I caught my breath, the ragged sobs began.

~

Bless her heart, Shayla knew just what to do.

She didn't argue with me about how bad I ought to be feeling, but she did take away my phone and laptop so I couldn't jump further down the black hole of reading more posts and comments.

I cycled through the emotional stages rapidly, with the bargaining stage lasting only about an hour.

During the anger stage, we planned out revenge on Brooke Summer. Shayla had been seeing her dining at the restaurant she managed, and had already given her full-fat milk in her latte instead of skim a few times. And that was before the fake interview with me, just for being a c-word.

I started to feel better, and then got hit with another wave of what felt like... everything. It wasn't fair. I pushed Shayla out of my bedroom, locked the door, and buried myself under my blankets. Barely able to breathe, I sobbed.

I'd come so far in the last few years, with my body image. I'd come to accept that I'd never have a thigh gap—that triangle of space between the upper legs that skinny girls have. I had a healthy body that functioned well, and took me places, and even gave me pleasure. I enjoyed my curves, and was only a little self-conscious about certain views while nude—something even my skinny girlfriends said they felt, too.

On bad days, I accepted myself; on good days, I even loved how I looked, and how I rocked certain outfits, like my red leather pencil skirt.

Now these strangers had taken this little bit of progress away from me. The hurt was fresh and raw, like no years had passed, and I was fifteen again, a victim of the disconnection between me and my body.

I stopped breathing, but the pain still found me.

~

Late Sunday afternoon, I emerged from my bedroom on shaky legs. After a longish hot shower (as long as our water tank would allow), I felt better. Not great, but better.

I joined Shayla downstairs, and we ordered pizza for dinner. We swivelled the couch in the front room around so we could watch the window for the delivery guy's arrival.

"I'm going to phone Dalton," I said. "Gimme my phone."

It was fully charged, but Shayla took a minute to clear through the alerts from our friends about the crap they'd seen online. She stayed next to me as I called Dalton, insisting she wasn't being nosy, but had to stay so I didn't read horrible things.

I frowned at her as Dalton's line rang and rang, then went to voicemail. I tried him three times, getting voicemail each time.

I left a message. "This is Peaches Monroe calling for Dalton Deangelo. I'm sorry I ran off yesterday. I didn't mean to be so flakey, but... things got a little intense there. I don't know how long you're in town, but I do want to see you again. I... um... I like you. Bye."

After I hung up, I stared into Shayla's amber eyes for clues. Had I sounded desperate? Needy? Clingy? And all those horrible things people say about girls, just because we have feelings?

"He'll call," Shayla said.

"No, he won't. He doesn't want to be photographed with Miss Porky Poundcake."

"I need to confess something."

I crossed my arms and waited. Her tone frightened me.

She continued, "I was a little jealous of all the attention you were getting. Yesterday, when the news crew was on the front lawn, I knew they were there, and I answered the door like that on purpose. Dressed in almost nothing."

She put her face in both hands.

"Why would you do that?"

"I'm a terrible person," she sobbed between her fingers. "I put on makeup before I answered the door."

I bit my lower lip, fighting back the urge to laugh.

"You put on makeup, but not pants?" I asked.

She nodded, her face still in her hands.

"You thought this was your chance to get fifteen minutes of fame?"

More nodding, still sobbing.

I patted her knee. "Hang in there. I'm sure if you keep doing stupid stuff, you'll get your chance to have strangers vote on mean nicknames for you."

She sniffed. "You think?"

226

"Oh, absolutely. These days, it's basically inevitable. How about you volunteer to tutor at the high school and seduce a teenaged boy who's just the other side of legal? That could be a good scandal."

She dried her eyes and stared at me, blinking repeatedly as she tried to figure out if I was joking or not.

"Or maybe two boys," I said.

"Brothers." Her eyebrows gave away that she was kidding along with me.

"Definitely twins. Super hot."

She made a gagging face. "Speaking of twins, remember how I made out with Golden's brother, Garret?"

"Yes. You guys were in the bathroom all night at that party, and I had to pee super-bad. I hated you that night."

"What I didn't tell you is Garret had terrible back and chest acne. We had the light off in there, and he took his shirt off. I guess he thought I wouldn't know, but I could feel it. I could feel all these gross cystic pustules under my hands."

I covered my mouth with my hands. "Ugh."

"But it was kinda hot, you know? Like making out with a monster. That mix of revulsion and attraction."

Giggling, I tossed a couch pillow at her. "Stop! You're making this up."

"I totally gave him a hand job with one hand tugging, and the other hand stroking across his acne-covered shoulders. He loved it, too. Guys love it when you accept them completely, warts and all."

"I guess… I can relate."

"And also when you make them come. Hand, mouth… thigh crease."

"Boobs," I added.

"Who?"

"Toby."

She got quiet, nodding. We didn't usually talk about Toby.

Outside, a man with a pizza box walked by, looking confused. We jumped up and ran to the door together.

The pizza from DeNirro's was the best in town, but the delivery driver had some sort of cosmic block that prevented him from locating our house.

We got our pizza and spent the rest of the evening eating and sharing details of dark sexual escapades. I thought I knew everything there was to know about Shayla, but there were some fantasies we'd not yet delved into.

I caught her up to speed on what had happened at the hot spring and Dolphin Falls, but I didn't have to go over what happened Saturday morning when I was riding *Lionheart*. We'd accidentally left the door open and she'd gotten the general idea, even with her pink noise-cancelling headphones on.

CHAPTER 21

Monday.

Kirsten at Java Jones was practically undressing me with her eyes as she made my mocha.

"Let me guess," I said. "You saw the photos."

She gave me a flirty look. "You should be proud! You were rocking that lacy bra. He's a lucky guy. What's it like dating a famous actor?"

"We're just friends," I lied, the goofy grin on my face probably giving me away.

Damn it, I was proud. My curves were all over the internet, and I was dating a hot actor. This was my life now! It was terrifying and also awesome.

"How did you meet him?" she asked.

"He just ran into the bookstore, Saturday before last. A TV crew was chasing him and he found—"

Kirsten interrupted with, "Sanctuary. In your arms."

"I was the one who fell into his arms, but sure. Sanctuary."

She handed me the mocha and gestured for me to wait a moment. She opened up the glossy celebrity magazine she was reading and showed me a picture of Dalton's gorgeous face, his jaw speckled with a three-day beard. They'd done something with his eyes to increase their intensity and lighten them to a pale green.

"Sanctuary," Kirsten said with a sigh.

Next to his photo was a quote from what I assumed was an interview:

The darker aspects of a role are no small things. When you pretend to be evil, even if it's just for the camera, it robs you of a drop of your soul. Even a lake can be drained, one drop at a time. That's why the thing I value most in a lover is the sanctuary they give. Only in loving arms can I feel my soul replenish.

I looked up at Kirsten's expectant face.

"He does have a flair for the dramatic," I explained.

She looked like she wanted to hear more, which was exactly why I needed to get the hell out of there.

I grabbed my mocha and was getting a matching lid when I noticed someone skulking nearby. She was trying to hide, with a baseball cap pulled down to her eyebrows, and she would have passed as a teenaged boy, but she made eye contact with me for just a second, and I knew.

"Alexis," I said, striding right up to the table where she was sitting. "Trying to get another photo of me to sell to the highest bidder? I hope you didn't give me away for nothing."

"I'm sorry," she muttered, confirming my suspicions. That was all the proof I needed.

"Just great! Maybe later I'll have my pants off, and you can get a nice, big one of my bare bottom. If they pay by the size, that should get you a lot more than you made selling my chest off to the highest bidder."

Some seniors having coffee at the next table over perked right up and trained their ears our way.

"It's perfectly legal," she said, not meeting my eyes.

"So is me telling you my opinion that you're a parasite. You don't do anything of value to society. You just take, and destroy."

Kirsten called out from behind the counter, "You tell her, Peaches!"

I leaned down and put my face right in front of hers. "What's your problem with Dalton Deangelo? Why are you in his business?"

She finally looked up at me, her eyes wide with fear.

"Because he left us," she said.

"Left who?"

She shook her head. "Can't say. Not allowed."

I snorted. "You hide in bushes and sneak around photographing people without their consent. You're not exactly a credible source."

"I didn't send all the photos I had," she said. "I couldn't do that to you."

"Oh." I put my hand on my hip. "You didn't send all the photos you took of me without my permission. Well, gosh. Let's be best friends. Come over tonight and we'll give each other pedicures."

And then, because there's nothing you can say to top premium sarcasm, I turned and walked out.

I crossed the street, opened the bookstore, and tried calling Dalton's phone again. Still voicemail.

I called Shayla and asked her to check if there was anything new online about me, or him. We'd installed an app on my phone to block my browser. She assured me nothing else had shown up. I could hear keys tapping in the background. We had internet on the computer at Peachtree Books, but I wasn't going to risk googling myself and having another meltdown.

"That's interesting," she said.

"How bad is it?"

"Not bad at all, actually. A couple of prominent bloggers have picked up on the story and are talking about... oh, the usual stuff. Fat-shaming, bad; body acceptance, good. Evil media conglomerates, bad; bloggers who run the exact same advertisements on their websites, good."

As she talked, I dumped the pens out of the can and started sorting them. "I'm not a person to them, am I? You know what? Seriously, forget the internet and everyone on it. Bunch of losers need to get their own lives."

Shayla gasped. "Noooo! You love the internet!" More keyboard tapping. "Oh, you're a meme, apparently. Like with the funny text over your photo."

I swore like a truck driver.

She giggled.

I sorted the pens on the counter by color and shape, the yellow vintage phone cradled between my ear and shoulder.

"Any good ones?" I asked.

"The usual assortment. Hah! That one's good. It says, 'My peaches. Let me show you them.'"

"People suck! They suck so hard right now."

"Did he call you back?"

"No," I said, then I caught her up on my run-in with Alexis at Java Jones before work.

She said, "That girl needs to leave town, and find a new career."

A male customer in a business suit came in, so I quickly said goodbye to Shayla and hung up the phone.

The man came right up to the counter and lay a folder on the surface between us.

"I have something for you to sign," he said.

"Get out!" I pointed to the front door. "I'm not signing some skeevy printed-out photo of me in my bra, you molestor. Those photos were taken without my consent. Actually, give me your name, and I'll eventually get around to suing you, as well."

He chuckled, as amused as I was annoyed. "I work for Dalton Deangelo, and I've come to collect your signature for an NDA. That's a non-disclosure agreement. This is a very common and completely normal protocol with actors."

My jaw dropped open with shock. I was half-naked on the internet, and now this?"

"Oh, hell, no," I said. "There's the door. Don't let it hit you on your way out."

"I also come bearing..." He shoved an open envelope full of crisp bills—a money sandwich—my way. "Incentive," he finished.

"You brought a bribe, to get me to sign a piece of paper to not say whatever, when I was already preparing to not say a word, for no additional fee?"

"Good! You're a smart girl. We won't have to spend long going over the terms."

"Is this happening because my breasts are all over the internet now? Plus that badly-edited video where it seems like I'm admitting to sleeping with Dalton? Because I'm afraid the horses have left the barn."

"Horses and barns notwithstanding, we would prefer things do not escalate."

I sighed and looked around me, at all the books lovingly stacked on bookshelves all the way up to the ceiling. So many words, so much wisdom, and what did I know? Nothing.

I thought of phoning my father, who was just down the street. He'd negotiated plenty of contracts, and he'd know what to do.

The man opened the folder to show me the NDA was a "short" three pages, and "not too scary."

"You're shushing me," I said. "I don't like being shushed. I can't believe Dalton would do this to me."

The man didn't reply.

"Was this all his idea?" I asked. "Does he want me to sign this? Is that why he hasn't called me back?"

The man withdrew a fancy pen from within his suit jacket and handed it to me.

"This need be but a simple matter," he said.

My blood was rushing into my head, making it harder for me to think straight. I certainly wasn't going to blab about Dalton to anyone, so what difference did it make if I signed the paper?

I took the pen and initialed the boxes on each page, then signed and dated the back page.

He handed me the envelope of cash, a satisfied smile on his face. "Don't spend it all in one place," he said.

"I don't want the money. I signed that for Dalton's peace of mind. You'll tell him that, won't you?" I pushed the envelope across the counter, back his way. "I really don't want this cash."

"Then give it to charity." He handed me a copy for my own records, and walked back out the door. He was so smooth, the bells didn't even jingle.

For the rest of the morning, I organized the shelves and helped book customers in the regular fashion, but nothing felt regular. At every moment, I was sure if I turned around, there'd be people watching me, and people with cameras just outside the window.

They say when you shiver for no reason, it's because someone's walking over your future grave. What do they call that unsettling shivery feeling you have, when you know the world is talking about you on the internet? Besides paranoia?

Whatever it was, the only cure was to keep myself busy.

I probably would have gone completely bonkers by the end of the day, if Dalton hadn't phoned me around lunch time.

"Are you through with me?" I asked.

"That depends on how angry you are, and if you're through with me."

I sighed. "It's good to hear your voice."

"The NDA was not my idea, but it is standard. And I wanted to be sure everything was taken care of for tonight."

"Tonight?" A warm feeling was creeping through my body, which was a welcome relief from all the crazy.

"Vanity Fair is doing a photo shoot with me tonight. It's all happening around sunset, after we wrap shooting for the day. It's going to be a long day for us, but I was hoping you'd come along and be my girl."

I didn't say anything in response, because I was too busy smiling. *Be his girl?*

He continued, "I'd love you to meet the director. He's a great guy, plus the rest of the crew. It's a small production, but full of talent."

"Are they all standing around you now?"

He laughed. "Actually, I'm alone. And I have another favor to ask you, but I'll wait until you're here, because I'm more convincing in person."

"You sure are."

"But when I turn my back, you disappear."

"About Saturday," I said. "I'm sorry I ran off like that after you told me your secret. You took me by surprise."

"I'd rather not discuss that matter," he said curtly.

"Oh." Now I felt like a jerkbag for bringing it up.

Gently, he said, "Vern showed me a bit of what's going around with your pictures today. I'm really sorry that's your first taste of the spotlight. It hurts like someone punching you in the guts with a knuckle full of rings, but you get used to it."

"I guess the money helps." As soon as I uttered the phrase, I regretted it. I hadn't meant the money I got for signing the NDA, but earnings in general, from being a star. I opened my mouth to explain, but he cut me off.

"Hey!" he said. "I'm holding everyone up. I have to run, but I'll send Vern to pick you up at your house at eight. Sound good?"

He barely waited for me to agree, and he was gone.

~

Here's the problem with every woman's wardrobe:

The person who buys the clothes is not the same person who later has to wear them.

Perhaps it's a brain disorder? A type of split personality? Rampant, unfettered optimism?

I swear the girl who buys my clothes weighs about ten pounds less, and stands two inches shorter. Why else can the rise of my pants and the hem of my shirt not meet somewhere over top my middle? Perhaps with a slight overlap?

I know what you're thinking: *Peaches Monroe, you wash your clothes in hot water.*

But I don't! Our washing machine isn't even capable of washing on hot, because it's not hooked up to the tank. And I don't use the dryer, choosing instead to string up all my clothes on an indoor drying rack.

With few viable options for attending a *Vanity Fair* photo shoot, I finally settled on a pair of jean shorts, paired with my layered black and white camisole, and then my green lace tank top on top. The front of everything dipped down to show an appealing view of my peaches, even if the back view was nothing to write blog posts about. I topped the outfit with blue-framed sunglasses.

"Too casual?" I asked Shayla.

"You look like you're going to the beach."

"Right." I switched my black sandals for a pair of flats with a floral pattern. Nothing I wore matched anything else, and for some reason this struck me as funny. It was the exact opposite of the way refined older ladies dressed, with everything in matched sets.

"Did you pack some condoms in your purse?" Shayla asked. We were standing in the kitchen, and I was picking sliced vegetables off the cutting board as she sliced them for her big salad.

"Condoms, yes. And your big bottle of lube," I joked.

"That's too bad. I was planning to do crazy things tonight." She held up a large zucchini from Mr. Galloway's garden.

"Right, vegetables. And definitely not your boss."

She grimaced. "We're off again. He's trying to have a baby with his wife, and he needs to reserve all his seed."

"His *seed*? If he calls it that, there's the first reason you shouldn't be sleeping with him."

"Who should I be sleeping with?"

"Call Golden's brother Garret and see if the back acne's cleared up."

"He's dating Chantalle Hart. Didn't you know? Pretty casual, but Golden walked in on them going at it in their parents' bed."

"Ugh. Why always the parents' bed? What is wrong with people?"

"Taboo is fun."

"But why?"

She shrugged. "Must be some human drive, to screw everything, everywhere. Our horny ancestors had more babies than the ones who had a bunch of hang-ups. We come from a long line of horny people with no self-control."

"One of them being our great-grandfather."

She grinned. "God bless his horny soul, or none of us would be here today."

"And this house would be on Larch Street, not Lurch Street."

"Sex makes the world go round." She grabbed a cherry tomato and closed her eyes as she chewed it. My mouth watered, imagining the soft flesh bursting in my mouth.

"Enjoy your salad," I said.

"Enjoy your meat," she replied.

"I'd share if I could."

"Ugh. I need to get laid."

The doorbell rang, and we both leaned to peer up the hall at the window, where butler Vern was silhouetted against the tall window next to the front door.

"He's gay," I said.

"His loss." She popped another tomato into her mouth.

~

Vern was all smiles and chuckles as he held open the door of the car for me.

"What's shakin'?" I asked. "Are you excited about this photo shoot thing?"

"I guess." He stood at my door for a moment, like he wanted to ask me something, then he shook his head and gently closed my door.

Once we were driving, I pressed the green button overhead to speak to him. "Thanks for coming to pick me up," I said.

"That's my job, miss."

"I appreciate it, though. You make me feel like a lady, even though I'm wearing jean shorts."

"Everyone here is so nice," he said over the speaker. "I've been here almost two weeks now. I thought I'd get tired of all the trees and nature, but now I don't know if I'll be able to leave. I've made some friends, thanks to your suggestion."

"I'd offer you a job being my butler, but I think Dalton would be mad."

"Oh, miss, I don't think you could ever do anything to make Mr. Deangelo angry. He really likes you."

"Thank you." Damn. If making me like Dalton even more was part of his job, he sure was good at it.

We drove for a ways, past Dragonfly Lake and then still a bit farther. The car turned onto an access road with a metal gate, the upper arch reading Double D Ranch in wrought iron letters, with horse shoes on either side.

I hugged my chest and smiled at the quiet joke that my own Double Ds were getting their very own ranch. A few years back, I'd looked online and discovered there were a number of ranches across America named Double D. The ranch names came from the brands the farmers used to put on their cattle, back in the Wild West days, and then from the time of community pastures.

Another thought occurred to me: Dalton Deangelo was also a Double D. So, that was a funny coincidence.

We parked next to a fence, where some horses grazing on the other side eyed us with curiosity.

I stepped out of the car and went to pet the gorgeous beasts. Most of them had glossy red-brown coats plus black manes and tales. One horse with a white lighting stripe down her face took a real liking to me, smelling deeply along the side of my head and brushing her velvet lips against my cheek.

Vern joined me in petting the horses, his eyes wide and his hands timid. He squealed as a young colt reached his head through the fence to nibble at his black trousers.

The horses paused as a group, sniffing the air. I heard the sound of an engine, then turned to see a helicopter was approaching. The horses snorted and took off at a gallop, disappearing over a hill.

The helicopter landed, whipping up dust from the dry, dirt road. A group of four people stepped out, and then the helicopter lifted up again and flew off.

"That's the photographer," Vern said to me. "And her three assistants. They aren't staying here tonight, as far as I know." He waved toward the largest building nearby, a thing one might be tempted to call a cabin, as it was apparently made from logs. The enormous ranch house really was more of a castle, by the size of it.

Vern saw me looking and waved to the ranch house, explaining, "Some of the filming takes place inside there, but we've also got a smaller cabin at the back, and that's where this evening's photo shoot is happening."

I turned and held my hand up to block the glare of the sun. "We're losing light, so I guess it's happening soon?"

"It sure is. Follow me."

There were two dozen vehicles parked along the front road, and close to a hundred people milling about, all talking on phones or walkie talkies and looking really busy and annoyed.

Vern pointed out people and explained to me which ones were part of the indie film crew versus who was there for the Vanity Fair shoot. I was beyond relieved to have him at my side, explaining everything.

I spotted some attractive young women who weren't looking busy or annoyed, but enjoying some late-day sunshine on lounge chairs. "Who are they?"

"Extras. They're only in a scene or two, but they're kept around so the director has some tail to chase around and doesn't bother the leading ladies."

"No!"

He held up his hands, grinning. "Standard practice. I imagine this is all rather sordid compared to running a bookstore?"

"Scandalous."

"You'll get the hang of it," he said.

We walked up to the smaller building, which was also made of logs, and could safely be called a cabin, though it was still rather majestic. Speaking of majestic, my eyes didn't spend much time on the cabin, because a muscular torso drew my attention. A shirtless man in plaid shorts and a brown, wide-brimmed hat brushed past us, bumping into me hard enough to make me lose my stride.

"Sorry, miss," he muttered.

CHAPTER 22

I sniffed the air, detecting a familiar musk, and wheeled around. "Dalton?"

Dalton Deangelo stopped and pulled off the hat, grinning. "So much for my disguise."

"I'd know that chest of yours anywhere. I probably know your nipples better than your face."

He frowned and looked over at Vern, who was struggling to maintain composure.

"I didn't mean it like that," I said.

Jokingly, he frowned and said, "I'm just a sex symbol to you girls. The way you fetishize me. It makes me feel dirty."

"Sir, may I fetch you anything else?" Vern asked.

Dalton grabbed me and pulled me against him, my back to his front. He wrapped his arms around my torso possessively and rested his chin on top of my head.

"You've brought me everything," Dalton said. "You brought my Peaches, and she brought her peaches, and that's all I need."

"You're so bad," I said, spanking his forearm as I chided him. The girls in the lounger chairs were looking our way with interest. My anger flared up momentarily as one pulled out her phone, and I imagined her taking my picture and posting it on a gossip site.

Vern excused himself to go check on some details, and I was alone with my guy again. *My guy*. Because I was there as *his girl*.

Turning around to face him, I said, "I signed that NDA for you, not for the cash. I'd rather have your trust than your money."

He glanced around, then kissed my forehead, right over my eyebrow. "Good. Let's go smooch behind a tree for two minutes, before you have to get into hair and wardrobe."

"What?"

"Smooch. It's sort of a slang word for kissing." He tugged my hand and led me over to a big tree, pulling me into his arms on the opposite side of the crowd of people milling about.

"What do you mean, hair and ward—" He didn't shush me, but he did press his lips firmly against mine, which made my knees as weak as ever.

He hadn't answered my question, but I understood the favor he was asking me. With my pictures all over the internet, and me being *linked to* him, having me in some of today's *Vanity Fair* photos would be good for publicity on the film. I still hadn't figured out what the movie was about, exactly, but if he cared about it, that was good enough for me.

His lips did most of the convincing. And then his tongue helped, as did his bare chest, his flesh hot and wonderful under my hands. With my back against the rough tree bark, I savored his kisses and his gentle, passionate touch.

He rubbed his lightly-stubbled cheek against mine and murmured in my ear, "It's a shame we only have one more minute. We could do a lot of damage to each other if we had maybe five minutes."

I pulled him close, my palms flat on his back between his shoulder blades. "Five minutes? But you have me all night."

"So you'll pose for a couple of photos? It would really help me out."

"I will do anything for you, baby."

He grinned and took my hand, guiding it down to feel his hardness.

"Feel how hot you make me."

I squeezed his rocket. "You've got quite the situation in those shorts."

"Don't plan on getting any sleep tonight."

I stroked the length of him, feeling equally engorged myself. "I think I'm making your situation even worse." I squeezed the head, pressing my thumb into the groove and feeling everything through the thin fabric of his plaid shorts.

For a second, I remembered his confession about being in the adult films when he was younger. Stereotypical porn images flashed through my mind, and it didn't turn me off at all. It made me feel frisky. So frisky, I could have screamed.

He pressed up against me suddenly, pinning me to the tree and grinding himself against my hip bone and stomach. Nuzzling my neck, he murmured, "Tonight."

"Tonight."

He took my earlobe into his mouth and sucked, hard. I whimpered as electric feelings shot through me.

After two more nibbles on my sensitive earlobe, he whispered, "Hair and makeup is in the yellow trailer. You'd better run, because you're late, naughty girl."

He pulled away, turned quickly, and jogged off in the direction of the smaller cabin, his hat off his head and held casually in front of his shorts.

I staggered toward the trio of mobile dressing rooms, drunk on lust. Two of the trailers were brown, and one bright yellow, so at least that part was easy.

The next part, however, was not so easy.

Inside the trailer, I was introduced to about a dozen people, each of whom passed me on to another person. Finally, a buxom girl with coal-black hair and tattoos up and down both arms shook my hand, and suddenly the two of us were alone in the trailer.

"I guess you're stuck with me," I said.

She winked, her full cheeks rising merrily. "We're stuck with each other. Is this your first shoot?"

"Not counting the ones I didn't know I was a part of, yes."

She gasped. "You're Peach Tits!"

I nearly slapped the bitch. I probably should have. That's grounds for slapping someone, isn't it?

She continued, "I'm a huge fan! Me and my girlfriends are all Team Peaches."

And then, as she said my name again with her particular accent, and I heard it: Peach-tchiss.

"We looooove Peach-tchiss!"

I clapped my hands to my face. "I nearly slapped you. I thought you called me Peach Tits."

Her snow-white face grew even more pale.

I fanned my face, saying, "Phew! Just give me a moment to get my bitch dialed down. It shot up to eleven there, but we're okay. We're cool."

The young woman pulled back her silky black hair to show me a hearing aid. "Some of my words come out different from other people's, because of how I hear them."

"I'm sorry I thought the worst. I'm a little trigger happy since I read all those nasty things online."

"I'm Finn," she said, offering me a delightfully plump hand to shake. "Short for Dolphin, but spelled with an F, in case you're wondering."

"We're sisters in the weird name club."

She glanced down, taking in my full figure at the same time as she stuck one round hip to the side. We were sisters in the BBW club, too. She could have played my body double, if not for the tattoo sleeves up both of her arms. Her ink was a mix of macabre and sweet, with the skeletons of cartoon animals mixed with flowers, sailboats, and antique keys, plus one yellow French's mustard squeeze bottle. Surely there was a story to that one, I figured.

"Come to my lair," she joked, leading me over to a swivel chair in front of three mirrors. We squeezed past several racks of clothing packed into the narrow trailer, and I took a seat.

As the perfumed scent of the makeup hit my nose, the gravity of the situation began to sink in. I was going to be shot for *Vanity Fair*. Shot, stuffed, and mounted in a display case for all the world to see.

"You have good hair," she said.

"Thanks."

"My instructions are to go Country Bumpkin, but screw them. Let's go Sexy Farmer's Daughter."

"What's the difference?"

"About a mile of false eyelashes and a push-up bra, plus a gorgeous pinafore dress instead of overalls."

"Honey, you had me at false eyelashes."

With a confident smile, Finn started opening packages of makeup and prepping fluffy brushes. She worked on my hair and makeup, then helped me try on a few outfit options. She knew exactly what to put on my body, from her own experience, and even loaned me her own silver belt when I confessed that none of the wardrobe options were nearly as nice as hers.

I found myself wishing my mother could have been there, as she would have gotten a kick out of the whole thing. *Next time*, I thought, then I laughed at myself for thinking there would ever be a next time.

After some frenzied last-minute makeup touches, while people kept popping their heads in the door to urge Finn to hurry up, I emerged from the trailer in my glamorous Sexy Farmer's Daughter getup.

The pinafore dress we tried didn't have the seam integrity to handle my curves, so I was in a sturdy and eye-popping polka dot dress, red and white. They actually had a lot of dresses my size in the wardrobe department, which surprised me. A stiff crinoline spread the skirt about a mile wide, and made my curvy legs, exposed from the mid-thigh down, look positively dainty amidst all that fabric. Around the high waist, I wore Finn's lovely silver belt, which was a snake biting its tail. At the top of the boned bodice, my breasts were high and proud, round and ready like two well-inflated bouncy castles.

My blond hair was styled in two braids, but artfully voluminous around my face. The makeup was comically heavy, especially the round blush apples on my cheeks, but Finn assured me it was necessary, because the bright lights would blanche half my color out. My earlobes were burdened by heavy clip-on earrings. My ears aren't pierced, so Finn didn't have many choices, but we both agreed the shiny silver earrings brought out the blue in my eyes.

As I followed some unnamed assistant to the set, I was glad for the earrings pinching my lobes, as they helped keep me from floating out of my body amidst the surreal scene.

My mouth dropped open as we came around the corner and I saw the scene in front of the log cabin. A seven-man band, all in red and black lumberjack-flannel jackets, were getting into place with musical instruments. A man with a long, red beard played the stand-up bass contentedly as people milled around.

The guy at the drum set, whom I recognized as Shayla's cousin from the other side of the family, Lester, gave me a wave. That's when I realized I was looking at the Bushy Beaver Tails, Beaverdale's almost-famous band.*

*Be careful when you type Bushy Beaver Tails into a search engine, that you don't have image preview turned on.

Lester cupped his hands around his mouth and shouted, "Go, Peaches!"

I felt myself blushing under my thick makeup.

When Dalton tapped me on my shoulder, I threw myself into his arms. "Hold me, I'm scared!" I wailed, mostly joking.

"I'm not Mr. Deangelo."

I squeezed him tighter, pressing my body against his, but careful not to smear my makeup on his crisp, green button-down shirt. "Then why do you smell like him?" I asked, nuzzling the neck of the man I assumed was Dalton.

With his hands firmly on my waist, the man pushed me back from him. "I'm the stand-in," he said, his blue eyes twinkling.

For an instant, I was amazed Dalton had turned his green eyes blue, but then realization smacked me in the face repeatedly (the way realization always does).

I apologized to the attractive young man, and he laughed and told me he would take my error as nothing but a compliment.

The realization I'd nuzzled this stranger's neck was still smacking me in the face as we got our instructions about where to go for the photos.

The Dalton look-alike was going to pose in the images with me, and then the real one would come join us at the end. As we talked a bit more, I found out that Charlie (that was his name) wasn't there just for the shoot, but also had a small role in the movie, as Dalton's character's brother.

The shoot itself was about as strange as you'd expect. They brought in some bales of hay for us to sit on, and Charlie and I sort of danced* while the Bushy Beaver Tails actually played music, and then we all acted terrified when a trio of people in teddy-bear suits interrupted our party.

*Charlie was a fine dancer, whereas I merely pretended to dance while trying not to look down and get a bunch of chins.

The photographer said nothing directly to me, but whispered to her three assistants, who then directed me.

And how did I enjoy my first major magazine photo shoot? I hated/loved every minute. It was the worst/greatest thing, ever. I felt hideous/gorgeous and the work itself was easier than selling books.

The time whizzed by, and I did a quick wardrobe change into a puffy white blouse and my own jean shorts for the next series. Charlie disappeared, and *my guy* strolled onto the photo set on the lawn of the log cabin, looking every bit the star. He wore an expensive-looking suit with a tie the same color as his gorgeous green eyes.

The next part was the most challenging: we had to pose like we were about to kiss, without actually kissing. Having Dalton's lips just out of reach was tantalizing torture. He dialed up the pain by eye-sexing me the entire time. I nearly died.

And then, it was done.

Well, first there was a tedious amount of hand-shaking and release-papers-signing, but eventually it was done. The sun disappeared behind the rolling hills, and that was the end of our light. The silent photographer and her three assistants disappeared in a helicopter, and everyone else drove off.

Dalton and I lingered behind to pet the horses, and before long, we were alone.

The horses eventually got bored of us, deciding we had no sugar cubes, and wandered off into the dusky night.

Vern had gone to wait for us in the car, where Dalton assured me he was taking a nap.

"Should we go somewhere?" I asked. "Back to your trailer? We're not allowed to hang out here with nobody around, are we?"

He laughed. "We're not trespassing. Help me block out a scene, will you?"

I didn't know what that meant, but I followed him back to the smaller log cabin, the dark sky cozy around us. Back in the main building, the large one behind us, lights were on and the windows showed human activity. Most of the production crew were staying there, with the family who owned the ranch. There was a personal connection between some of the crew and the ranch owners—a connection I didn't care about, because Dalton had my hand in his, and that was everything.

Oh, I nodded politely as he told me about the budget overruns, and how today's photo shoot was saving their bacon because they had no promotion money, but his gorgeous body paired with my freak-girl lust was stealing my attention. Was it the suit and tie? I couldn't wait to get him back to my place, or even to his ridiculous Airstream trailer.

I was quite surprised when he led me into the log cabin, then to a small room, where he started kissing my neck like he meant business. We were in a room full of cameras, with a bed in one corner.

"What are you doing?" I moaned as his lips traveled up and down the side of my neck.

"Blocking out a scene." He reached for my layers of tops and lifted them up. My hair was still in braids, but I'd changed back into the green lace top I'd arrived there in, what seemed like days earlier but was in fact only hours.

Down to just my bra on top, I shivered in the cool evening air. The room was lit by just one table lamp, next to the bed, and the house was eerily silent.

"You cold?" he asked. "I'll warm you up." He rubbed his palms together, the sound like fine sandpaper, then rubbed his hot palms up and down the outer edges of my arms.

With a nudge, I was backing up, stopping only when the backs of my legs touched the bed.

I whispered, "We can't mess up the film set."

"A bed can be re-made." He reached for my jean shorts and deftly unfastened the button and zipper. The denim hit the floor, the sound resonating through the empty cabin. Dalton's eyebrows shot up. "Uh-oh."

I glanced over his shoulder, at all the cameras and equipment, staring at us with their dark eyes. All the power was off, but the devices were still menacing. Watchful.

"We could go to your trailer," I said, my voice hopeful.

A shadow passed over his green eyes, already dark and mysterious in the low light of the room. "I can't wait that long."

"Mr. Impatient."

"Undress me." He stood absolutely still before me.

Okay.

I reached under the suit jacket, finding his heat trapped beneath the fine wool and silky lining. Slowly, I removed the jacket and lay it on the bed behind where I stood. The tie came off next, and I got flustered because of how he was staring at me. I lay the green tie on the bed next to the jacket.

Next, I unbuttoned his shirt, slowly revealing his perfect body. I pulled the fabric away and then draped it gently on the bed as well.

"Should I put your clothes somewhere other than the bed?" I asked.

"That's fine."

What did he mean? It was fine that we'd be rolling around on the clothes, or that we weren't going to be using the bed, or what?

"Keep going," he said.

Silently, obediently, I started unbuttoning his trousers.

"On your knees," he said.

I thought about it for a moment, then got down on the wood floor, on my knees. He was already thick and hard for me as I eased down his trousers and boxers.

Slowly, enjoying the torture of drawing it out, I draped the remaining clothes on the bed.

He didn't say a word, and his mouth didn't twitch with any expression.

I could smell the musky scent of his pubic hair, his smell intoxicating. He was rigid and pointing at my lips, the bead gleaming.

Leaning forward, I took him into my eager mouth, relishing the slightly bitter tang of his fluid, followed by the earthy, saltiness of his flesh.

"There's my girl," he murmured, and he buried his fingers in my hair as I took him deep in my mouth. He didn't push my head, but encouraged me to bob faster, then slower.

He groaned as I sucked his gorgeous length. I could hear the lip-smacking sounds of my mouth on his flesh, and the noises only turned me on more.

He groaned and clutched his hands more tightly at the base of my skull.

"I'm going to come," he said, which wasn't news to me based on how pressurized and big he felt.

"Mmm," I moaned, my mouth full of him.

He murmured, "Look at me."

I tilted my head to the side to make eye contact, my lips still around his thick rod.

"I want you to touch yourself for me," he said. "Touch yourself the way you wish I was touching you."

I didn't have to think about that request for long. My hand practically dove down into my panties. I whimpered again as fingers slid easy into my silken crease, back and forth across my flesh.

The flesh in my hand and mouth matched the heat between my legs, and soon everything was in motion.

Just as I began to release, the delicious waves of toe-curling pleasure pulsing through my arms and legs, he also began to pulse in my mouth. With a groan, he thrust against me, captive of his own sweet ending.

After I swallowed, he relaxed in my mouth, conforming to my shape, his balls now loose in their skin. I gave them a gentle tug, and he moaned again, then let out an embarrassed laugh.

I pulled him out and finished with a kiss, right on the winking little eye. I'd already pulled my hand out of my underwear. Resting back on my heels, I gazed up at him, waiting for what he'd say next.

Would he make a joke about not having to make the bed, after all? Would I say something about the cameras, and surprising footage they could have shot?

He tilted his head to the side, and simply said, "Your house?"

"Sure. My house. My roommate's there, but she won't mind if we make a little noise."

He looked around, then gathered up his clothes and started getting dressed. I took his cue and gathered my clothes as well.

Once I had my clothes back on, he grabbed me and pulled me in for a kiss.

"I hope that wasn't too weird," he said, grinning at me. "I was watching you with that other guy, Charlie, during the photo shoot. I got all these feelings, like I wanted to grab you by the hair." He looked away from me, as if embarrassed. "I don't know why I say stuff like that to you. I think you bring out my inner porn star. I hope you're not too disgusted."

He was so tall, and my floral ballet flats weren't helping me get up to where he was. I reached up with both hands to tilt his face so he was looking at my eyes.

"Don't sweat it," I said. "I think everyone has a little porn star in them."

"You'd make a great porn star." He reached down and cupped my buttocks, pulling me closer in our embrace. "You already have a great name, and you could totally be a star, but don't get any ideas, because you're mine now, and I ain't sharing."

I wheezed with laughter over the idea of being a porn star. "Right. Like people would pay to see me bounce around."

"They would! There's a huge market for..." He trailed off and didn't finish.

"BBW?"

"Hot, confident women," he said.

"Let's not pretend my body shape doesn't put me into a certain category. A certain fetish. And one you seem to have, yourself, mister."

"Honestly, Peaches, once upon a time there was someone in my life who was a bit like you. Maybe I do have a fetish. It's complicated. But it's been years since I've dated..."

I tried to guess where he was going, and rattled off a few things girls like me get called.

He shook his head. "I was going to say *regular girl*, but now I'm worried even that's going to come out sounding wrong."

I shrugged. "You're my first pretty boy."

He grimaced. "That's emasculating."

"So ver-y pret-ty."

He made an amused noise as he crossed past me to flick off the lamp, blinking the room into darkness.

His voice soft and disembodied in the blackness, he said, "How pretty am I now?"

"About as pretty as I am big."

"I don't like that word," he said, and we both knew he didn't mean pretty.

"Dalton, tall people are tall. Short people are short. It is what it is. I'm okay with all the words, because I'm okay with myself. But are you?"

"Some days I hate every single thing about myself."

My eyes adjusted to the darkness of the room, and I could make out the whites of his eyes and the moon light from outside the window glinting off them.

Every fiber of my being wanted to make a joke to fill the awkward silence. To say something flip, and change the subject.

Instead, I asked, "Do you really hate yourself?"

After a pause, with our breathing as the only sound in the room, he said, "No, but it would explain a lot. I guess I've been working so hard, for so long, that I forget what it is I wanted in the first place."

"I thought you were doing this indie movie because you wanted the challenge of a different acting role."

"Sure, but to what end? Maybe get an award? So I can get bigger roles and work even harder?"

"Dude, I work in a bookstore. In the morning, I live for getting my mocha from Java Jones. And then in the afternoon, I live for locking up and going home to read or hang out with my friends, or maybe even less. The night before I met you, I was cat-sitting for one of my mother's friends. My mother didn't even ask if I was available before she pimped me out. It was just assumed I had nothing else going on Friday night. So, let me ask you this, Mr. Dalton Deangelo, famous actor, do you really think I, Peaches Monroe, responsible cat sitter, have all the answers?"

He drew me to him in the darkness, a warm body in a cool, dark room.

"You seem so happy," he murmured.

"To you, sure. I'm happy whenever you're around, you big, stupid monkey."

He took in an audible breath. "That may be the greatest thing anyone's ever said to me."

"Good." I reached up on my tiptoes and kissed his lips in the dark. "Now take me back to my house and do some seriously nasty porn star stuff to me."

"Careful what you wish for."

CHAPTER 23

He took my hand and led me out of the dark room, moving slowly so we didn't trip over the many cables stretched across the pathway.

Outside the cabin, we made our way toward the car by the light of the moon. Along the way, Dalton popped into one of the trailers to "liberate" a bottle of champagne for us from craft services.

As predicted, Vern was napping in the car, sleeping like a kitten behind the tinted windows. It took a moment of us rapping on the windows to wake him up.

Dalton and I climbed into the back seat, and I snuggled next to him for the ride home.

It had been just over twenty-four hours since I'd seen those photos and awful comments, yet it felt like a distant memory. Being with Dalton made me feel like fame was our problem, shared, and not mine or his to worry about alone.

"Do you like champagne?" he asked.

"I'm not sure. Isn't it just sparkling wine?"

"Hah!" He popped open the bottle of champagne, the cork banging into the rounded ceiling and ricocheting into my forehead.

"I've been shot!" I joked, then I acted out a dramatic death.

"Oh no," he said. "My girlfriend's dead, and what's worse, we don't have any glasses to drink from."

I sat up and swiped the champagne from his hand, raising it to drink from the bottle.

"You are one classy dame," he said as I was drinking. This made me nearly spew champagne all over him, but luckily I fought the bubbly drink down.

Wiping my mouth with the back of my hand, I said, "I've never been a dame before, much less a classy one. I like it."

"Cheers." He tipped up the bottle and drank noisily.

"Who needs glasses, anyway," I said.

He turned and gave me a sly look. The world beyond the car's windows was black and cozy, and inside we were lit by pale blue interior lights, from an LED panel running along the ceiling. Dalton's skin looked cool and blue, his eyes shining.

"You've got the perfect champagne glass," he said, eyeballing my cleavage.

"Naughty boy."

Another sexy look, his eyes shining.

"I want a taste of your sweet, sweet champagne," he said, still eyeballing my cleavage like mad.

"Are you waiting for an engraved invitation? Come get some."

He slid closer, then tipped up the bottle and poured champagne between my breasts, where it pooled in the small triangle next to my chest.

I squealed as the cold champagne trickled down between my breasts, to my stomach and the hem of my jean shorts. My champagne glass wasn't water-tight, but did hold, somewhat.

"Better drink fast," I said.

He grabbed my breasts with both hands and started lapping at my bubbling boob-crack.

I shook with giggles. "You sound exactly like Howie, this old wooly sheepdog we used to have."

"Ruff, ruff." More slurping.

The cold champagne and his hot mouth and tongue were not an unpleasant combination. The front of my tank top was now completely drenched in sweet booze, and the damp layers of fabric weighed down at the front, skimming below the edge of my bra.

He pulled back. "Your turn."

I shook my head. "Oh, baby, you don't even have one squishy bit, let alone two to squeeze together." I pulled up his shirt and probed his shallow navel playfully with my finger. "This little valley wouldn't hold much more than a teaspoon full, but I suppose we could try."

We pulled his shirt up, and he lay back on the bench seat. I got on my knees on the dark carpet interior of the car, feeling wet and sticky from the waist up, and even more wet and slippery from the waist down. My P-town was ready for visitors.

Vern the driver continued to smoothly steer the car toward my house on Lurch Street, taking corners ever-so-slowly. I was pretty sure he knew we were up to hanky panky in the back seat, but I didn't care. In fact, the whole having-a-driver situation was starting to feel almost normal to me. Good things are surprisingly easy to grow accustomed to.

Dalton's smooth, muscular abdomen was certainly a good thing. I poured champagne into the valley of his navel, and then got to work slurping it out. Now it was my turn to sound like a wooly old sheepdog, between giggles.

After my third or fourth refill of the valley and subsequent lapping, I said, "Despite the inadequate size of this champagne glass, I think I may be drunk. Or drunk-ish."

"I'm confiscating this," he said, swiping the bottle from me and polishing off the remainder himself.

Our timing was perfect, because we'd just pulled up in front of my house, and after all that sexy licking, I needed a good rogering.

In my most dramatic, breathy voice, I said, "Would you like to come in for a nightcap?"

"I have to be back on-set in nine hours, which means I can only come in and do you for eight and a half straight hours."

"Then I guess we'll skip the nightcap and get right to the main event."

He growled as he pushed open the door. Cool, moist air filled my lungs. I stepped out to find it wasn't raining, exactly, but the air was dense with that misty Pacific Northwest humidity that hangs in the air, like rain in slow motion.

Dalton took a moment to give instructions to Vern about picking him up in the morning, and then we ran together into the house.

Shayla wasn't home, because she was working a split shift and closing the restaurant. I knew she'd be a while, since the staff usually partied together on Monday nights after closing. (And Tuesday nights, most Wednesdays, every other Thursday, alternating Fridays, plus Saturdays if someone's birthday fell within the previous or following week.)

"Here we are again," he said as we entered my bedroom.

This time, I was mindful to close the door in case my roommate came home. There's absolutely nothing shameful about riding your studpony and calling him Lionheart, unless of course, someone finds out.

The overhead light was too bright, so I clicked on the adjustable lamp I used for reading in bed. That was a little too bright for nude viewing of someone who eats carbohydrates, so I peeled off a damp layer, the green lace tank top, and draped it over the lamp.

"Mood lighting," I said as the room took on a cool, green cast.

Dalton pulled out the drawer next to my bed. "Good. We'll need all of these."

I clapped my hands. "Balloon animals?"

He stripped down without delay. Grinning, he said, "I'll show you balloon animals. Get those sexy little take-me-in-the-barn denim shorts off and bend over that bed."

I gulped, and then I did exactly as ordered. Naked from the waist down, I gathered my pillows for support and bent over.

He came closer, and I freaked.

"Music," I said, standing upright again and running to the dresser. I pushed the books off my stereo, and set it to the playlist I usually used for... let's just call it relaxing.

The sultry sounds of Justin Timberlake (don't judge me, I know you like him, too) came out through the tiny speakers with the surprisingly big sound.

His voice bordering on stern, Dalton said, "Stop stalling and get your sweetness over here. Time for those dirty porn things you requested."

"Eep!" I returned to the side of the bed and bent forward.

"Just one, small adjustment."

Something hard tapped against my heel. I lifted my foot, and he slid a good-sized hardcover book under my right foot, and then repeated the same with my left foot.

"Perfect," he said, tearing open a condom wrapper.

"Eep!" I repeated, my whole backside exposed and practically quivering with excitement.

With my pulse pounding in my ears, I awaited what would come next.

He didn't go straight for it, though, but massaged me with his fingers. His touch felt so good, as always, and soon he replaced his fingers with the head of his sheathed rod. I moaned with pleasure, my body flushing with heat.

He nudged harder and filled P-town.

First he stroked in and out, his hands firmly on my hips. He paused to withdraw and slide his length along me, between my lips and bluntly across my sweet spot. The whole area between my legs became one throbbing hotspot of sensitivity.

He took me to the edge, but neither of us slipped over. We were holding out, but not holding back. Not vocally, at least.

"Oh, Lionheart," I moaned.

"You're so beautiful when you're wrapped around me."

He thrust hard.

"Lionheart!"

"You want more? You want me to do you like a porno-pony?"

"Yes! Take me, you porno-pony."

And then… then it was party time.

He slowed down, thick and almost ready to explode deep within me. Slow to the point of stillness, he pushed up the white and black camisole I was still wearing, and his hands stroked up and down my back. He kept grinding into me as he rubbed my back, which was so sexy, like I was an extension of him, my torso branching off from his body at the hips.

I groaned in frustration, wanting to come. Hot. Swollen. Wet. Wanting.

He withdrew from me and began to tease me, until I begged for mercy.

Between the lube on the condom and my excited juices, he slipped back in easily, at a different angle. A whole new set of bright lights flashed on behind my eyelids.

"You feel so good."

"Mm-hmm?"

"Can you take it all?"

Nervous giggles.

"Laughing?" His tone was light with amusement. He grunted, "I'll give you something to laugh about."

He thrust deeply, his balls hot and prickly against me now.

With encouraging grunts from me, he sped up.

"Harder, faster," I said. (Classic!)

He really gave it to me, harder and faster and harder again.

Our bodies slapped together amidst animal noises for a spell, and we changed positions a few times, finally getting into a more relaxed situation, lying on our sides on the soft bed.

He kept grinding into me from behind, sending stars all through my body. I propped one leg up for access, and he reached over the side of my hip to find my sweet wetness with his fingers. With a gentle touch, he played me like the world's tiniest bongo drum, and then worked me like his fingers were a tiny bulldozer trying to flatten a stubborn anthill.

I came with a wail, alarmed at the force. I broke like a dam, and, ladies and gentlemen, it was a gusher.

He grunted and pulsed, coming right after me, and I enjoyed the sensation of his firehose blasting into its sheath, deep within me, but with all the gushing, I was just a little alarmed that I'd somehow broken my vagina.

After he withdrew, I cupped my hand down there to catch the strange flood of mystery fluid. I wriggled my way off the bed and darted straight out the door and into the bathroom next door.

What. The. Hell.

I'd half-expected to find a bad surprise, maybe from my cycle starting early, but it was just colorless, odorless fluid. Not urine, but something else.

I sat on the edge of the tub and pondered this new discovery.

I was a squirter?

I'd heard of girls shooting out fluid during deep g-spot stimulation, but hadn't exactly believed.

Dalton tapped on the door. "You okay?"

"Fine! Gimme a sec and come join me in the shower?"

Uh... sure, I was fine. Never mind that I felt like a teenage boy who just had his first wet dream and was scared, confused, and possibly aroused again. I had a squirting orgasm?

"Sure, I'll join you," he said. "Should I bring anything? Are you hungry or thirsty?"

I stared at the interior side of the old, wooden door. It had been orange and blue when we moved in, and we'd repainted everything inside, but skimped on a final coat. You could see the blue through the cream color. It really needed another coat.

I put my face in my hands. What the hell was I doing? Distracting myself from this scary situation by thinking about paint. That wasn't good. *Eyes wide open.*

"Peaches?"

"Just give me five minutes. Help yourself to anything in the kitchen." I looked at my blotchy face in the mirror, my eyes looking wide and frightened. "And bring me up a beer."

"Will do."

After he walked away, I splashed some cold water on my face and tried to pull myself together. I used the toilet and checked. Yes, my pee was still yellow, and not at all like the other fluid. My butt was tingling and happy, but not juicy, thanks to the condom. So, that squirting thing had really happened.

Huh.

I got the shower running, and a few minutes later, Dalton joined me, two unopened cans of cold beer in his hands. He pressed them against my buttocks to make me shriek, of course.

"You're so bad," I said.

"You make me want to be bad. Now kiss me like I'm dangerous."

I complied, enjoying his lips on mine, in the shower, our intimacy so casual and right.

He cracked open one of the cans and passed it to me. We took turns standing under the hot water, doing the two-person shower dance.

Some of the shower water was splashing into my beer, so I drank deeply before it got watered down.

"Gotta replenish your fluids," he said, grinning.

What was that supposed to mean? Guardedly, I stared up at him.

"Do you have to work in the morning?" he asked.

The morning. Work. My morning mocha at Java Jones.

"I ran into that girl, Alexis, this morning," I said.

He looked annoyed. "That's too bad. I would have thought she'd take her money and get lost."

"How do you know her, exactly?"

His head nodded under weight I couldn't see. "For a while, she was like my sister. Remember I told you I ran away from my parents with a woman?"

"She was someone in the porn business, right? I mean *adult film* business."

"Don't be politically correct on my account, but, yes. Her name was Katherine. Everyone called her Kiki. She had more charisma than common sense, and like an idiot, I went straight from trying to date two high school girls at once to losing my virginity to a porn star."

I ran my free hand over his wet chest as he took his turn under the shower. "I hate that she took advantage of you when you were young."

"We all take advantage. It's what people do."

A lump caught in my throat. I never liked it when someone said bad things about human nature. It was as if they were paving a future bad road with excuses.

He continued, "Kiki was Alexis's mother."

"Was?"

"Kiki hung herself."

I put my empty beer can on the edge of the tub, then turned back to hug him. I whispered, "I'm sorry."

He looked genuinely sad. "Kiki hung herself the week after I moved out and broke up with her for good. I said I was done with the adult film industry, and I honestly wished her the best. I thought she was going to be okay, but she wasn't right in the head."

I gazed up at him. Now we both had our arms wrapped around each other, and I couldn't tell you who was supporting whom. I worried that if I let go, we'd both fall away.

"I thought of Alexis as a sister," he said. "We were practically the same age, so I couldn't see myself as a father figure."

"She seemed so angry at you."

"People misplace their anger. Her mother's dead, so all that pain had nowhere to go. Grief is like a heat-seeking missile, and it burrows into the nearest heart."

"It's been a few years, though. She needs to move on and leave you alone."

"When you're famous, people refuse to disappear. Even when you give them money and they promise to be quiet, they keep coming back."

I thought of the NDA I'd signed that day and pulled back.

Was I just a future problem for Dalton Deangelo?

Was that how he saw me?

Dalton had been staring down at our feet in the tub, and now he looked up at me. Water from the shower streamed down his face, and his eyes were red, but I couldn't tell if he was crying.

Despite my fears, I felt my eyes water with sympathy tears at his pain.

"What about your parents?" I asked.

"My mother died of a drug overdose two years ago," he said.

I mouthed the words "I'm sorry," though my voice was cut off by emotion.

"Not as sorry as I am," he said. "It was my hush money that fueled her utter collapse."

The water cooled down, the hot water tank in the basement reaching its limits.

"And your father?" I asked, hating myself for my insensitive curiosity.

"The checks keep clearing, but we've not spoken directly since the fight we had the day I left with Kiki."

I stood shivering as the water turned from cool to cold. I reached around Dalton to turn off the tap, since he hadn't seemed to notice.

He chuckled, his voice hollow in the echoing bathroom now that the running water was stopped. "I told him I was going to be a big star one day, and I'd buy a big mansion and they'd beg me to live in the guest house."

I pulled two towels from the cupboard and handed one to him. He seemed confused, then after a few blinks, started to slowly pat himself dry.

"I'm sorry about everything with your family," I said.

"Your parents seem so perfect. I was watching them at the wedding, and during the speeches, they kept looking at each other with so much tenderness."

I laughed, thinking of their current argument over my father's ratty old recliner, and now the buckets being tossed down on the bushes.

"There's more than meets the eyes," I said. "I know I'm lucky, though. They've been more than understanding. They saved my life."

"How?"

My throat closed up, and then I was crying, barely able to catch my breath.

Sometimes, it just hit me like that.

I moved my jaw, thinking about telling him, but then I remembered the paperwork I'd signed that day. I'd signed *his*NDA, but he hadn't signed mine. So he didn't need to know. Nobody did.

"It's been a long day," he said gently, pulling me into a damp hug and wrapping his big towel around both of us.

"A very long day." I smiled, the waterworks finished.

"Sleep with me," he said. "Join me in the darkness, walk through my dreams, and hold my hand in the morning light."

I nodded, because what can you say after something as beautiful as that?

We spent a few minutes brushing our teeth and getting ready for bed, just like a regular couple, then I climbed into my bed next to a very sleepy-faced, droopy-eyelid-having Dalton Deangelo.

Join me in the darkness, walk through my dreams, and hold my hand in the morning light.

MIMI STRONG

CHAPTER 24

I was groggy in the morning when Dalton woke me.

"Five more minutes," I moaned, snaking my arm around him. He was fully clothed, which I did not like, but at least he was in my bed.

He kissed my cheek.

"Just a few more days, and we'll wrap this movie. Then I'll be able to sleep in, too."

I opened my eyes, suddenly awake.

"A few more days?" We hadn't talked about how much longer the movie shoot would be, but I'd hoped for more time than that before I lost him to LA.

"Yeah. Do you want me to send Vern back here to give you a ride to work this morning?"

I rolled over and squinted at my clock. I didn't have to be at Peachtree Books for another two hours.

"No, thanks. I always walk."

"Every day?"

"I have a couple of umbrellas for the winter."

He nodded. "I should have known you walk to work. But I didn't. And I don't know your middle name, either."

"Luanne."

"Favorite color?"

"My favorite color is your gorgeous eyes, Dalton Deangelo."

He cracked up. "Have fun at work. I don't know when I can see you again, but I'll call you."

"Sure," I said, and then I watched him roll off the bed and leave.

I listened to him walk down the steps and close the front door. A thought struck me: our goodbye had felt like a final goodbye, despite the casual words spoken.

Was this the end?

Part of me was sure I'd never seen him again, and that same part of me was relieved. He'd not just kept me up late. He'd disrupted my life, inserted himself into my every thought.

He and his whole life and personality were so damn big, where did that leave me?

And if we were done now, or in a few days, how long before the internet forgot all about me and left me in peace?

And one more thing: who was that moaning?

I lay still in my bed, listening.

It sounded like someone was...

I pulled my pillow around my head, because someone was moaning, and that someone was Shayla. I could still hear her, through the pillow. And now a guy's voice, as well.

Wow. Go, Shayla!

~

I didn't get to meet the guy who was getting Shayla to make such musical sounds, because I threw on some clothes and left the house early. If she was nailing her boss again, that was the last thing I wanted to be a witness off. If it was someone else, I'd meet him if he made it to a second audition. (A *callback*, as Shayla sometimes joked. She did have a string of one-night hookups in her past, because guys rarely got a callback from her, unless they were unavailable.)

I wandered around downtown with my thoughts, and by the time I opened the bookstore, mocha in hand, I wasn't even early.

The yellow phone on the wall was ringing when I walked in the door, and after I turned off the alarm, I answered it with a breathless, "Hello?"

"Peaches Monroe?" came a woman's voice.

"Speaking."

She started talking, and I know she was speaking English, but it was difficult to comprehend her words, because they were so ridiculous.

I had to keep asking her to repeat herself, and I pulled out an envelope from the drawer and scribbled on the back of it:

New underwear line

Full figured girls with personality

Team Peaches

Wednesday

Photo shoot

$$$

Fly? LA

WTF???

I jotted down the woman's phone number, told her I'd have to talk it over with my family, and hung up the phone.

"WHAT?" I said to the empty bookstore.

The houseplants on top of the shelves peered down at me in silence.

"Me, an underwear model," I said. "Me."

My father walked in the door just then, a welcome sight in his plaid, short-sleeved shirt and khaki trousers. His curly red hair had been freshly trimmed, which I noticed because he had that cute summer feature of a pale margin of skin on the back of his neck, where his now-gone hair had prevented a pink sunburn the previous day.

"Dad!" I ran out from behind the counter and nearly bowled him over with a hug.

"It's chilly in here. You don't have the air conditioner running already, do you? Open the front door and get some airflow."

I pulled away and gave him a good look. He was the perfect person to ask for advice, because he was always so sensible (about everything but his recliner.)

"Did you come by to check on our power consumption?" I asked.

"I've got some epoxy curing back at the shop. Figured I'd save some brain cells by not sniffing it."

"Good choice," I said, then explained about the phone call I'd just received.

He seemed really hung up on the fact the job was *underwear modeling*. We got past that, by working through the concept that

269

underwear covered the same stuff as a swimsuit, and he wouldn't be worried about my modeling swimwear.

"Why wouldn't they get a professional?" he asked.

"They want regular girls."

He snorted. "No, they don't. It's the whole celebrity endorsement thing. You've got your image all over the place, in your underwear from that one time, and now they want a piece of you. If you'd sent in your pictures last week, they wouldn't have even called you back."

"You know about the half-naked photos?"

"How could I not? People keep telling me. I had an old college buddy call me out of the blue."

"I'm sorry I embarrassed you and Mom and Kyle."

"Kyle doesn't know. And he's not going to." He gave me a long stare, the look in his blue eyes softening by the second. "And don't you dare be embarrassed. You're a beautiful girl, and you look beautiful in those photos. Plus you didn't do anything wrong."

His love nearly made me cry.

I looked around, double-checking that we were still alone in the store. "Dad, is this it? Is my life starting to happen?"

"Your life has been happening for a long time now."

"You know what I mean. Life outside of Beaverdale."

His eyes went wide, and he joked, "Take me with you?"

The garbage truck passed by outside the window, its weight making the whole building rumble.

"Mom would never let you go, and you know it."

He grinned and said, "Let me have a look over the modeling contract, and I'll tell you what I think."

~

I called the woman back and asked her to fax me a contract to the bookstore.

By the time the contract came in by fax, my father was already back at his shop with all his radio-control helicopter parts, so I faxed it to him.

He strolled back in around lunch, saying, "This is not written to be in your best interests at all."

My face got all disappointed, as did the rest of me.

"You won't let me be a model?"

He gave me a cute Dad-knows-best look. "I know you're excited, but you can't jump into opportunities blindly, or they have a way of becoming disasters."

My cell phone beeped with an incoming text from Dalton. "Speak of the devil," I said. "Here's a message from my current disaster. Did you know there really is a hot spring on the Weston Estate? Dalton took me to see it."

"Hot springs sometimes disappear and reappear after earthquakes."

"I know, Dad. You bring that up every time someone talks about a hot spring. And you know what else? That's the same thing Dalton said."

"Smart guy."

"He claims he isn't."

"Playing dumb can work to your advantage. Not that you'd ever try it."

"Hah! I got you to help with my contract, didn't I?"

He frowned over the papers. "You should have an agent for this. This matters. As far as the other stuff goes, dating and whatever, you're only twenty-two. Date whomever you want. It's not like you're ready to get married."

"Really. You don't say." I put my hand on my hip, the attitude working its way through my suddenly-in-demand, voluptuous body. "And at what age am I ready to get married?"

"Twenty-nine. You'll wear a big, white dress. Too expensive, of course. Your mother and I will pay for everything, and we'll book the same hall as we had for our wedding."

I honestly didn't know whether to chew him out for being so bossy, or hug him and kiss him for having given it so much thought.

"Dalton seems nice enough," he said, nodding.

I threw myself into his arms. "You're a good daddy."

"All I want is the best for you." He patted my back. "What temperature do you have the air conditioning set to? Seems a bit chilly."

He went off to fiddle with the settings for the HVAC system.

Some customers came in, and I helped them with their shopping. My father slipped out, the contract in his hand.

Once I was alone again, I remembered the text message on my phone that I hadn't read yet.

Dalton: *This lunch the catering truck made us today is insane.*

Me: *You're making me hungry!*

Dalton: *Haven't had lunch?*

Me: *I'll get something from the coffee shop soon.*

Dalton: *Don't bother! Vern is bored out of his mind here today. He's going to bring you over lunch.*

Me: *How would you feel about dating an underwear model?*

There was a long delay with no response. Over half an hour. Then I got this:

Dalton: *I don't know what you mean, but I'm not seeing anyone but you.*

Me: *An underwear company called me this morning, about modeling their new plus-size line. Do you think I should do it?*

Another delay, maybe ten minutes.

Dalton: *I don't want you to get hurt.*

I typed a whole bunch of responses and deleted them all without sending. I appreciated his concern, but I wished it didn't make me feel like he thought I was an idiot. It was bad enough I had my father working on the contract, like I was some child who didn't understand consequences.

If Dalton had been dating someone skinny, who got asked to model non-plus-size clothes, would he say the same thing?

I guess the worst part about my father and Dalton both being apprehensive was how they introduced more doubt to my mind. Right after I'd talked to the woman, my mind had whirled with dreams coming true. I'd get pampered, take instructions for a photo shoot or two, then gather my big stack of cash and buy the brand new house that was for sale down the street from where I lived. Then it would be goodbye to the grotty old rental house with "character" and scary spiders in the basement, and hello to long, hot showers in my new house. Shayla would still be my roommate, and we'd have a formal dining room and tons of fancy dinner parties.

STARDUST – PEACHES MONROE #1

Oh, and my books! I'd line the formal dining room with bookshelves.

What the doubts did was rain all over these dreams. I'd have bookshelves, but wouldn't enjoy them because I'd be sobbing on the bathroom floor over hate mail and awful things about me on the internet. If people started to dig—really dig—they'd find a gossip goldmine. *People* magazine would want to write a feature story about me, and then everyone would know everything.

The door jingled, and Vern came into Peachtree Books, looking every bit a butler with a silver-lidded tray in hand.

With a flourish, he revealed the lunch sent over from the movie set. It looked like spaghetti and meatballs, but the healthy version, where half the pasta was stir-fried vegetables.

"What are these?" I asked, sampling a green vegetable that looked and tasted like asparagus, but rolled into a circle at the tip, like the fiddlehead on a fern.

"Fiddleheads," he replied.

Of course.

"I'll watch the door while you eat," he said, and he started browsing through the new releases on the front table.

I took a seat back at the table where I usually unboxed new orders, and scarfed down the meal as I texted Dalton.

Me: *These meatballs are really good. Thank you!*

Dalton: *I'll show you meaty balls.*

Me: *I'll bring the peaches for dessert.*

Dalton: *Stop it. This scene doesn't call for wood.*

Me: *Are you in that room we visited last night?*

Dalton: *Yes. And I keep thinking about you on your knees, with your sweet lips on my...*

Me: *I do love meatballs.*

Dalton: *Back to your previous question. If you want to be an underwear model, then I say go for it. Opportunities are good. One should always make the leap when Fate winks.*

Me: *Leap?*

Dalton: *Leap! Gotta go. Very long day and long night ahead of us.*

I said goodbye and was putting the phone away when I got one more message.

Dalton: *I can smell you on my skin, you little minx. XOXO*

With a huge smile on my face, I put away the phone and chased the last bit of noodle from the plate. I'd never had someone send me lunch at work. The beautiful flowers he'd sent me were now enjoying their final day, looking gorgeous in their decay.

Flowers or lunch, or even just a text message, it all showed he was thinking about me. I'd been so concerned about him getting into all my thoughts that I forgot I'd gotten into his.

And now I lived in his mind, along with his script lines, his fancy life, and his awful memories of a lover who killed herself, a vindictive stepdaughter/sister, and a mother who overdosed on his money.

He had a lot to worry about, so I vowed to myself that no matter what happened with the underwear modeling, I wouldn't add to his problems.

~

Friday.

On Tuesday morning, I'd gotten the call about modeling an as-yet-unnamed underwear line.

By Friday, the details had been ironed out, thanks in no small part to my father's savvy negotiating.

It had been his idea to lend not just my image, but my name to the underwear line. That's how I found myself acting as the "consulting designer" on the Peaches Monroe line of plus-sized bras, panties, and body shapers. Me! A fashion designer! Specifically, I received a FedEx packet of fabric samples and chose five colors from the ten samples; I was assured my involvement was very important.

I would be paid for a few days of modeling—decent money, but not buy-a-house cash—but the real perk was getting equity in the company itself. If things went well, I could stand to get a bunch of money, plus a lifetime supply of underwear, of course. No more wearing the ratty old ginch and saving the pretty lacy ones for special occasions. No, ma'am. Starting in a few months, I'd have Date Panties on every damn day of the week.

Was I nervous about the upcoming photo shoot?

In a word, eep!

My flight to LA, where the company was based, was booked for Saturday morning. On Friday, they called to tell me the "good news." They'd increased the marketing budget, and were whipping together a national TV commercial, to be shot the next week while I was in LA.

That put a damper on my plans to spend time relaxing in LA with Dalton. He was wrapping the film shoot Sunday, and would meet me down in California a few days after I got there.

I'd be staying in his gorgeous house in the Hollywood Hills, "warming" his bed by sleeping nude in his fancy Egyptian Cotton sheets until he arrived.

We hadn't discussed what would happen after my vacation days ended, but I imagined it would be more of this, with both of us flying between the two cities as our schedules permitted.

A few days earlier, I'd been sure he was about to dump me, and now I was thinking about The Future. What had changed? The modeling contract.

Becoming a model changed everything.

See, my theory is that people don't just get confident by acting confident and believing in themselves. You have to accomplish things, reach goals. Once I became the manager of the bookstore and had staff (even if it was just Amy and the occasional part-timer or student getting work experience), I gained the confidence of someone who was a boss. I acted like a boss because I was a boss.

Now I'd had my photo taken for *Vanity Fair*, and was about to be rocking my curves and wobbles for an underwear line.

And that wasn't nothing!

I was in a celebratory mood, and Shayla was taking all my good news with more grace every day.

"Good things are happening for us," she'd say, as if the rising tide that was lifting my boat would also lift hers. And maybe it would.

She was so enthusiastic, in fact, that instead of staying quiet Friday night and getting a good night's sleep before I took a long bus ride to the nearest city and then flight to LA, I agreed to some drinking Friday night. Not *partying*, mind you, but specifically *drinking*. Starting with cucumber gin and tonics at our house.

275

The house started filling up around eight o'clock, when I was still playing Tetris with my suitcase contents. Did I need to bring a blow dryer, or would Dalton have one at his house? I didn't want to text and bother him with such a dumb girlie question, since he was working late, and I'd already asked so many questions already.

The music started up downstairs, and Shayla came up to put a cool mason jar full of ice, gin, tonic water, and sliced cucumbers in my hand. The sweating glass felt cool against my skin, and the drink went down like a refreshing waterfall that carries away all your worries—your worries about blow dryers, keys, and setting off the alarm system of a fancy house in the Hollywood Hills.

Mmm. Gin. Time to party.

CHAPTER 25

"Golden is here," Shayla said. "And she's got huge, epic news."

I rolled my eyes. "The last time I saw her, she gave me the *epic* news that she'd joined a book club. Where ladies discuss a book and drink wine. Honestly, you'd think she'd just invented the printing press the way she went on about it."

Shayla snickered. "But she's sweet."

"Yes. She is sweet. And maybe this time her epic news is actually epic."

Shayla patted me on the shoulder and winked. "Hey, not everybody gets to be a role model for girls, modeling underpants and dating a hot actor."

I swirled my ice and cucumbers, wondering where all the gin went. Somebody drank it! I would have to find another one.

"I'm no role model," I snorted. "Just because I'm full-figured and somebody famous wants me doesn't make me any better than anyone else. I didn't cure a disease."

"Please don't say the full-figured. Yuck."

"Okay. We'll call my hips... too wide for narrow minds."

"People on the internet are calling you *juicy*, and *real*."

I put down my empty glass so I could cover both ears with my hands and sing, "La la la! I'm not listening! I already have enough voices in my head, la la la, and I don't need more!"

She got bored of my crap and walked out, going downstairs to join the party. I thought about finishing my packing, but then realized I was also bored of my crap, so I went down to the party.

The first person to accost me was Golden. She's a tiny little teacup poodle of a girl, with big eyes and a round head on a skinny neck. She was born with a full head of golden hair—hence the name—and her locks were still wavy and radiant, augmented by chunky streaks ranging from pumpkin spice to platinum. You would think people would have teased her and called her Goldilocks, but they rarely did.

"I have something to confess," Golden said, clutching my arm just above the elbow, her fingertips digging in.

"Do I need to sit down to hear it?" I joked, for no benefit but my own, since my sarcasm was usually lost on her.

"I have a crush." She blinked at me, her lashes emphatically cute across her doll-like blue eyes.

We stood near the door of my house, and my employee Amy came in with some friends her age. They all had on heavy makeup and ripped fishnet stockings, like they were fifteen going on fifty-year-old-hooker. Amy, with her blue hair and pale blond eyebrows, scurried past me like she was crashing the party and didn't know whose house it was.

Actually, I didn't remember inviting her, so maybe she was doing just that. Kids!

Ah, I felt so grown up, about to fly off to LA for my second photo shoot ever.

My living room was full of people talking over the music, and leaving their wet beverages on surfaces without using coasters. The urge I always got when we had a party—the urge to kick everyone out, or hide in my room—returned. The only cure was another cucumber gin and tonic.

Golden was still talking to me about her crush, and about how talking about the crush *would jinx it*. Because jinxes were real things.

I started making my way through the crowd, stopping only once to ask someone to smoke their joint on the porch and use the Ninja Turtles ashtray.

Golden stuck with me, so I started making both of us drinks in the kitchen.

A tall, blond man walked in, followed by the intoxicating scent of his cologne. Adrian Storm.

"Two Fridays in a row, Peaches." He winked at me as he stole some cucumber slices from the cutting board.

"Don't flirt with me. I'm dating Dalton Deangelo. I assume you're aware of that, since you also knew about this party, and you're a pretty sharp guy."

"Ouch." He took the knife from my hand and worked on slicing the rest of the cucumber. "Wait. Does that mean if you weren't dating that guy, you'd welcome me flirting with you?"

Golden gyrated her hips as she leaned forward, her elbows on the part of the counter that jutted out from the wall in a peninsula. "You could flirt with me," she said.

"Maybe just for practice," he said, a twisted smile on his sexy lips.

She shrieked, "You're so bad!" As he laughed, she flailed away at him, her tiny hands whacking his broad, muscular chest.

Suddenly I felt like the awkward third wheel, even though it was my house.

How dare Adrian stare down at tiny Golden with that dumb I'm-getting-a-boner look on his face? His IQ was totally dropping by the minute, along with reduced blood flow to his brain.

Meanwhile, Golden had an equally dumb look on her face as she gazed up at Adrian's chiseled cheekbones, then down at what he was wearing, which seemed to be one of his formerly-oversized band shirts.

I swirled my mason jar full of Easygoing Fun Girl Juice and asked him, "What's with the band shirts? Why haven't you updated your look since high school?"

He looked down at the emblem on his chest, pretending to be surprised by it. "Oh. This. My parents had a bunch of my old clothes in the attic, and let's just say the two-seater car I drove back to Beaverdale didn't exactly have a ton of cargo space."

"That's a bit sad. So, you're that broke, huh?"

Golden gyrated a little more. "I think it's cool you're starting from scratch," she cooed.

Adrian gave me a frosty look, his blue eyes stormy with irritation. "There are plenty of opportunities right here in The Beav, if you know where to look," he said.

"I'm sure," I said.

He popped another cucumber slice in his mouth and crunched away. "Oh, but why am I telling you? You're the one who found herself a movie star."

"What about you?" I asked Adrian. "Weren't you hot in the underpants for some actress? What happened with that?"

"It was all an act," he said with a weird smile.

"Actors aren't like regular people," I said. "At least you had some fun."

He gave me the most heartbreaking look. "Not really."

With that look, my heart plummeted. I felt bad for Adrian, and worse for me. What was I getting myself into?

"Movie stars," I said with a shrug, as if that explained everything.

Golden said, "Hey Peaches, that Deangelo guy is really more of a TV star than a movie star, wouldn't you say?"

I shrugged. "We'll see about that after this new movie comes out."

Adrian chewed on the cucumber slices, his gaze still locked on me. "Do you even know what this movie is about?"

"No. Do you?"

"Of course I do. I know everything."

"I'm sure I'll find out soon enough, but why don't you tell me what you know?"

He didn't answer me, but turned to Golden, a sunnier look on his face. "Is it cool to dance at a house party? This song is the best."

She threw her arms in the air and whooped. "Dance party!"

She led the way out of the kitchen and back to the front room, where we'd set up my little stereo and cranked the speakers to maximum. Adrian followed, his round buttocks particularly eye-catching in the tight jeans that he used to wear five years ago, when he was a scrawny semi-goth with a lip ring.

Wait. Why were his buttocks still so appealing to me? I thought my ancient crush had long since expired, but apparently it had been taken out of the mothballs in Adrian's parents' attic, along with his band shirts.

I stood in the doorway to the kitchen, watching through the crowd for glimpses of Adrian dancing. He was loosening up by the second, dancing like he was just a regular guy at a house party in his hometown, which he was.

All the people there were just regular guys and gals, which was why they were at a house party on Lurch Street on Friday night, and not out at the Double D Ranch filming an indie movie.

It's not unusual for me to feel isolated when I'm at a party. After all, you're never as alone as when you're surrounded by people having fun you can't relate to. This night, however, it was different. I felt like I was on the verge of gaining something truly amazing, but in order to grab it, I had to let go of everything else.

~

According to the flight attendants, the trip to LA was smooth.

According to my stomach, it was not.

I did not throw up, but I did locate and clutch my airsickness bag for a few minutes, just in case.

The man sitting next to me on the flight reminded me of my father, which both comforted me and made me miss him.

The man said, "Hey, do you know why airplane travel is the safest form of transportation?"

We'd just gone through a rough patch in the little airplane, and I was breathing slowly, willing my guts to either be calm and hang on to the donuts I ate before boarding, or just get it all over with and purge those calories already.

He continued, "In all the years of airlines traversing the skies, they've never left anyone up here."

I stared at him, waiting for actual safety statistics that never came. A full five minutes later, I realized it had been a joke, but by then he was engrossed in his paperback, ignoring the mean girl who didn't laugh at his joke.

At least the flight was mercifully short, and soon we were landing. I smiled at the merry metallic chorus of seat belts unfastening around me.*

*This was my third time on an airplane, which explains why I sound like a total pro, right?

I'd brought just my small carry-on suitcase, so I was saved the adventure of awaiting luggage, and headed through the airport toward the exit and taxis.

I tried not to gawk at everyone around me and out myself as a tourist, but my eyes still bulged, because everywhere I looked, I saw big, round breast implants. And hair extensions, huge sunglasses, skinny tanned girls packing bottles of water bigger than them.

I hadn't felt so frumpy since, well, never. I've got some skinny friends, but in the town of Beaverdale, I'm average size. There are just as many girls wider than me as narrower. LA? From what I'd seen so far, not-so-much.

My mother had offered to come down with me, paying her own way, but I said I didn't want to take her away from Kyle. (We both knew the real reason was so she didn't chaperone my time with Dalton, but she was discreet enough not to call me on my fibs.)

As I made my way through the airport, I was attracting attention. Blame my paranoia, but it seemed like every set of eyes hidden behind sunglasses were trained on me. I'd worn a comfortable outfit for traveling: a red shirtdress with a black belt, over black leggings and a newer pair of Keds. On top, I wore a lightweight denim jacket to protect my pale arms from sun and exuberant air conditioning. What I should have worn was black, from head to toe.

I kept my head down and walked as quickly as I could without breaking a sweat.

As I stepped out of the glass doors, the heat coming off the asphalt walloped me. I dove for a taxi like an action hero dodging into a cave to avoid fireballs.

When I gave the address of Dalton's house to the driver, he didn't say a single word. He just pulled the car out of the queue and started driving.

"Is that a good neighborhood?" I asked sweetly. (Okay, I was looking for some sign he was just a tiny bit impressed. Call me shallow, but it was my first time address-dropping a place in the Hollywood Hills, and I was dying to get *something* in the way of a reaction.)

"Many movie stars," the driver said, eyeing me warily in the rear view mirror. "You're not stalking someone, are you?"

I laughed, probably too loud, in the exact manner of a stalker trying to sound casual.

"Just my boyfriend," I said.

His eyes narrowed, crinkling deeply at the corners. "Does he know he is your boyfriend?"

I crossed my legs and glared out the window, wishing we were in a fancy car, with the glass between us.

"Just teasing," he called back over his shoulder. "I can tell a stalker right away. You don't seem like one."

"I'm not a stalker. If you must know, I'm here for a modeling contract."

He frowned as he reached over to turn up the volume of music. "Music okay? Light rock?"

"Sure." I sat back in the seat, my arms crossed.

Business cards. I would have to get some business cards printed up, to give to people who didn't believe me. What would the cards say?

I ran through some options:

Peaches Monroe, Bookstore Manager, Plus-size Underwear Model, and Fashion Consultant.

Peaches Monroe, Girlfriend of Dalton Deangelo and Veteran Airplane Traveller.

I'm Peaches. My Business is None of Your Business.

~

We pulled up in front of Dalton's next-door neighbor's home, where I was to get a key and a quick tutorial on how to turn off the alarm system.

After the rude taxi driver, Dalton's neighbor was as pleasant as sweet tea on a hot day. She looked about seventy, and fit, wearing a trim suit that if I had to guess I'd say was Chanel.

"How was the flight?" she asked as she closed the thick wooden door to her house and waved for me to follow her around the side of the house. She had a thick yellow envelope in one hand, which I assumed might be some of Dalton's mail.

"Bumpier than expected, but the pilot was good, and he didn't leave anyone up there."

She turned back to give me a smile, perfect teeth visible between her pale-lipsticked lips.

"I can see why he's so fond of you," she said.

She opened a gate and led me through from her backyard into Dalton's garden. "These two houses were built at the same time, back in nineteen sixty four. The husband, a well-paid but not very famous director, lived on one side, with the children, and his wife lived in the other house, with her lovers. The gate was so the children could slip back and forth easily."

"Which side was the woman's?"

The platinum-haired neighbor lady, whose name was Jessica, smirked at me. "Spend the night, and in the morning, you tell me." She stepped carefully up some stone steps, then waited for me, smiling the way someone does while you're unwrapping a birthday present they're particularly proud of.

"Oh!" I said when I got to where she was. We were now above the tree line, and LA lay in one direction, stretching out of sight across the valley. In the other direction, a wall of glass stood like a cliff face, overlooking a shimmering swimming pool. Unlike the hot spring I'd skinny dipped in with Dalton, this pool was clearly man-made, lined with sparkling, teal-blue tiles. The landscaping all around was lush, with leafy palm fronds, blossoming flowers, and at least three spots set up with chairs for comfortable lounging.

Jessica asked, "Do you have gardens like this in Beaverdale?"

"Gardens, yes. Not like this. I mean, I have some geraniums. Red, in terra cotta pots, of course."

"Of course," she said, nodding. "Shall we?"

I followed Jessica as she showed me how to use the remote control button to disarm the security and unlock the doors. It wasn't nearly as complicated as Dalton had made it sound, but I appreciated having Jessica there with me.

As she took me on a tour of the house, I asked her if she was an actress herself.

"I was a continuity girl for many years. They call it a script supervisor these days. It was my job to notice the details."

"Sounds like a cool job. Noticing things. I try to keep my eyes open, but it's work."

"Noticing is a good skill to have. One day I noticed that the producer had stopped wearing his wedding ring. And that is how I came to live next door."

I grinned, unsure of the appropriate verbal response. That usually doesn't stop me from saying something, but Jessica was so refined, and so gracious, I didn't want to offend her.

She turned to look at her house from a small window at the side of the room. "We were the second owners. New kitchen in nineteen ninety-eight, but other than that, it's all original. Gorgeous spanish tiles everywhere."

I looked around the room we were standing in, with the polished concrete floor, high ceilings, and giant ceiling fans that looked like airplane propellers.

"I'm guessing this house has been renovated a time or two."

She lay the yellow envelope on a glass coffee table in front of a white, leather sectional.

She winked at me. "Like many gorgeous things in LA, this home's had a little work."

I thanked her again for making me feel at home, and then walked her out. After my exciting journey, I was feeling the after-effects of the cucumber gin and tonics from the night before.

As soon as I was alone, I sent Dalton a cute photo of myself nearly naked and about to get into his soaker tub overlooking the valley. The photo was cropped, showing me only from the shoulders up.

He messaged me back immediately, demanding to see "the rest of the photo."

Me: *I'm feeling shy now, so I guess you'll have to hurry home soon.*
Dalton: *Did you like Jessica? She's hilarious, right?*
Me: *She's very nice. I guess we both have good neighbors.*
Dalton: *Send me a picture of your sweet peaches.*
Me: *You first.*

A moment later, I received a photo of a nipple, surrounded by a few short, dark hairs. Honestly, I was relieved it wasn't a photo of his wang. His was truly gorgeous, but, like food, you need to know how to photograph that stuff so it looks appealing.

I returned his message with a shot of my cleavage, my breasts cupped by the red satin of my bra.

Dalton: *No wonder you're a model. I would buy exactly one million of those bras.*

I blushed, pressing my hand to my cheek. Who knew you could get flustered and embarrassed like that, even when nobody was around to see it?

We exchanged a few more messages about the weather, and then he had to get back to filming.

I climbed into the soaker tub and had the hottest and greatest bath of my adult life.

After, I dried off with the fluffiest, softest towel I'd ever touched. The experience was not unlike being gently patted dry by a hundred fluffy white bunnies. In other words, in case you're not picking up on my subtext here, *a girl could get used to this kind of luxury.*

The food situation was equally appealing. Dalton had arranged for his housekeeper to stock the kitchen with "a few simple meals" for me. Apparently to Dalton and the housekeeper, this meant a refrigerator jammed full of beautiful cheeses, salads, a half-dozen steaks, desserts, and a basket full of fruit so exotic, I didn't know the names of half of them.

I made myself dinner in the palatial kitchen, with Shayla on speakerphone the whole time, so I didn't feel lonely.

As I described the food and the house itself, she played along and described our kitchen back in Beaverdale, trying to put a positive spin on everything.

"I just found at least one third of a cucumber," she cooed. "It's been out on the counter all night since the party, but I think if I cut off the wrinkled end, I could use the crumbled potato chips from the bottom of this bowl and make some fancy hoover-doovers."

(Hoover-doovers is our term for *hors d'oeuvres.* I know, pretty cute, right? Try not to barf in your mouth over our cuteness.)

"Girl, we are living it up!"

"Tell me something," she said. "When you turn the kitchen tap off, does it stop right away?"

Giggling, I tested the tap. "Oh my god. The stream stops immediately. No dribbling. And there's no water leaking out of the base."

"I'm so jealous," she moaned. "Okay, finish up dinner so we can go snooping around."

"I can't violate Dalton's space."

"Sure you can. It's easy. Just think about where you would hide your good stuff if you lived there." She gasped. "What if he asks you to move in with him? I can't pay the rent here by myself."

"Hang on. Don't jump on the train to Crazy Town yet. I've known the guy two weeks."

"I should have been nicer to him so he would be generous to his girlfriend's bestie. I should have screamed when he tried to scare me with his vampire teeth." She let out a stream of swear words.

"Calm down. One swear word at a time, Shay."

"Okay." She sniffed. "I'm totally not crying."

"Change is scary."

"I love you, P."

"I love you more."

She sniffed again.

"Time for a little light snooping," I said.

I picked up the phone, took it off speakerphone to conserve battery, and started wandering around the house, giving her the tour.

I opened a door to what I expected was a closet, but discovered a set of stairs going down. Here I thought I was on the bottom floor, but apparently the house had a basement.

CHAPTER 26

I climbed down the narrow stairs, lights flicking on overhead on their own. "Must be motion sensors," I said.

"The house is aliiiiiive," she joked.

"I'm opening a door."

"Probably a wine cellar."

Lights flicked on overhead automatically. "You're not wrong!"

"How's the spider situation?"

"I'm not screaming, am I?"

"How many bottles of wine?"

I counted the number of bottles in the row, and then the column. "At least four hundred, plus there's—OHMYGOD."

"What?"

I took a closer look at the framed art along the cool, cement wall. The pictures were Polaroid photos, from the sixties and seventies by the look of the hairstyles and clothes. The same woman was in all the photos, usually naked. She was voluptuous, with long, heavy breasts falling to either side of a softly protruding stomach. Her blond hair was teased up, and in the seventies-era photos, she wore thick black eyeliner and lurid blue eyeshadow.

I recognized the view in the outdoor photos, as well as the placement of the pool. These photos had been taken in and around the house I stood in. The woman was kissing or hugging about five different men, plus one woman, in the dozen framed pictures.

Shayla howled in frustration for me to tell her what was going on, so I took some pictures with my phone and sent them to her.

"Wow, that chick looks like you," she said.

"No way." I giggled. "Her bush is five times bigger than mine."

She snorted. "Two birds could live in that bush and never meet."

"Olden days look so fun." I sighed. "This must be exactly what Dalton's neighbor Jessica was teasing me about finding. Apparently this house was where the wife and her lovers lived."

"If you tell her you know, then she'll know you snooped."

"This isn't snooping." The thick yellow envelope waiting on the coffee table upstairs popped into my mind.

Shayla yawned audibly, then said, "My ear's hot, which means this phone call is giving me a brain tumor. Gotta go, toots."

We said goodbye and ended the call.

I thought about bringing one of the wine bottles upstairs with me, but a car was coming to pick me up in the morning, early. My first official underwear modelling photo shoot would be challenging enough without a hangover.

Then again, a glass or two might help me sleep.

I selected a bottle from the middle of the wall, careful to leave the really dusty ones undisturbed. I was no wine aficionado, but I did know wine collectors loved the dust, and that those bottles were for special occasions only.

Back up in the master bedroom, I finished my glass of wine as I checked email and whatnot on my laptop, using the wireless password Jessica gave me during the tour. I was pleased to see Dalton's network was named Paradise, because it really suited the home.

One of his neighbors had a network called Free Kittens and Candy in 218, and another had For The Love of Decency Please Draw Your Curtains. A third one, Big Guns Tight Buns, made me giggle.

After I'd exhausted my usual internet haunts, I shut everything down and snuggled into the enormous bed to get some sleep. Dalton had requested I sleep naked, so naked I was.

Half an hour later, I still couldn't sleep. I flicked on a light, poured another glass of wine, and pulled on a fluffy robe to go in search of the library.

I didn't get to the books, though, because the fat yellow envelope on the coffee table called me with its siren lure. It wasn't sealed or labeled, and I shook out a thick stack of paper.

A movie script.

The Post-It note on top read:

What a wonderful project! I can't wait to come to the premiere. - Jessica

This had to be the script for the movie Dalton had been so tight-lipped about. The second page described the setting as a small town in Washington.

For all of about half a second, I worried Dalton would be cross at me for reading the script, but then my curiosity took over and said surely it was fine.

I padded back to the bedroom with the manuscript and settled in for a good read.

The title was We Are Made of Stardust, which made me laugh out loud. Dalton had said all those corny things to me when we first met, about us being...

Actually, there it was, right on page five. Word for word, exactly what he'd said to me. In the script, the main character's name was David.

~

David: Let's just be two souls tonight. Two souls who are made of stardust, and found their way back to each other, the way they were destined to.

Harper: You left me here. You wouldn't have had to find your way back if you hadn't left in the first place.

David pulls Harper into a passionate embrace.

David: Kiss me like I'm dangerous.

Harper: Up to your old tricks?

David: Kiss me like I'm bad for you.

~

I put the script down and stared at the blotchy abstract art on the wall in Dalton's palatial bedroom.

The second part was exactly what he'd said to me the night we had dinner at DeNirro's. Our dates had been scripted. Well, his side had been.

This unsettled me, but not enough to stop reading.

I read on, and I lied to myself and said it was just a good story, and that was why.

The truth is, every page was cutting me. Deeply. My sorrow grew with every line I read, that I'd also heard come from Dalton's lying lips.

Line after line he'd fed me, and I'd gobbled it down.

The character, David, had returned to his hometown and discovered the love of his life dating his estranged brother, and sporting an extra fifty pounds. He still felt something for her, but... *it hurt so bad for me to read his dialog with his friend...* he didn't know if he could be physically attracted to Harper anymore. He was a wealthy tech company owner, and used to dating, in his words, "hotties."

Later in the script, he told his friend that maybe being with a full-girl wasn't so bad after all. He said hurtful things that his idiot character meant to be positive, but were not positive at all.

I read all the way to the end, which included the stupidest ending for any movie, ever.

Harper hired a personal trainer and got her butt skinny enough to climb back into her prom dress, and she and Dalton—I mean, David —attended their high school reunion.

And they lived Happily Ever After.

If I'd had a knife nearby, I would have stabbed it through the manuscript, the way it had stabbed through my heart.

These were all the actions and words of fictional characters, but I read Dave's words as though every word was coming from Dalton's lips. I'd already heard so many of the lines.

I heard horrible sounds, like a woman howling in pain, and I realized it was me.

It was four in the morning.

The darkest hour for the human soul.

~

THE END of Book 1

Continues in Peaches Monroe #2
STARLIGHT